THE HOUSE BUILT ON SAND

An Emad Almasry Mystery

Peter Townsend

Contents

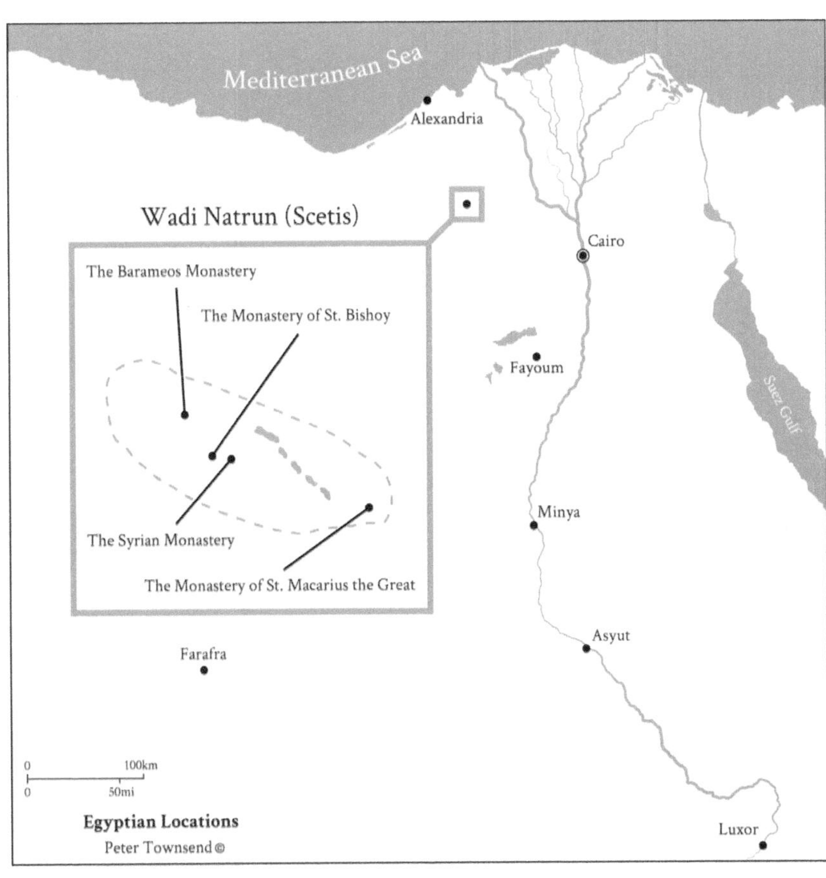

Mediterranean Sea
Alexandria
Wadi Natrun (Scetis)
The Barameos Monastery
The Monastery of St. Bishoy
The Syrian Monastery
The Monastery of St. Macarius the Great
Cairo
Fayoum
Suez Gulf
Minya
Farafra
Asyut
100km
50mi
Luxor
Egyptian Locations
Peter Townsend ©

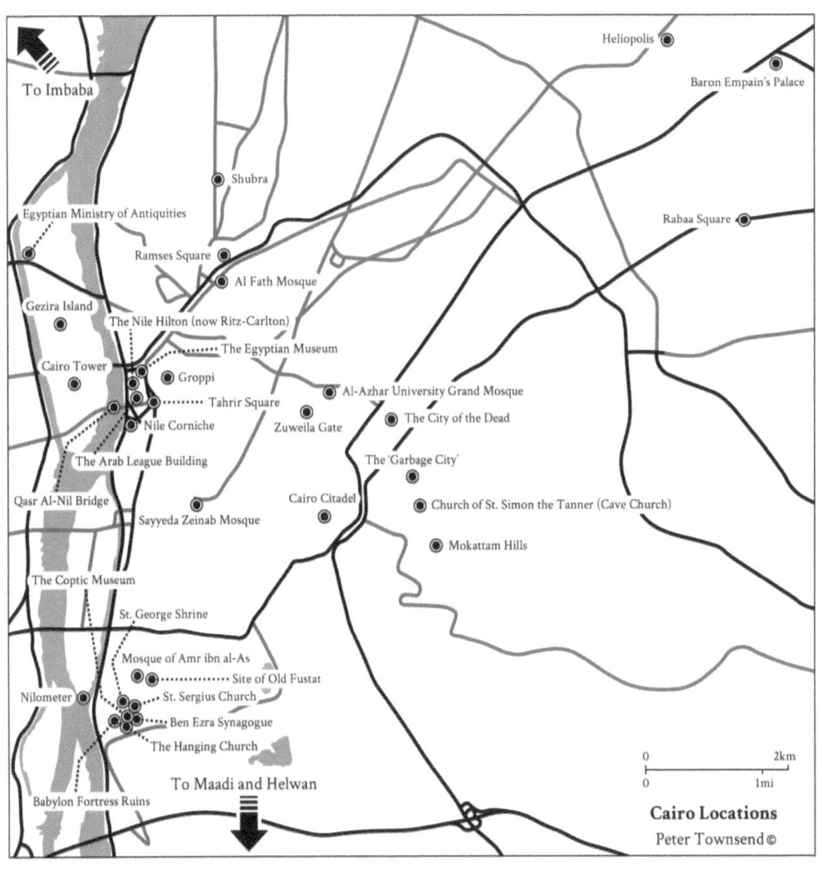

To Imbaba
Heliopolis
Baron Empain's Palace
Shubra
Rabaa Square
Egyptian Ministry of Antiquities
Ramses Square
Al Fath Mosque
Gezira Island
The Nile Hilton (now Ritz-Carlton)
The Egyptian Museum
Cairo Tower
Groppi
Al-Azhar University Grand Mosque
Tahrir Square
The City of the Dead
Nile Corniche
Zuweila Gate
The Arab League Building
The 'Garbage City'
Qasr Al-Nil Bridge
Cairo Citadel
Church of St. Simon the Tanner (Cave Church)
Sayyeda Zeinab Mosque
Mokattam Hills
The Coptic Museum
St. George Shrine
Mosque of Amr ibn al-As
Site of Old Fustat
Nilometer
St. Sergius Church
Ben Ezra Synagogue
The Hanging Church
To Maadi and Helwan
Babylon Fortress Ruins
0   2km
0   1mi
Cairo Locations
Peter Townsend©

Chapter 1

"Who struck the jackpot this time?" Emad Almasry cracked a wry smile at the message that just pinged its way into his Inbox. Not a week goes by or someone, somewhere in Egypt, is convinced that he made a discovery to rival the 1922 opening of the tomb of Tutankhamen in the fabled Valley of the Kings.

There is a pattern to such excitement, a certain formulaic inevitability. It starts with breathless speculation as soon as something looking remotely ancient is yielded up by the earth. Phone calls follow, 'experts' are consulted, castles made of dreams are built. Then, the bureaucracy. All the excitement eventually gets turned into a flashing electronic envelope on Emad's desktop. Hopes, dreams, and aspirations reduced to strings of code.

Still, any find, no matter how seemingly trivial, must be investigated by the Egyptian 'Ministry of State for Antiquities', and the task of doing so, often lands on Emad's desk.

As an archaeologist with the ministry, much of Emad's life consists of trooping out to dusty building sites or plowed-over fields to deal with people who are utterly convinced that they were about to get filthy rich on the back of some overstuffed tomb beneath their feet. Almost as regularly, it is his painful duty to deliver the sad tidings that the object that sparked dreams of wealth and glory was available for less than $10 on the antiquities black market.

Even after seven years behind this desk, Emad was still amazed at how saturated the soil of Egypt is, to the point of bursting, with ancient objects. Whenever someone claims to have found something utterly unique, Emad's thoughts turned to the millions of jars containing animal mummies still lying unopened at Saqqara just south of Cairo. There are so many urns, filling roof-high shelving more than a mile in length in a specially built mausoleum, that the archaeological community had mostly given up on attempts to catalog them all. In fact, during colonial times some of the cat mummies had even been exported back to England by British authorities to be ground up and used as fertilizer. Against the backdrop of this kind of super-abundance of archeological artifacts, the chances that something new and unique will emerge are vanishingly small.

"Ah well, better see where I'm heading to next" Emad quickly scanned the details of the email. He was surprised to see the word 'Fustat' at the top of the document. At least this job will be slightly out of the ordinary and, more importantly, not in some godforsaken and flyblown village hundreds of miles from Cairo. Spending days traveling along dusty roads, only to find the ancient Egyptian equivalent of an IKEA dinner service at the other end must be his least favorite part of his job. Fustat, on the other hand, is well within the Cairo city limits and he should be able to make it there with a short taxi ride from the headquarters of the ministry on Gezira Island in the middle of the Nile.

You could almost say that Fustat used to be Cairo, or instead, that modern Cairo was built right on top of it. It was the first capital created by the Muslim invaders shortly after they overran Egypt with the message of the Prophet in the year 641. It fulfilled this role for about 500 years until a new Muslim dynasty, the Fatimids, who conquered Egypt in the name of Shi'a Islam, decided to move the center of Muslim rule to a site that would be easier to defend from expected Crusader attacks. So, in 1168 the sultan's vizier, Sawar, had Fustat burned to the ground. The new capital was established further to the north at a much more easily fortified spot that was called, in a not so subtle reminder to the native Egyptians of who was in charge, Al-Qahira ('The Victorious').

Losing its status as capital to Al-Qahira (Cairo), not to mention being gutted by fire, had a devastating effect on Fustat. There were some efforts at rebuilding, but over time the erstwhile capital declined into obscurity. Even its famous mosque, the Mosque of Amr, the oldest in Africa, lay in ruins for centuries. Things are a bit better today. The urban sprawl of Cairo has overtaken Fustat, but at least the carefully restored mosque is recognized as one of the most prominent Islamic sites in Egypt. The curious and the devout regularly flock there to see its ancient splendor, or rather the impressions of later generations of what it must have looked like before being destroyed. The area also contains many churches and synagogues, with the part of it closest to the metro station known as 'Coptic Cairo.'

Emad was slightly perplexed by the report of a 'find' in Fustat. Since it is such an old part of Cairo, very little new building work is undertaken there. The request form had the answer. A tunnel was being dug to help relieve Cairo's chronic traffic congestion, and it passed under a corner of the suburb.

"The new laws must be having some effect," he thought. In the past, it was a rarity for big contractors to send work the ministry's way. The 'big guys' would often quite literally bulldoze their way through sensitive sites knowing that it was always easier to beg forgiveness than ask permission. They also relied on the fact that in Egypt, there are few things that some judiciously distributed backhanders cannot smooth over. All of this was changing, with some new brooms at the ministry, and a few successful prosecutions of flagrant offenders.

Improved compliance did not mean that contractors suddenly started to appreciate what they've always viewed as unnecessary meddling by the ministry. Unlike small builders, most large contractors knew that it was highly unlikely that they just bumped up against 'the big find.' Visits to their sites were therefore quite different from Emad's regular inspections. He knew that he would be expected to get in and out as quickly as possible and that his report allowing work to continue needed to be completed 'by yesterday.' On the upside, no one made giddy with gold fever would be looking over his shoulder while he was working. "Better get cracking," he sighed as he turned to the first port-of-call for the 21st-century archeologist.

CHAPTER 2

Emad gave an exasperated sigh. Things had come a long way from having to pore over dusty survey maps to do initial assessments, but Howard Carter, who discovered the intact tomb of King Tut, did not have to deal with his tools 'freezing'. In ideal circumstances, he would see Google Earth zooming into Fustat at lightning speed. However today it was going there at walking pace. He glanced up at the iconic photograph above his desk of Carter sporting what looked like a condescending smile as he stood in front of the treasures he unearthed. "You would think the ministry in charge of some of the most important archeological sites in the world would have a few spare dollars to provide their staff with better equipment," he thought as he reached for the restart button.

While he was waiting for his computer to go through its cumbersome restart ritual, his phone rang. It was Maryam. Over the years Emad had come to expect these little "How's your day going?" calls from her. For some reason she never made the transition to text messaging and still insisted on calling, even for seemingly trivial matters. Emad liked it that way. It was always good to hear her calm and pleasant voice as he navigated his working day.

It turned out that the call was not entirely trivial. She wanted to let him know that she heard about an apartment that might be going for a reasonable price. "Where is it?" he asked. "About 25 minutes from the Helwan metro station". Emad grimaced. The traditionally industrial suburb of Helwan is at the southern endpoint of Cairo's north-south metro line. Commuting 25 minutes to Helwan station and then for more than an hour by metro and on foot to Zamalek on Gezira Island sounded like his idea of torture. Still, they had to do something if they wanted to get married anytime soon.

In Egyptian society, couples are often engaged for years and years, with the family of the bride only consenting to go ahead with the marriage ceremony once the groom can provide a fully furnished apartment and a suitable dowry. Emad had been engaged to Maryam for almost the whole time since he came back from the UK seven years before and it felt like he was no closer to meeting the demands of her family than he was when they celebrated their engagement. A combination of skyrocketing property prices, salary freezes at the ministry and the Global Financial Crisis saw to that. Knowing that there were millions of Egyptian couples in their early to mid-thirties in the same position only added to his frustration.

"Let's go and have a look on Friday," he said as his eyes were drawn to his freshly restarted computer "Got to go; I'll call you when I'm done here." As someone who is generally preoccupied with much more ancient technology, what he calls 'the magical restart' was the only card up Emad's sleeve when it came to computer troubles. Thankfully it seemed to have worked. The familiar spinning globe spun vigorously this time, before descending at the speed of a parachutist in deep trouble into Old Cairo.

Emad scanned the disorganized warren of streets and alleyways that looked crowded and jumbled, even on a satellite photo. This part of the city is known as 'Old Cairo,' which reflects the fact that Fustat is about 500 years older than the rest of Cairo, and its age can be appreciated even better when viewed from above. The irregular pattern of the narrow streets stood in sharp contrast to the cube-like shapes of modern high rises to the east and the multi-lane Cairo Ring Road to the north. It was to link these new developments with the ring road that a new tunnel was needed under a part of Fustat.

Two large open spaces broke the irregular pattern on the satellite image. These were the courtyards of the two significant and historic mosques in the area, the mosque of Amr Ibn Al-As and the more extensive and newer (although still more than a millennium old) mosque of Ibn Tulun. It was to the mosque of Amr Ibn Al-As that Emad's eyes were immediately drawn, as it was near to this site that the tunnel-project workers made their find. Little remains from the original site plan of the oldest mosque in Africa, as the mosque had been subjected to countless 'improvements' over the ages. Still, being able to see the site from the air helped him to form a general idea of the lay of the land in its current state.

The next step was to access the ministry's extensive database of historical maps and site plans. A few years ago, this would have called for a trip to a dusty archive, housed in the basement of the ministry's headquarters. Thankfully the entire collection had recently been digitized with the help of a grant from UNESCO, and all it took was a few mouse clicks before the various layers of the history of Fustat appeared on the screen.

Once again, the pattern was the same — a chaotic mess of narrow streets, broken by the rectangular spaciousness of the two large mosques. As Emad looked at some of the older images, he could not help thinking that something was not quite right. It was the feeling that he often got when presented with counterfeit Egyptian antiquities. Sometimes these pieces were incredibly well executed and, if asked to explain himself, he would typically be unable to verbalize the reason behind his discomfort. However, his initial snap judgment almost always turned out to be correct upon closer investigation of the piece.

Being an expert in Egyptology rather than classical Islamic architecture, Emad pushed his sense of unease to the back of his mind to jot down a few initial notes. The Fustat area is filled to the brim with ruins and with objects related to the Islamic conquest of Egypt. It could well be, therefore, that the investigation would have to be handed over to an expert in Islamic antiquity. If there was indeed something to investigate that is.

It was, of course, possible that something from the age of the pharaohs could be unearthed, but this part of Cairo is not on the list of Egyptological 'must-visits.' Several locations in the Cairo area like Giza, Saqqara, and Heliopolis can lay claim to having been centers of pharaonic power or worship during different stages of the history of Egypt. Fustat, with its strong Islamic connections, is not one of them. Still, as they were often told during staff pep talks, no find was too small to ignore.

After printing out some of the maps, Emad picked up the phone and dialed the number on the request form. A very professional-sounding secretary answered. "Can I please speak to Mr. Bassem Fakry?" Emad asked, only to be firmly requested to state his business. They ran a tight ship over at Quwah Corporation Ltd. After being satisfied that he was not about to invite her boss to participate in some Ponzi scheme, the secretary put him through to Mr. Fakry, site manager for the Fustat Tunnel Project.

Emad barely had time to introduce himself before being brusquely cut short with, "So when can we get this over and done with?" Efficiency obviously trumped the joys of painstaking archeological research for Mr. Fakry. This indeed came as no surprise to Emad although this did not keep him from almost contributing to an abrupt rise in the harassed executive's blood pressure by suggesting that the ministry had a six-month waiting period for this kind of case. Thankfully he stopped himself at the last moment. Cairenes are famous for their excellent sense of humor, but he was sure that Mr. Fakry would probably not have appreciated any attempt to make light of his burning desire to keep his project running according to schedule.

"I can be there tomorrow at three," Emad said with a slight smile playing at the corner of his mouth, "Please make sure that the find remains undisturbed until then." The call was over less than two seconds later, with only a single "Fine" emanating from the other side before the connection was cut. Mr. Fakry was not a stickler for proper telephone etiquette.

This was panning out exactly as Emad expected. In his mind, it was a tossup whether dealing with corporate indifference or quashing the expectations of untold riches of the 'little guys' was most frustrating. He probably preferred the former. At least it allowed him the opportunity to get on with his work with a minimum of interference.

The rest of Emad's afternoon was spent reading up on the history of Fustat and of previous digs in the area. It quickly became apparent that dating artifacts would be relatively uncomplicated. The burning of the city in 1168 acts as a fixed point. Anything above the resultant layer of charred remains must date from after this date and *vice versa*.

His concentration was finally broken by the steady increase of movement in the corridor outside his office. Another workday at the Ministry of State for Antiquities was ending. After jotting down a few final notes, Emad got up to join his homeward-bound colleagues. As he left his desk, his eyes were drawn, as happened almost every day at this point, to an action figure of Indiana Jones, whip in hand, that he kept on a shelf above his computer.

The plastic 'Dr. Jones' never ceased to elicit a smile, coupled with a slight twinge of regret. It was his only remaining link with another world and an unrealized alternative future.

It was a gift from Lucy.

CHAPTER 3

Lucy and London felt like half a world away, and in many ways, they were. His life was in Cairo now.

Eleven years before, he had received a prestigious scholarship to study at one of the most famous Egyptological departments outside Egypt, located at the School for Oriental and African Studies (SOAS) in the heart of London. Emad immensely enjoyed his time at SOAS and would eventually be awarded a doctorate based on his research on changes to Egyptian worship practices during the ascendancy of the 15th, or Hyksos, Dynasty.

Walking the streets of Bloomsbury, he often reflected how far he had come from his humble village in Upper Egypt. Identified as particularly bright by an eagle-eyed teacher, he was sent to a high school in Asyut, one of the largest cities to the south of Cairo. Although this inevitably led to extended periods away from his family, it did mean that opportunities for further study opened before him. To him, it always seemed obvious that such further studies would have to focus on the ancient history of his country.

The 'Upper' in Upper Egypt refers not to a point on the compass but the location of this part of the country upstream along the Nile from Cairo. This fact is something that often confuses foreigners as they puzzle about why something called 'Upper' is to the south on a map. Many pharaonic dynasties had their power bases in this part of the world, and it is, therefore, impossible to escape the glorious past of Egypt as you travel along the Nile in Upper Egypt. Not that Emad wanted to avoid the past. He positively relished growing up in such a history-haunted part of the world. When the time came to go to university, it was to the Egyptology Program at the University of Minya, the largest city in Upper Egypt, that he applied for admission.

A few years buried in his books, coupled with extended field trips and even some digs at pharaonic sites around Upper Egypt, eventually saw him gain entrance to Cairo University for a master's degree. Leaving the Upper Egyptian landscape with its palm trees, rice paddies, and water buffaloes (with the Nile trailing through it all) for the big city was quite a shock to Emad's system.

In English, 'Egypt' and 'Cairo' are two different words. This is, however, not the case in colloquial Arabic. Very few Egyptians consistently use Qahira when speaking about Cairo. Instead, both the country and the city are called 'Misr' in Arabic. For the twenty million or so Cairenes this blurring of city and country is self-evident. Cairo is Egypt and Egypt is Cairo. Emad did not share this view while growing up. Coming from outside the capital, from what he still regarded as the 'real Egypt,' it took him ages to adjust to the fast pace, the congestion and the pollution that form the inescapable backdrop to life in Cairo; he was glad that he did.

The city was now well and truly home. Yes, it could be dirty, noisy and run-down, but it also pulsed with an energy and zest for life that you would be hard-pressed to find anywhere else. His first reaction on walking the streets of London was to ask: "Where are all the people?" Even London's Oxford Street on a busy day seemed sedate compared to Cairo. Where else, after all, is it possible to stand in line to buy a freshly squeezed mango juice at 3 am?

Emad was very conscious of the fact that many people making the journey from Upper Egypt or the Delta to Cairo were chewed up and spat out by the capital. Millions of them could be found on the edges of the city, living in shoddily built apartment buildings while trying to eke out a living on a few dollars a day. He was thankful that his journey turned out very differently.

He greatly enjoyed his time at Cairo University. Not only because of the research opportunities, but also for the contact with students from other universities that it offered. Halfway through his master's degree, he met some students from the American University in Cairo (AUC) who came to Egypt to study Egyptology on-site. This led to several 'language exchange' arrangements where his new friends would help him improve his English, while he tried to teach them the basics of Arabic. Given all the sitting around in coffee shops solving the world's problems, it is a miracle that any 'language exchange' took place, but somehow it did. He became quite at home in the English language, although he would be mercilessly teased during his time in London as the 'Egyptian-American', due to the strong accent that he picked up because of getting his English from AUC students.

In London, Emad found a place to stay with some other Egyptian students in Surrey Quays, about 4 miles southeast of the city center. The archeologist in him relished the opportunity of seeing an area transforming from one use to another. The Surrey Docks used to be part of the beating heart of British trade but repeated bombing raids during the 'Blitz' in WWII, the decline of UK manufacturing and the increasing bulk of container ships all contributed to the eventual closing of the docks. Many of the warehouses, at least those not damaged beyond repair, have been turned into apartment blocks. At first Emad was disconcerted with how quiet everything was, until he realized that just about everywhere else was quiet compared to Cairo. He eventually grew to love the fact that artifacts from the area's maritime past were not buried underground but were available for all to see. Turn a corner, and you were likely to find a colossal anchor mounted in the middle of a sidewalk or vast stretches of water previously used to accommodate boats or cargo. Somehow these tangible links with the past pleased him.

Across the River Thames from Surrey Quays was a sight that acted as a visible reminder of home. From the 1980s onwards, London's second financial district sprang up at the top end of the Isle of Dogs, a peninsula jutting into the Thames that used to act as royal hunting grounds. At the heart of this development, known as Canary Wharf, is a building that for about 20 years (until the completion of 'The Shard' in 2012) was the tallest in the UK. Atop this building, officially known as *1 Canada Square*, was the ultimate symbol of the reign of the Pharaohs: A vast glass pyramid. On many a walk next to the Thames with Lucy, Emad glanced up at this reminder of home suspended 600 feet above the river, and raised an ironic smile at this shining glass and steel combination of old and new.

The Canary Wharf pyramid, one of the icons of London, symbolized for Emad the predicament that haunted most of his time in the city. Lucy was one of the librarians at SOAS. She was, in fact, one of the first people he met in London, as she was given the task to show him, as one of the new doctoral students, around the library. Perhaps she felt a particular sense of affinity with someone who was so obviously an outsider, since her background in the valleys of Wales and the University of Aberystwyth was quite different from that of the rest of the staff at SOAS.

Emad sometimes worried about how her 'small-town girl made good' background caused her to be just that little bit too trusting. Because of SOAS' reputation as a treasure trove of information on the ancient world, there were far too many 'hangers-on' at the library who were undoubtedly not there primarily for the sheer joy of learning. Indeed, some of the archeological and documentary information and skills that you could pick up at SOAS would be just as useful when it came to entering the black market in illegal antiquities. Emad prided himself on spotting the 'mercenaries' (as he called them) rather quickly. Mostly because they always seemed to fixate on the dollar and cents values of whatever they were studying. Lucy, however, regarded everyone who stepped through the doors of her library as merely interested in learning for learning's sake. He tried to warn her a few times that she may be leading people to information that could be used for shady purposes, but he was mostly met with a blank stare of incomprehension. He later realized that you probably had to have come from a place, like Egypt, that had been comprehensively plundered of its greatest treasures to be alive to the possibility that not everyone interested in the ancient world approached the subject with the purest of motives.

His worries about her too-trusting nature did not stand in the way of Emad and Lucy becoming fast friends, and perhaps a little more. During his time in London, Lucy performed many heroic feats of investigation as she helped him to source texts that could only be described as extremely obscure. In the process, their conversations gradually moved from the academic to the personal.

The knowledge that their relationship could progress from friendship to something more, and that Lucy would welcome it if it did, was one of the bittersweet themes of his time in London. Through it all, it was as if the pyramid towering over their walks reminded him that Egypt, and Maryam, were calling him home.

"A call duly answered," he thought to himself as he walked out into the leafy streets of Zamalek. On Gezira Island, the hustle and bustle of the 'real' Cairo could sometimes feel a world away. This was, however, the world that Emad gradually re-entered as he started to head home. He made the first part of the journey on foot, partially because he needed the exercise, but also because, after all the years, it still gave him a thrill to cross the Nile.

One of the first phrases that every Egyptian student is taught, is: 'Egypt is the gift of the Nile.' Not many of them will perhaps be able to identify this as a line from the Greek historian Herodotus, but all of them understand the sentiment behind it: No Nile, no Egypt. If it were not for the river, all of Egypt would be like the murderous sandy deserts that make up most of its territory. Instead, the Nile supports a narrow ribbon, fanning out into a delta, of the most fertile farmland in the world. It is this narrow strip of land that the vast majority of Egyptians call home.

As he walked across the 15th of May Bridge towards the right bank of the Nile, Emad mentally tipped his hat to one of the world's great rivers. Leaving the bridge behind he walked for a while along the road right next to the river, the *Corniche*, and smiled at the many courting couples who were doing their best to get as close to each other as possible, while staying on just the right side of what would be deemed acceptable behavior for unmarried couples. If Egypt had religious police (this was, in fact, a dream of the recently ousted Brotherhood government), this is where they would probably come to fill up their cells. As it was, the expectations of a conservative society were still enough to keep most couples from doing more than sharing the odd stolen kiss.

Emad loved the Corniche this time of day. The knowledge that the working day was over, and the sun playing on the water, combined to create an atmosphere that could almost be described as festive. This mood was accentuated by smoke rising from a multitude of braziers on which all sorts of snacks were cooking. A firm next-to-the-Nile favorite is corn-on-the-cob, barbecued to just the right midway point between slightly warm and charcoal. Emad bought one and marveled at how the vendor could complete the transaction without for one moment ceasing to fan the coals with a massive chicken-feather fan.

As he sat down to eat, Emad reflected on how many hundreds of generations of people have ended their workday beside this river. How many cultural influences contributed to the society that he called his own? Ancient Egyptian, Nubian, Greek, Roman, Coptic, Arab, French and British overlords all came and went. Still, Egypt remains, with the Nile as seemingly the only constant. The next day he would have the opportunity to participate in the peeling back of some of the layers hiding artifacts from one of these civilizations. In his more glamorous moments, he felt like a detective with a casebook stretching back centuries. He sighed as he got up to walk back into the somewhat less exciting realities of real life.

CHAPTER 4

Of all the qualities that you need to survive in Cairo, an indifference to the very notion of 'personal space' is very near to the top. During his time in England, Emad saw a few rugby matches on television. It seemed to him that the rules of the game require that all the players collapse in a colossal heap now and then. He had always thought he would have been entirely at home on the pitch, as the same kind of thing happens on Cairo's bus system every day. This was once again the case as he braced himself against the impact of what felt like a hundred bodies swaying in time with the Cairo Transit Authority bus, belching and rattling its way towards Shubra.

When he finally wrestled himself free from the heaving mass of humanity on the bus, he stepped into a world that could not be more different from genteel Zamalek. Shubra is one of the largest suburbs of Cairo. That is if you can call a district with 3 million residents a mere 'suburb.' Ironically the name 'Shubra' can be traced to the Coptic word *Sopro* which means small village. This 'Sopro' has left its village roots behind, to the extent that it is home to more people than the entire population of many countries.

Bustling and busy are probably the two most accurate words with which to describe Shubra. Emad rented a back room in one of the more run-down sections of the suburb and had to fight his way through what in most other parts of the world would be regarded as semi-apocalyptic early evening traffic to make his way home. On his way there, he passed one of the many thousands of mosques in Cairo. Some of these are buildings on the grandest possible scale. Others, like this one, were wedged in between other buildings or housed in storefronts.

As he passed the mosque, the call to prayer suddenly began to sound from the giant speakers attached to the roof. As soon as the first *'Allahu Akbar'* faded, the call was taken up by all the other mosques in the area. Soon a wave of sound swept over the city pouring out of tens of thousands of speakers. The sound of the city being blanketed by the faithful being exhorted to bow towards Mecca in submission to Allah is probably one of the 'exotic' things that many foreigners will always remember from their visits to Cairo. To locals, who have heard it five times a day for as long as they can remember, it probably does not evoke the same response. It is merely something that happens with predictable regularity. Unless you are very devout of course. In this case, the calls of the *muezzin* form the fixed points by which you organize your life.

Emad would certainly not number himself among the devout. Sure, he did go to the mosque most Fridays, and like most Muslim Egyptians, he also kept the fast during Ramadan. However, he had not prayed five times a day since he was a teenager. Initially, he rationalized his slackness as a logical response to the general busyness of life. Eventually, prolonged exposure to other beliefs and ideologies during his time in London contributed to moving him away from dogmatic adherence to his faith.

Then there was Ali. He met Ali within a few weeks of arriving in London and was astounded to hear him declare that he had turned his back on Islam. Ali was the very first apostate from Islam that Emad ever met. If they were both still in Egypt, the fact that Ali had turned his back on his religion would have had severe consequences. In London, he felt free to declare his unbelief, and he did so repeatedly and loudly. Emad tried to debate him on occasion, but the Imam in his village mosque when he grew up was barely literate and could not do much more than instill the basics of Islam through rote learning. This meant that the religious education he received did not equip him to engage in high-level theological debates. His usual approach towards Ali was, therefore, to allow him to recite his string of reasons for leaving Islam while not offering much by way of a reply. Like a furious volcano, Ali would eventually fully vent his frustration, although not without making some annoyingly good points along the way. Emad managed to ignore these and continued to regard himself as a believing, if not particularly devout, Muslim.

His lack of zeal was turning into more and more of a problem with Maryam. Their practice, or rather lack of consistent practice, of Islam, had initially been quite similar. However, things were changing. Her brother, Yusuf, had recently transformed himself from the family playboy to being ultra-devout. Out went the Western clothes for what he termed 'proper' dress and a long bushy beard. All-night parties on boats on the Nile were replaced by extended periods of prayer in the mosque. He was keeping this up to such an extent that he was well on his way to developing what Cairenes jokingly call a 'raisin': A callous on the forehead that is the ultimate mark of piety, as it is caused by repeatedly pressing your head to the ground in prayer.

Yusuf was not keeping his deepening devotion to Islam to himself. He had taken to openly accusing Maryam's father of failing in his Islamic duty by not maintaining tighter control of his daughter. He would most importantly have liked to see her dressing much more modestly. Maryam already wore a veil covering her hair in public. Pressure from the wider Muslim community to do this had become so intense over the past few years that you could almost guarantee that a woman going unveiled in public is from the Coptic Christian community and not a follower of Islam. Yusuf wanted Maryam to do much more than cover her hair, however. If it was up to him, she would discard all Western clothing and would also wear the full-face veil, the *niqab*. Emad was horrified at the very idea, and he said so on numerous occasions. Naturally, this had created significant tensions between him and Yusuf who was convinced that his sister was engaged to someone little better than an unbeliever. All of this was translating into subtle hints from Maryam that he should be a bit more consistent in fulfilling his religious obligations, if only to keep her brother happy.

For a moment Emad played with the idea of going into the mosque for evening prayers as a first step towards working on his levels of observance, but he quickly realized that a few extra prayers here and there would never satisfy Yusuf. He was in any event not looking over his shoulder. Besides, he had a big day ahead. With a little pang of guilt, he crossed the street towards his neighborhood *koshari* shop for the second part of his dinner.

Koshari is the cheapest hearty meal that it is possible to eat in Cairo. It consists of a mixture of rice, lentils, and pasta with lashings of tomato and onion relish. This is dished up from massive bowls that are piled high at the beginning of the day, to be whittled down by hungry customers until there is nothing left by late evening. Emad practically lived off the stuff when he was a student, and it was still an essential part of his diet since it is so cheap. This was not a bad thing for their 'Save for an Apartment' fund.

As he sat down to a steaming bowl of *koshari,* Emad pulled a copy of Egypt's largest newspaper *'Al Ahram'* ('The Pyramids') from the other side of the table. His mood immediately darkened as he scanned the front page. "Another day, another beheading," he thought to himself as the image of a bright orange jumpsuit jumped out at him. He did not need to read the actual report to know that the 'Islamic State' was up to its old trick of 'beheading for maximum effect'. A swirl of emotions jockeyed for attention in his head as he looked at the face of the person about to lose his head: pity, anger, disgust, fear and even revulsion at the fact that he'd heard many attempts to justify this kind of action in the past few days. This included a justification from his soon-to-be brother in law, who launched into a long lecture on the importance of recreating the ancient Islamic system of governance, the caliphate. On that occasion, Emad just nodded and walked away, but it pained him to think that he would soon be related, if only by marriage, to someone who saw nothing wrong with the image splashed across the front page of *Al Ahram*.

"Better turn to the sports pages," he thought as he flipped towards the back of the paper to check up on the exploits of his beloved Zamalek. Zamalek is one of the largest football clubs in Egypt and happened to be based on Gezira Island, where Emad went to work every day. He always found it ironic that the team is so strongly supported by millions of working-class people while carrying the name of a suburb that cannot by any stretch of the imagination be given that description. Satisfied that the preparations for this weekend's match against Al-Ahly were sufficiently rigorous, and having finished his koshari, he closed the paper, got up and walked a few doors down the street to complete the rest of his evening routine by sitting down at his usual spot in the local coffee shop.

Cairo's coffee shops (known as *ahwas*) are very different beasts from what passes for coffee shops in the West. You will find no hi-tech machines and fancy coffee descriptions. Instead patrons, almost always men only, sit at tiny tables where they consume ridiculously strong cups of coffee or tea into which they stir teaspoon after teaspoon of sugar. If anything, ahwas are spaces designed for conversation, and anyone who enters hoping to snatch a few quiet moments to get some work done will invariably attract tuts of disapproval. The other way in which Egyptian coffee shops are radically different from their Western cousins is in the fact that they can just as well be called 'smokehouses.' Large water pipes stand ready for anyone who would like to access the most potent legal 'high' available in a society where most people shun alcohol. The sweet smell of waterpipe tobacco is, therefore, a much stronger indication of the presence of a coffee shop than the smell of coffee being roasted.

Most ahwas do not bother with anything as fancy as a name or distinctive decor. Many of them do, however, have reputations for attracting different clienteles. Emad's 'local,' for example, had a reputation of being something of an intellectual hangout. Many university lecturers and teachers spent their evenings there. It was often jokingly called 'The Professor's Club' because of the practice of one of the waiters to greet everyone with a smiling, "Evening Professor", as they sat down for their evening coffees. As Emad walked in someone pulled up a chair for him, and the conversation resumed without skipping a beat. It was always pleasant to be among friends, but Emad was almost immediately sorry that he did not go straight home. As might be expected the topic of conversation was the latest ISIS beheading, as if he needed another reminder of it. Predictably the opinions ranged from outrage, through wild conspiracy theories, to tacit expressions of support.

With a sigh, Emad drained his coffee and got up to leave. As an archaeologist, he preferred his wars to be of the ancient variety.

CHAPTER 5

One advantage of living in a Muslim city is that you do not need to invest in an alarm clock. The local mosque will gladly do the job for you, as it did for Emad the next day. The morning call to prayer explicitly states that: "*To pray is better than to sleep.*" Even though he was not about to go through the full prayer ritual, Emad appreciated the sentiment. He also enjoyed the opportunity to have a few moments of peace before the day began in earnest.

As he gradually woke up, Emad quietly surveyed his surroundings. Like most Cairenes, he lived in an apartment complex, although the term probably obscured the prosaic reality of his living conditions. It is perhaps fair to say that many, if not most, of the apartment buildings in Cairo, were hastily constructed by builders who cut as many corners as possible to maximize profit. Add to this the fact that it is notoriously difficult to raise rents in older buildings, due to them being frozen by the Nasser government in the 1960s, thereby removing any incentive for landlords to invest in building maintenance. These factors combined to ensure that Cairo presented a rather scruffy face to the world.

The apartment that Emad woke up in was somewhat schizophrenic, like so many others all around the city. On the outside, the building was as dilapidated as any other in Cairo. To step inside was to enter another world, however. This space belonged to one of Emad's maternal uncles and his wife who also made the journey from Upper Egypt. Shortly after his arrival, his uncle achieved modest success as a shopkeeper. Emad rented a room that became available once their last child left home. His aunt was as house proud as it was possible to be, and her style of decorating seemed designed to prove the point that the former country bumpkins had indeed 'arrived' in the big city. In Cairo society, this means lots of baroque furniture combined with heavy drapes and a multitude of little ornaments, yet another bit of evidence of the profound impact of French culture on Cairene society. In this case the France of the 'gilded age'.

Emad walked past the little 'salon' that his aunt created in their living room to the bathroom. Once there, he turned on the shower and began the customary three-minute wait for the water to reach their part of the building. Almost every Cairo apartment block plays host to a ludicrously underpowered pump to get the water to the upper levels. The valiant efforts of these pumps often lead to loudly banging pipes and very unimpressive results at the business-end where the water is required. Emad often wondered at the fact that the modern descendants of the pyramid builders could be so spectacularly bad at plumbing.

While he waited, he stared at himself in the mirror. Looking back at him he saw what he supposed was a typical Egyptian, cast in the pharaonic mold: Olive skin, dark hair in which a few traces of grey were beginning to show and a nose that his friends often described as aristocratic. The picture was completed by a pair of penetrating brown eyes that were usually safely ensconced behind a pair of rimless glasses. Keeping fit and staying healthy is notoriously tricky for Cairenes, given the combination of high-calorie foods and a lack of exercise opportunities. Most people are not keen to go for a jog in one of the most crowded and smog-filled cities in the world. Emad was therefore somewhat dismayed to notice the beginning, but thankfully only the beginning, of a middle-aged spread.

After his shower, he went to the kitchen to eat a typical Egyptian breakfast: *Ful* and bread. The '*ful*' part of this combination consists of kidney beans that are mashed and mixed with salt, pepper and lemon juice. This is regarded as such an essential part of the Egyptian diet that some of Emad's friends seriously suggested to him that they disliked overseas travel because they cannot get ful when abroad. The bread is a kind of pita that is sold all over the city. During the 1960s the government of President Gamal Abdel Nasser decreed that the price of bread must never go up. 'Government Bakeries', therefore still dish out bread at the ridiculously low price of 5 piasters (a few cents) each. However, the individual loaves of bread are now about a quarter of the size they were in Nasser's time. There is also a commonly held belief that the flour is contaminated with all sorts of nasty fillers to bulk up the bread. There might be truth in this as it is widely reported that a diet with 'government bread' as the staple ingredient is liable to wear down the teeth of those who subsist on it. Emad's uncle saw it as a point of honor that his family should not eat what he calls 'cheap junk,' so Emad's breakfast was ful and some of the very best bread sold in his uncle's shop.

Leaving the apartment, he retraced in reverse his journey of the previous evening, this time in too much of a hurry to even notice the faithful prostrating themselves in the local mosque as he rushed past. On reaching his office, he quickly printed out a few more maps, the investigation request form, and his notes before going down to the street to hail a taxi.

There must be tens of thousands of white taxis buzzing around the streets of Cairo. All with multiple dents and scratches and most with inoperative fare meters. Upon entering one, you will almost immediately learn whether your ride will be a religious experience or whether you will get an immersion in Egyptian popular culture. Some taxi drivers keep Qur'anic recitals going all day, while others have the latest Arabic pop hits on loop. There is no question of asking the driver to turn the volume down or to change the content. The taxi is the domain of the driver, and the passenger must make his or her peace with what is being served up.

"How do you address an Egyptian taxi driver?" runs a popular joke in Cairo. The answer: "Doctor." It is a sad comment on the Egyptian economy that people can often earn much more by driving taxis than they could as doctors, dentists, or engineers. Emad's current driver came from a humbler background, but he did conform to another Cairo taxi driver stereotype. He drove like a demon. Another favorite Cairo joke states that there will be many more taxi drivers than imams in heaven. The reason: People sleep while most imams preach and pray when most taxi drivers drive!

Emad's driver beamed when he asked him to drive to the mosque of Amr Ibn Al-As in old Fustat. He was obviously in the religious camp, given the fact that the words of the Qur'an were pumping through a variety of speakers scattered around the vehicle. Upon being told that Emad was not conducting a mini pilgrimage to the mosque, the driver hardly missed a beat but continued to speak of the glories of Islam. His chosen theme was the fact that the Qur'an is supposedly the repository of all sorts of scientific 'miracles' and that this proved that the book must be from Allah.

Listening to this, Emad could almost hear the sneers of Ali back in London, as this claim was one of his ultimate bugbears. "Selective treatment of the evidence, wishful thinking and ignoring that the supposedly 'scientific' Qur'an teaches that the earth is flat," he would quickly say to anyone talking about 'Qur'anic science.' Not the snappiest line ever, to be sure, but a clear indication of his thoughts on the matter.

Not wishing to enter a debate, Emad tried to concentrate on his notes while the driver wove in and out of the traffic. It was only when the driver started to praise the efforts of the brave *mujahideen* ('those who struggle for the faith') of ISIS seeking to create a society obedient to Allah that Emad's ears pricked up. "Is there no escaping this stuff?" he thought before saying to the driver: "Don't you think they should seek to honor Allah in ways other than fighting?" The driver stared at him with the look of one whose mother had just been insulted. "There can be no better way of honoring Allah," he said with deep conviction. As if to reinforce his point he fiddled with the CD player. Obediently the melodious voice of the reciter shifted to a different part of the Qur'an:

"Not equal are those believers remaining [at home] - other than the disabled - and the mujahideen, [who strive and fight] in the cause of Allah with their wealth and their lives. Allah has preferred the mujahideen through their wealth and their lives over those who remain [behind], by degrees. And to both Allah has promised the best [reward]. But Allah has preferred the mujahideen over those who remain [behind] with a great reward."

Emad listened in silence until the taxi pulled up outside the mosque. He paid the fare and walked away fuming. "What hope for peace with people like this?" he mused as he strode briskly to the entrance. A nagging realization that Ali back in London would have phrased the question as "What hope of peace with a book like this?" but he had no time to turn this thought over in his mind. He had work to do.

Already waiting for him at the mosque was a foreman, along with a team of workers sent by the ministry. There were several such teams that ministry archeologists could call upon on short notice. They played a vital role in investigations, as they were familiar with the basics of archeological excavations and could be relied upon not to charge into sensitive sites with all spades blazing.

After greeting Emad, the foreman led the group to a temporary building next to the perimeter wall of the mosque. It was next to this site-office that an impatient Mr. Fakry was waiting for them. With his hard hat, fluorescent vest, and iPad he was every inch the personification of a busy site manager. "You're late," he said, hardly pausing for the standard (and very credible) response: "Traffic."

On entering the site office, it was apparent that the entire project was managed to the highest possible standards. Not only were they all given an extensive safety briefing, but they were also issued with the latest in safety equipment before being escorted, under Mr. Fakry's watchful eyes, to the location of the find. This meant entering the main tunnel through a smaller service tunnel. Emad was thankful that he was not claustrophobic, something that could be quite an occupational impediment in his chosen profession.

Once they reached the main tunnel, the visitors were awed by the scale of the project. With so much dirt being shifted it was no surprise that they uncovered some artifacts from the ancient past. "There it is," Mr. Fakry said, pointing towards a part of the tunnel that was sealed off with plastic tape. Almost at once the area was illuminated, as several hardhat lights all focused on the same spot. This would, however, not be enough. "Could you please rig up some lights?" Emad asked. Mr. Fakry, ever organized, merely flicked a switch and the entire area was bathed in light.

Wedged into the dirt, were some clay jars. Two or three of these were damaged by digging equipment, but to their credit, the workers immediately stopped when they realized that they encountered something out the ordinary and most of the twelve jars were intact. Near the jars, some solid brick-like stones indicated that they must have been in a building of some sort. The jars were of the type that was used to store all kinds of objects in the ancient world. They were, therefore, undoubtedly worth investigating.

The next few hours were a blur of activity as every inch of the site was photographed and measured. A call would have to be made later, hopefully not too much later, from the perspective of *Quwah* Corporation Ltd, on whether the site would have to be more fully excavated, but in the short term a decision had to be taken on what to do with the jars. After a few telephone discussions with his superiors, Emad gave the order that they should be lifted and transported to the ministry's warehouse of recent discoveries.

Those who had the chance to observe the ministry's workers marveled at how these roughhewn laborers could carefully, delicately and methodically remove objects from their ancient resting places with a minimum of disruption or damage. This day was no exception. In a relatively short time, all twelve jars were covered in the industrial equivalent of cotton wool and safely ensconced in wooden crates.

The ministry owned several trucks with modified suspensions to ensure that precious objects could be transported with the absolute minimum of bumps and hops. It was while waiting for one of these trucks to arrive that Emad had a chance to take a closer look at the jars. Almost as soon as he did so, he observed something that struck him as slightly curious in this bastion of early Islamic Egypt.

As he wiped the dust away, he was startled to find that the inscriptions on the jars were written, not in Arabic, but in the Coptic language.

CHAPTER 6

"It's going to be one of those evenings!" Maryam Abbas realized this as soon as she carefully opened the door to the family apartment. As expected, she was almost immediately greeted with a terse, "Where have you been?" Her brother Yusuf had recently taken to waiting for her to come back from work to ensure that she did not stay out too long and get into mischief.

The absurdity of doing this to a woman in her early thirties escaped him. As far as Yusuf was concerned, their father was failing in his Islamic duty to keep control of the women in the family, and he was stepping into the breach. He would not dare do this with his mother, who would quickly put him in his place. But ensuring that Maryam stayed on the straight and narrow was another matter.

"I met a friend on the way back from school, and we chatted for a while," she mumbled as she loosened her headscarf, as a close male relative Yusuf could see her hair. "You know I don't like you dawdling" Yusuf sneered. If it were up to him, Maryam would resign her job as a kindergarten teacher and spend her time at home, but the family needed her income. So, the only other alternative, in Yusuf's mind, was to ensure that she spent as little time as possible outside of the home. Maryam was about to, once again, tell him what she thought of his attempts to control her life in this way but thought better of it. It would only result in one of their very regular blazing rows.

Maryam realized that she should attempt to understand Yusuf on his own terms, but this was an incredibly hard thing to do. Yusuf showed much promise at school and was eventually able to gain a sought-after place to study engineering at Ain Shams University. He did very well in his studies and had big dreams of helping to build Egypt as a civil engineer. In the end, however, these dreams were frustrated by a combination of the reality that Egypt's universities were churning out way too many graduates and the fact that despite the best efforts of their father, his family could not access the right strings to pull to get him a job as an engineer.

Like so many other recent Egyptian graduates Yusuf, therefore, ended up with an excellent qualification but minimal prospects of ever working in his chosen field. The best that he could do was to earn some money working as a part-time math tutor for a few hours per week. This, however, did not bring in nearly enough money for him to strike out on his own, let alone even contemplating the thought of marrying and supporting a family.

One of the effects of Yusuf's enforced leisure was that he could spend lots of time at the local coffee shop. It was there that he met Abdullah. Abdullah had a very similar story to Yusuf's, except that he was a qualified dentist. One who also could not get permanent employment. Out of frustration, he began to volunteer at clinics operated in slum areas by perhaps the most significant grassroots movement in Egypt, *Ikhwan Muslimeen,* or the 'Muslim Brotherhood.' Over time, Abdullah's work in the slum led to conversations with some committed, not to mention persuasive, 'Brothers' and the developing of a firm conviction that the Brotherhood's key slogan was exactly what Egypt needed: *One Solution, Islamic Revolution.*

Yusuf was initially skeptical, especially as he correctly perceived that a firmer commitment to Islam would cramp his rather free-spirited lifestyle.

He did eventually start going along to the clinics when it was pointed out that he could use some of his professional skills in the slums. Over the next year or so, he had many sessions with slum dwellers about improved drainage and building energy-efficient coal-fired stoves. In the process, he also picked up a hefty dose of Brotherhood ideology.

Yusuf's family watched with bemusement as his involvement with the Brotherhood transformed him. His father, Muhammad, raised his children with a healthy respect for Islam and was personally quite devout. He was, however, in a junior position at the health department under the Mubarak government, to which the Brotherhood acted as a vast grassroots opposition. Any family links with the Brotherhood was bound to be problematic. Yusuf and his father had many arguments about this, but in the end, these always circled back to Yusuf's insistence that obedience to Allah (which he increasingly equated with supporting the Brotherhood) trumped all other loyalties, even loyalty to your own family.

Over time, Yusuf's ever-deepening commitment to all that the Brotherhood stood for became evident to all. He started to be scrupulous in praying five times a day; he also grew a bushy beard and spent long hours memorizing the Qur'an. Then there was the fact that he began harassing Maryam to be a better Muslim woman. Initially, this took the form of pestering her to be more consistent in wearing a headscarf, but with every concession, a new demand would emerge. To the point that he now seemed to monitor her every move.

For a while it seemed that Maryam would escape his attention, the 'Arab Spring' saw to that. This started as a broad-based pro-democracy movement aimed at toppling President Hosni Mubarak, Egypt's dictator of twenty years running. When this objective was acheived, the Brotherhood sprang into action. As the best-organized grassroots movement in the country, it called upon its extensive network when the time came to elect a new parliament and president. A Brotherhood candidate, Muhammad Morsi, was elected to the presidency in 2012.

Many of those involved in the anti-Mubarak uprising saw Morsi's election as a total betrayal of their ideals since it was widely believed that a Brotherhood government would ignore democratic principles and human rights. For Yusuf however, Morsi's election was a moment of triumph and hope. It also led to an almost immediate change in his fortunes.

After the elections, the Brotherhood moved swiftly to change the make-up of government departments to get more sympathizers into positions of power. With his record of helping with Brotherhood projects in Cairo's slums, Yusuf had an inside track to fill one of these positions. It was, therefore, no surprise when he was appointed as a junior engineer in the Department of Public Works. For a few months, he went to work, genuinely believing that he was contributing to building a better Egypt where the principles of Islam would be consistently applied. In the process, he was so busy that Maryam was able to breathe a sigh of relief. He was hardly ever around to check up on her. There was even talk of him moving out and getting his own apartment.

Many Egyptians did not entirely approve of their experience of political Islam at the levers of power. So, a popular uprising in July 2013 toppled president Morsi and replaced him with a military-backed government. Yusuf almost immediately lost his job as the new government implemented restrictions against the Brotherhood that were much more severe than those in existence during the Mubarak era. As a vocal Brotherhood supporter, he never stood a chance.

So, there he was, back at square one. Or perhaps even before square one because now he also had to deal with the knowledge that many of his friends were in prison, a fate he narrowly avoided by being late for a demonstration where many of them were 'picked up'. Some days all that sustained him was burning anger at what he saw as the betrayal of Islam by the people and the military. In responding to this anger, Yusuf's world became ever smaller. He did not attempt to go back to tutoring and increasingly stayed at home, especially since he knew that his full beard would immediately mark him out as someone to whom the police should pay particular attention. His daily routine was reduced to going down to the mosque, just a few doors from their apartment, and then spending the rest of his waking hours on the internet listening to sermons. This was apparently what he did as he stormed back to his room after 'welcoming' Maryam at the door.

Except, the sounds coming from his room did not sound quite like a sermon. Instead, Maryam heard the hectoring tones of someone delivering a speech in English before shouting *'Allahu Akbar.'* Some unearthly screams and then silence followed the shout. To her utter horror, it dawned on her that Yusuf was watching, presumably with approval, the ISIS beheading of the day before. A moment later, another speech, clearly by the same person, started.

Knowing what was coming, Maryam ran to her room, flung herself on her bed and pulled her pillow over her head. Listening to the death throes of a fellow human being was not quite what she had in mind for her evening.

CHAPTER 7

Emad was so used to hearing the words 'Coptic Clay Jars' combined with two others that he could not help but feel a little excited by what had been unearthed under Fustat. Those words were *Nag Hammadi*. Nag Hammadi used to be just another dusty Egyptian village on the west bank of the Nile, until some clay jars stuffed with Coptic writing were found there in 1945.

It turned out that these jars contained the most extensive library, in the Coptic language, of so-called Gnostic writings ever uncovered. Historians always knew that early orthodox Christians were opposed by other Christians who held to a wide variety of teachings focused on 'secret knowledge.' Based on the Greek word for knowledge (*gnosis*), such Christians were labeled *Gnostics*.

Up until recent times, those studying Gnosticism had to be content with meeting the Gnostics through the writings of their enemies. Hardly the place where you would expect a fair and accurate picture of their beliefs. The Nag Hammadi discovery changed all of that. Suddenly several alternative 'gospels' were available. While these were much more recent than the gospels in the Bible, some of them, most notably the *Gospel of*

Thomas, achieved renown as providing a window on an alternative understanding of the early history of Christianity. Even as a Muslim, Emad could take pride in the fact that such a remarkable discovery had been made right there in Egypt.

There was, of course, no way of knowing whether the jars, now slowly making their way to Gezira Island, contained anything at all, let alone a significant find. Emad was not nearly patient enough to even contemplate traveling back to the ministry at a snail's pace. In addition to the modified suspensions of the 'archeology trucks', the drivers were also under strict orders to drive as slowly as possible. So, after the jars were loaded, he left a foreman in charge and hailed a taxi.

As he sank into his seat, Emad was relieved to hear that in this taxi it would be neither the Qur'an nor syrupy pop music. Instead, the instantly recognizable sound of the 'Queen of Arab Music' greeted him. For decades, until her death in 1975, Umm Khultum captivated people across the Arab World with her dusky voice and resonant lyrics. Even today, most Egyptians can quote the lyrics of her songs word-for-word. Emad closed his eyes as he listened to the final majestic strains of *'Lissa Faker'* (Do you remember?), thinking that it was all too appropriate for someone in his profession:

> *When you ask me, I will tell you*
> *It was in the past*
> *Do you still remember?*
> *It was in the past*

As he reflected on the fact that he was one of those whose task it was to reveal some of the secrets of the distant past, Emad could not help feeling the slight frisson of excitement that accompanied the possibility that he might be on the cusp of uncovering something significant. He allowed himself a smile. If he as a professional could not help but be enthused by the prospect of a substantial find, he should perhaps be a bit more understanding towards those who became giddy with believing that their lives were about to change forever because of some artifact in their backyards.

Upon arriving at the ministry's offices, Emad began to prepare the room where the jars would be received. After clearing a large stainless-steel table, he donned a white jumpsuit and waited for two interns to do the same. Together they would meticulously document every single step of opening the jars. The whole process would also be recorded on both video and still cameras. As he observed the hustle and bustle around him, Emad could not help but chuckle at the prospect that the jars might be empty. There was a chance that they merely represented the remains of the stock of some merchant who went out of business centuries ago. He had been through many such anticlimaxes in his years as an archeologist, but he realized that the experience might be rather devastating for his interns. They were graduate students at Cairo University who were participating in the cataloging of a find for the very first time. As it turned out, his worries about their possible disappointment were wildly misplaced.

Once the jars arrived, they were ever so carefully placed on the metal table. An assistant placed a paper containing a serial number and a printed ruler next to each one. For as long as it remained in the ministry's system, this number would continue to identify each jar. After being photographed with their numbers, the painstaking task of cataloging any defining features began for each jar. Emad would later reflect that even at this early stage, while the jars were still caked in dirt and dust, he knew that one of them was different. So it proved.

Most of the jars were a little rough and had phrases in Coptic carelessly scratched into them. The one that stood out was the result of careful craftsmanship and showed signs of having been glazed earlier in its existence. What was most curious, however, was a strange emblem that was evidently painstakingly etched into its side while the clay was still wet. As he carefully wiped away the dust to completely reveal this, Emad could not help but admire the artistry across the distance of centuries. What appeared under his hand was a set of scales, heavily weighted to the left. Above it, a few letters in Coptic probably acted as an explanation.

The Coptic language is an amalgam of ancient Egyptian and Greek and was widely used throughout Egypt until the coming of Islam. Even in the

21st century, it cannot be regarded as an entirely dead language. It still functions as the liturgical language for the 10 million or so Egyptians who belong to the Coptic Orthodox Church. Emad had to learn the Coptic alphabet as part of his studies, because some Roman-era burial sites contained inscriptions in this language. His knowledge of Coptic was, however, very rusty since he did not use it regularly. The bulk of his work was focused on earlier periods of Egyptian history, during which hieroglyphs were the standard form of written expression.

Still, he could at least piece together the word above the scales, as it consisted of only a few letters. It merely said: Micah.

Emad furrowed his brow. He vaguely remembered that this was the name of a Hebrew prophet. If so, what was this jar doing buried under a mosque?

CHAPTER 8

"And now the real work begins, better get going!", Emad gave himself a little pep-talk as he arrived for work the next day. While the cataloging of a find was sometimes viewed as the most exciting part of archaeological exploration, it only represents the first few baby steps of the process. The discovery had been safely transported and cataloged the day before. Now, much time would have to be spent in dating and assessing the artifacts spread out on the table before them. Given that all the inscriptions were in Coptic, Emad already suspected that he would have to pass this project on to someone with more experience in this area. It was, however, still his duty to undertake some of the initial assessments.

As to dating, he already noted that all the jars were found beneath the layer of charred soil that dates from the fire that destroyed Fustat in 1186, so the find must be older than that. More precise dating would still have to be done by experts.

He was, once again, strangely drawn to what he began to think of as the 'special' jar. "Might as well begin here," he said to the interns, Abu Bakr and Hana, as he put on a headlight of the kind sometimes used by dentists. Using a magnifying glass, he went over every nook and cranny of the jar. For the second time, he was deeply impressed by the intricacy of the image of the scales that was etched on the outside. This jar was obviously created for a special purpose.

Donning a pair of rubber gloves, he picked up the jar and took it over to the x-ray room. As Mahmoud, the ministry's radiologist, got ready to scan the jar, Emad quipped: "If there are broken bones in there, they're beyond help don't you think?" Mahmoud, who was keenly aware that his workday was very different from that of most members of his profession, smiled: "Well if there are, at least the owner can't talk back!"

Mahmoud took his time, way too much time in Emad's humble opinion, to scan the jar from every conceivable angle. Once the plates were ready, he called Emad over for a look: "Firstly, if you were hoping that this represents the end of your financial troubles I have to disappoint you! There are no metal or jewels in there. It seems to me that the jar is mostly empty." As Emad squinted to make sense of the picture, he had to agree. There was not much inside the jar. Then he spotted something: "What is that mass in the bottom left corner?", he asked.

Mahmoud leaned in for a closer look: "I don't know. It is certainly not made of metal or stone. It is too ill-defined. I would guess that it is some form of organic matter. Possibly leather?" Emad pricked up his ears. This was getting very curious. Why would someone use a costly jar to store something as simple as a piece of leather? "I think we have to make plans to open it," he said to Mahmoud. "Can't help you there," Mahmoud responded, "I only do the magical seeing-through-walls stuff!" Emad chuckled as he got out his phone to talk to his boss.

Escalating an archaeological inquiry can often take months of committee meetings, but Emad had been at the ministry long enough that his superiors implicitly trusted his judgment. It, therefore, took only a brief explanation of the find for permission to be given for him to open the jar. "I'm going to need your help," Emad said to the interns who had been hovering in the background. "Get suited up and meet me back in the investigation room." He picked up the jar and cradled it like a baby as he walked it back to its companions on the metal table.

Anyone who peered into the investigation room a few minutes later would have been forgiven for thinking that he stumbled onto a crime scene investigation. Three figures in white jumpsuits stooped over some strange object, studying it intently. The jar was about two feet high and had the circumference of a small wastepaper basket. It was topped with a lid, also made of clay. From experience, Emad knew that the lid would be sealed with pitch or some other adhesive substance. He also knew that just trying to pry the top off after a millennium, give or take, would result in it shattering into pieces.

Emad spent a few moments explaining the theory of removing the lids of ancient clay jars to the interns. From their wide-eyed looks, he could only surmise that they did not teach this kind of stuff in the archeology department at Cairo University anymore. "All well and good to be able to handle the latest technology but without the basics you're stuck," he said as he pulled a blunt chisel and a small wooden mallet towards him. For the next hour or so, only the 'tap tap tap' of the mallet could be heard. Leaning in closely Emad ever so gently nudged the bottom of the lid where it met the jar. The movements under his hands could be described as microscopic, but they were, nevertheless, occurring. Despite years of doing this kind of thing, he still inwardly marveled at the fact that he could soon be laying eyes on something that was probably placed in this jar more than ten centuries ago.

As he continued to observe the tiny movements of the lid, Emad reminded himself that the mark of a true professional in these circumstances was not to speed things up. Many a precious object had been destroyed because of undue haste when the goal was already in sight. So, he continued his soft, rhythmic, tapping until he was sure that he would be able to remove the lid by hand. As he did so, he inwardly beamed with pride at the fact that he was able to place a fully intact lid on the table.

"Flashlight, please," Emad held out his hand towards Abu Bakr. Like Hana, he was craning his neck to get a better view. Once he received the flashlight, Emad shone it into the body of the jar. It was, as was already determined by the x-ray, mostly empty except for something at the bottom. Emad was quite impressed with Mahmoud's judgment because it seemed that he was indeed looking at a piece of leather.

Before the art of papermaking made it to Egypt, most documents were written on papyrus, essentially the flattened-out insides of *Cyperus Papyrus,* which grows in abundance next to the Nile. The main problem with papyrus, from the perspective of ancient historians, is that it is not very durable. So, unless it is stored in near perfect conditions, documents written on it are bound to degenerate into illegibility over the course of a few centuries. When it was felt, therefore, that a document merited special care as far as its future preservation was concerned the ancients often shunned papyrus and opted for animal skin from which the hairs have been scraped, as the best alternative. Documents created using this process were known as parchments. As he stared down into the body of the jar, Emad realized that this was precisely what was in there, a small piece of parchment. Whoever created the jar, had a message that he or she wanted to resound throughout the centuries.

Reaching into the jar with a soft-tipped plastic tweezer, he gently pulled out the piece of parchment. "Get the camera ready," he said to Hana before placing the object on a plastic sheet that he had previously prepared for this moment. Against the white plastic sheet, it was easy to appreciate just how darkened with age the piece of parchment was. The writing on it was, however, clearly legible. As he waited for the parchment to be photographed, Emad's eyes were immediately drawn to the top section. Here, as clear as day, was the same image that appeared on the outside of the jar: A pair of market scales, very heavily weighted towards the left. Above it, the word 'Micah.'

As would be expected, the letters on the parchment were all in the Coptic alphabet. Although he knew that this would be the case, Emad was still disappointed that they had reached a dead-end for the day. It is one thing to figure out a few letters, but deciphering an entire page was entirely beyond his level of comfort with Coptic. As he wondered who he could rope in, on such short notice, to translate the words of the parchment, Emad's thoughts were suddenly interrupted by Hana: "Would you mind if I had a go, sir?" He quickly turned his head towards her with a look of slight irritation. Then it dawned on him that he knew almost nothing about her. Still, the clue was in her name, to which he should have paid more attention: 'Hana' is a common name among Coptic women.

Hana, who desperately tried not to be thought of as impertinent, immediately confirmed this. "I learned Coptic in Sunday School and later did an advanced course at the cathedral in Abasiya, sir." Ignoring her blushes, Emad smiled at her and stood aside. Hana leaned over the parchment with furrowed eyebrows. Finally, she looked up at Emad. "It is very strange," she said, "I can understand every individual word, but when they are put together, they do not make sense. It is almost as if it is a kind of riddle!"

"Let's hear it then," Emad said. The irony that someone who was both a woman and a Christian was at the center of the investigation at this very moment was not lost on him. Some of his colleagues may have blanched at allowing this, but Emad was happy to take expertise anywhere he could find it. Hana gave him another shy smile but seemed hesitant to begin reading for some reason. Finally, she cleared her throat, and started her translation:

In the blessed land
In the White Valley
From which many sought immortality
Where devotion was tested by sleep

At the place of the resurrection
She that walks will finally soar
The Saracens will be pulled apart
As the sons of Micah awaken

The Qibla of the Arabs
Will betray them
The Holy City of Islam
Shall be its downfall

If anything, Hana's blushes were even deeper after she finished reading. She searched out Emad's eyes, waiting for his rebuke of the ancient members of her community for their impertinence in making such statements against the followers of the prophet. "I'm sorry," she blurted out as if she herself was at fault. "*Maalesh*" (It's nothing), Emad said quickly. He could not help noticing the feeling of dread rising inside him. It seemed like he was haunted by the warfare of believers, even from the distant past.

He hid his unease behind a cheerful smile. "Thank you both," he said to the interns. "I think we've done quite enough for today. Please go and get ready for me to lock up". As they walked towards the changing rooms to take off their jumpsuits, Emad stared hard at the piece of parchment. His thoughts were interrupted by Abu Bakr, slamming the door to the men's room. It seemed that he did not share Emad's sentiment that the Coptic fighting-talk in the inscription meant 'Nothing.'

Emad could feel his heart racing inside his chest yet could not explain why. "Calm down," he thought, "It is just another find." Still, he did something he had never done before (and which was strictly against regulations). After a glance to make sure that he was alone, he took out his iPhone and snapped a few pictures of the parchment.

CHAPTER 9

Muhammad, Abu Bakr, Umar, Uthman, Ali.

Yusuf Abbas slowly recited these names in his mind. They represented the prophet of Islam and his four successors. O what bliss it must have been to be alive when they were! To be an eyewitness to the golden age of Islam. A time when the 'perfect example' and the *khalifs* (successors of the prophet) walked the earth. Yet, he believed that this golden age need not only be in the past. A new *khalif* arose, one who declared large parts of Iraq and Syria to be the new Khalifate dedicated to Allah.

"Then what am I still doing here?" Yusuf thought to himself. The modern-day *khalif* had made repeated calls for the 'Lions of Allah' as he called them to come and fight alongside the forces of the 'Islamic State.' If it were up to Yusuf, he would have been there many months ago. However, the Sheik and the Muslim Brotherhood had other ideas.

As might be expected with an organization that was forced to conduct its existence in the shadows, the Muslim Brotherhood developed some fascinating leadership structures over the years. A hallmark of this was the entrenchment of the ideal that leaders at each level of seniority would only have contact with their immediate superiors. In this way, the fallout from the capture of an individual member could be contained.

It was taken as a given that captivity would inevitably lead to torture to extract information about the organization. A favorite method of Mubarak's secret police was to file down the teeth of detainees until they were ready to cooperate. Under such circumstances, it would be logical to assume that at least some people would not be able to withstand the pressure and would blurt out everything they knew. Thus, the restriction of knowledge about the inner workings of the organization was an absolute necessity. This way, junior members of the Brotherhood would not be able to divulge damaging details about their superiors, even if they wanted to.

During his time with the Brotherhood, Yusuf had seen many superiors come and go as he rose through the ranks. These relationships were often fleeting, as it was strictly forbidden to make contact outside of Brotherhood activities. Once you were moved to a different area of operations, that also meant the end of a relationship. Then there was the fact that Brothers disappeared, sometimes literally so, into the not so fond embrace of the Egyptian justice system with alarming regularity.

Still, with most of his superiors, Yusuf was able to strike up something resembling friendship, to the point that he was on first-name basis with all of them, even if both sides knew that the name in question was a convenient lie. With the Sheik it was different. He was, and it seemed would remain, only 'The Sheik.' Yusuf understood the necessity behind this, but he did feel that some of the camaraderie that existed when he was a foot soldier of the Brotherhood was lost. Still, if this was the price to be paid for doing something great for Allah and his prophet, then it was a tiny one.

There was another thing that intrigued Yusuf about the Sheik, namely how he made it through the post-Morsi era unscathed. While the Brotherhood was in power under Morsi, it was, of course, only natural for senior Brotherhood operatives to emerge from the shadows to take up positions within the new administration. When Islamist rule was forcibly terminated by the will of the people and the military it was, therefore, the simplest thing possible for the secret police to spring into action and detain those who under Morsi's rule openly boasted of their Brotherhood connections.

It seemed that the Sheik was entirely unaffected by all of this. He had no profile under the Morsi government and was therefore not a target for arrest once it ended. Yusuf often wondered why this would have been the case. He was a talented and very senior leader. Why was he ignored? Could it be that the leaders of the Brotherhood kept some capable operatives in the background, as a kind of reserve force, for precisely the type of scenario that they were now enduring?

As far as Yusuf knew, the Sheik had never spent so much as a single night in prison, a rare distinction among Brotherhood operatives. Perhaps this had something to do with him being so deep undercover. With many members of the Brotherhood, there were some tell-tale signs of their commitment to a rigorous application of Islamic principles. The Sheik, however, believed that the cause also needed people who could hide their identity for a time. This would enable them to strike a devastating blow against the enemies of Islam when the right time came. So, if you saw the Sheik in the street, you could be forgiven for thinking that he belonged to the army of businesspeople who kept the wheels of the Egyptian economy turning. No bushy beard, calloused forehead or obsessive fingering of prayer beads for him. Instead, he looked like someone who would be totally at home in a Paris boardroom or on the trading floor of the Cairo Stock Exchange.

Some of Yusuf's compatriots occasionally grumbled about what they perceived to be the Sheik's lack of piety. But this usually lasted only for as long as it took for the Sheik to begin speaking. When he opened his mouth, it quickly became apparent that he was deeply conversant with the intricacies of Islamic theology and fully committed to the cause of establishing the caliphate right there in Egypt. The Sheik was particularly well-versed in the writings of Sayyid Qutb, the intellectual father of modern Brotherhood ideology. Qutb was executed in 1966 by the Nasser government who viewed him as a mortal enemy. He lives on in the minds of those, like the Sheik, who saw Islamic teachings as the foundation upon which to construct society.

Indeed, while listening to the Sheik, Yusuf often wondered at the incongruity of seeing someone apparently so westernized quoting long passages arguing for the necessity of jihad from Qutb's monumental 30 volume *'In the Shade of the Qur'an.'*

Given the necessity of laying low, his regular meetings with the Sheik had, of late, dwindled to the occasional hurried phone call. On this day he was traveling to see him for the first time in months. "Why now, after all this time?" he wondered. Something must be up.

As Yusuf stepped onto, Luxor Street, one of the main thoroughfares of his suburb of Imbaba, he felt a little twinge of pride that it was here in the north-western corner of Cairo that the Brotherhood scored one of its early successes. In 1992 some dedicated Brothers gained control over large parts of the suburb and proclaimed the 'Islamic Emirate of Imbaba.' It took 12,000 troops to put down the rebellion, and the majority of the instigators ended up dead or in prison. Their example acted as an inspiration to later generations of believers who saw that even the mighty Egyptian state could lose control in the face of those genuinely dedicated to Allah.

Almost three decades later, the effects of the uprising were still visible throughout the suburb, not least in the fact that there was a noticeably higher police presence here than in almost any other part of Cairo. Due to his tight finances, taking a taxi to his meeting with the Sheik was out of the question. So, Yusuf stuck out his hand to make the signal for Ramses Square, Cairo's central transport hub. Almost immediately, a *meekrobas* (microbus) pulled up next to him. He got in and handed his money to the guard. Once they got moving again, the guard, one of tens of thousands of teenage boys for whom this was his first job, hung out of the main passenger door to announce in a singsong voice where they were all heading. Pretty soon twenty people shared this tiny space. Hardly comfortable, but dirt cheap.

From his seat, at the window, Yusuf cast a wistful look at the city as it passed by. Cairo had every chance to once again become 'The Victorious' in the name of Islam. It had turned its back on this opportunity by spurning the Brotherhood. And for what? To lapse again into being the lapdog of Western imperialism? As they edged closer to Ramses Square with the traffic continuing to thicken into what seemed to be a knot that would never be untangled, his sense of anger mixed with desperation only heightened. It was here at the crossroads of Cairo, where so many road transport routes connect with the Cairo Metro and the central railway station, that many of his brothers made the ultimate sacrifice in attempting to keep the city and the country faithful to Islam.

In August 2013, after the pro-Brotherhood president, Mohammed Morsi had already been ousted, his supporters, many of them close friends of Yusuf, gathered in several Cairo squares and refused to leave. Yusuf winced again at the thought that he would have been there himself if it had not been for Maryam. This realization was mixed with both sadness and guilt. Sadness, because hundreds died, and thousands were imprisoned after the army moved in and perpetrated what became known as the Rabaa Massacre. Guilt, because he knew he should have been there, shoulder to shoulder with the other believers. He owed his life and his freedom, for what that may be worth, to his sister.

Yusuf's gloom deepened as the Al-Fath (*The Conquest*) mosque, which towers over Ramses Square, came into view. This mosque, boasting the tallest minaret in all of Cairo, celebrates the Islamic conquest of Egypt. With a bitter taste in his mouth, Yusuf reflected on the fact that from the perspective of the Brotherhood, this was where Islam itself was conquered.

After the Rabaa Massacre, a large group of Morsi supporters entered the mosque, which they turned into a field hospital, to care for the injured. Not even remotely respecting the sacred custom which forbids fighting in a mosque, soldiers stormed in and cleared its occupants out, thus effectively ending organized Brotherhood resistance to the military takeover. The fact that it was likely that at least some of the soldiers who snuffed out the flame of Islamic resistance inside the mosque could have been Coptic Christians (as Muslims and Copts serve side-by-side in the same military units) was enough to cause Yusuf something akin to physical pain. This was not how the world was supposed to be.

So, as he left the meekrobas Yusuf looked up at the impossibly tall minaret of the mosque and thought of what might have been. He also silently prayed to Allah that Islam would one day tower over every aspect of life in Egypt, just as this mosque towers over Ramses Square.

For someone with a fear of crowds, Ramses Square represents the ultimate hellish nightmare. It must surely rank as one of the busiest places on the planet. So overwhelming is the level of foot traffic that the solid marble steps of the overpass bridges have to be replaced regularly, as they get totally worn out by the millions of shoes treading on them every day. Yusuf, however, hardly noticed the crush of humanity as he approached the central railway station.

Since 1955 a giant 3,200-year-old statue of Pharaoh Ramses II had stood in front of the station, hence the name of the square. When it was found that the statue was decaying at an alarming rate due to the apocalyptic levels of air pollution around it, it had been decided to move it to Giza to be the centerpiece of the new 'Grand Egyptian Museum.'

Yusuf was glad that the statue was not there anymore. Like many other members of the Brotherhood, he was deeply ambivalent about the ancient past of Egypt. "Much better to leave idols in the past," he thought as he glanced back at the mosque. It represented the triumph of Islam over all the darkness that Ramses and other so-called gods stood for. Yusuf was sorry that the statue was only removed and not destroyed. If only they had more time. During Morsi's brief reign there were even serious calls from within Brotherhood ranks that he should use his presidential powers to do what Amr ibn al-As (the Islamic conqueror of Egypt) could not do and destroy the pyramids. Personally, Yusuf felt that their time would be better spent in building a new Islamic Egypt rather than in destroying ancient structures, but he was in favor of a total ban on visiting the pyramids. How could Muslim people make money from idolatry? Again, that was all in the past. The power of the Brotherhood to make that kind of decision was gone. But for how long?

As part of his early training in the ways of the Brotherhood, Yusuf learned some basic counter-surveillance techniques. Traveling through Ramses was part of this. If ever there was a place to lose yourself in the crowd, this was it. He did more than rely on the masses to grant himself anonymity, however. Heading to one of the overpasses he placed his body in a spot where he had a 360-degree view of his surroundings. Once he was confident that nobody was following him, he went into the station to visit a relic of a bygone age.

Under Nasser's Socialism of the 50s and 60s, it sometimes took as long as 15 years to get a phone line installed. In desperation many Cairenes turned to phone-shops where well connected, in more ways than one, entrepreneurs made banks of phones available (at a fee of course) to the public. With the coming of cell phone technology, most of these shops went the way of the dodo, but some like this one in Cairo's central railway station were still clinging to life. It was perfect for a situation where a cell phone might be more of a liability than a help.

Yusuf sat down at a phone whose keys closely resembled the well-worn marble steps that he had used to get there. After dialing the Sheik's number, there was the usual moment of rising panic as the phone rang. "Please tell me he hasn't been picked up by the police" Yusuf prayed before the Sheik's voice, exuding both confidence and authority, swept his dread away.

True to form, the Sheik was sticking to his doctrine of hiding in plain sight in setting up their rendezvous point. 'The Egyptian-American Society is just two blocks from where you are, meet me at the coffee shop next door in 15 minutes" he said, and with that, the call was over almost before it began.

"Not quite the belly of the beast but close enough to smell the sulfur," Yusuf thought as he saw the US flag swaying gently in the Cairo breeze in front of the American Society's offices. He walked past the entrance sporting posters depicting idealized images of American daily life. "All that happiness is just a charade," he mused, "No one can be truly happy without the message of Allah and his prophet. *Inshallah* (God willing) even the Americans will one day see that".

The coffee shop was a far cry from the kind of place that Yusuf typically frequented. All chrome, fancy machines and phrases in a language he assumed to be Italian. The Sheik, of course, looked right at home. He was for some reason mildly irritated by Yusuf's "Nescafe" reply when asked what kind of coffee he would like, but he quickly got down to business.

"This place is clean, a friend owns it," he said.
"So, you're not the only Brother orbiting close to the enemy?" Yusuf responded.

The Sheik allowed himself a quick smile, but he also seemed conscious that a meeting between two men who were so clearly from different rungs of the social ladder might attract attention, even there.

"I think you might like what you're about to hear!" he said. "We have given the matter much thought, and we think the time is right. The enemy dealt us a terrible blow, but even a wounded lion can give a bite that will never be forgotten."

Yusuf sat back in his seat with a swirl of emotions rising in him. He knew what was coming.

The Sheik looked straight at him: "I realize that many brothers are answering the call to go to Syria, but I want you to stay right here in Egypt. Get ready to leave your home at short notice. Wait for instructions. We are about to deploy you!"

CHAPTER 10

As Emad stepped onto the street outside the ministry's offices, he looked up at the Cairo Tower. One of the icons of the city's skyline, it was built in 1961 here on Gezira Island in the middle of the Nile. At more than 600 feet high it is by far the tallest structure in the city. Emad loved the fact that it was so very Egyptian, with its stylized lattice-like architecture modeled on the lotus, the ultimate symbol of Upper Egypt. He also could not help but smile every time he looked up at the tower. His smile had little to do with patriotism. Hilarity at the expense of Brotherhood prudishness was a bit closer to the mark. The tower had long been a bugbear of the religiously conservative part of society as they thought that it could induce sinful thoughts in Cairo's female population by reminding them of a part of the male anatomy.

"There's still so much work to do in dragging our people towards the 21st century", Emad mused, as he set off towards the river for the first leg of his journey home. Just then, his phone rang, it was Maryam. "You still okay for tomorrow?" she asked after some pleasantries. Emad's heart sank. He had been hoping to head back to the office to do some more work on the other clay jars. But he had promised that they would go and look at the apartment in Helwan, so that's what they would do. In common with most working Egyptians they both had Friday off, so it made sense that they would use this day for apartment hunting.

"Can we meet at Nasser Metro Station at 10?" Emad asked. They regularly traveled by metro from their respective suburbs of Imbaba and Shubra. Nasser Station is right in the heart of downtown Cairo, and this had been their rendezvous point for many years. "Yes, that's fine", Maryam said, with a note of hesitancy in her voice: "There's just one thing, Yusuf wants to come along."

Emad knew what was coming. Islamic law requires that women always be accompanied by a close male relative. He could only assume that Yusuf was tightening the screws on his sister even further. Letting her go to work was one thing. Staining 'family honor' by letting her go house hunting with someone she is not yet married to, quite another. He thought of telling Maryam that it was out of the question, but they do need somewhere to live sooner rather than later. He also knew that his refusal would give Yusuf more ammunition with which to undermine their relationship so that he could steer his sister in the direction of someone a little more serious about Islam. He sighed inwardly before saying, "That's fine, I'll see both of you at 10 am tomorrow then".

As Emad walked towards the Qasr el-Nil bridge, his spirit was lifted by the many 'party boats' on the river, each of them trying to outdo the rest with the decibel count of its sound system. In Cairo, Thursday evening was the start of the weekend and therefore the time to let your hair down. One of the best ways to avoid the accusing eyes of the super-devout had long been to take your party to the middle of the Nile. The party trade was frowned upon by the Morsi government, which had organized raids on several boats. The boats bounced back after his departure, and you would never believe from the level of pre-weekend celebration on the river that Cairo would come to a standstill with the prayers of the devout the very next day.

Emad stopped for a moment on the bridge to survey the scene. In addition to the mobile discos, many single sailed *feluccas* were also tacking back and forth across the river. Some of them were holding tourists, others Cairo families who merely wanted to get away from the crush of humanity that is their city, if only for a while. More likely than not, the tourists have heard the immortal words: "He who takes a sip from the Nile is bound to return to Egypt." Or should it be "Will never leave?" Emad mused. Drinking untreated water from the great river was not recommended.

When he finally reached his room after his usual evening routine, he pulled one of his textbooks on the history of Egypt from the shelf. Today's find made him think about the early interactions between the Coptic church and the Muslim invaders after the 7th-century Islamic conquest. The textbook was not much help. It merely spoke matter-of-factly of the 'Triumph of Islam' without going into too much detail. Yet, from an Islamic perspective, the 'triumph' was incomplete. Between 10-15% of the Egyptian population (depending on who you ask) identify as members of the Coptic (Egyptian) Orthodox Church. The Coptic church, with its millions of members, still form by far the largest Christian community in the Middle East.

"Of course, the percentage of Copts must have been substantially higher in the past," Emad mused, realizing that he had never given much thought to exactly how Islam gained the upper hand. It had always been presented in books, like the one open before him, as a historical inevitability that Islam would triumph. Given that assumption, the process through which it happened could be seen as rather unimportant. "Although, of course, this information would be rather helpful in the present circumstances," Emad thought, as he closed the book and got ready for bed.

The next morning, still barely awake, he began the long journey to Helwan.

Cairo's metro system was built in the 1980s with French investment and still betrays, albeit faintly, traces of France. French influence is evident in the train carriages, the little rectangular tickets reminiscent of the Paris metro and the commitment to turning some stations into artistic statements. This is nowhere more evident than in the central Cairo stations which all commemorate some heroic figures from Egypt's past. Nasser Station was, of course, named after Gamel Abdel Nasser, Egypt's post-revolutionary leader who took the country down a path to socialism in the 1950s and '60s. A vast mosaic of him dominates the platform wall. His left shoulder was Emad and Maryam's regular meeting spot. Emad was silently wondering what Nasser would have made of the fact that Cairo now plays host to the Middle Eastern headquarters of just about every capitalist behemoth you might care to mention, when he saw Yusuf and Maryam walking towards him.

Even from a distance, he could see that they had been arguing. He could guess why. '*Salaam Aleikum*' (Peace be with you), Yusuf said, taking care to use the proper Islamic greeting, instead of the more colloquial '*Saba al-Khair*' (Good Morning). Emad's guess as to why they were irritated with each other had been spot-on. The Cairo Metro has ladies-only carriages for women who want to observe the proper Islamic separation between the sexes. Yusuf was insisting that Maryam travel there. She usually would not mind as it is a great way to escape the harassment that can sometimes be part and parcel of traveling on Cairo's public transport system but given a choice she would rather be with her fiancé. They saw little enough of each other. Yusuf was adamant, however, so with an angry look in his direction she moved down the platform. Emad had learned long ago to stay out of their quarrels, but he soon wished he had not. Miryam's absence meant that he faced about an hour of appeals to be a better Muslim from his soon to be brother-in-law.

While Yusuf was offering some helpful hints on how to memorize large slabs of the Qur'an, Emad occupied himself by listing the names of the stations as they traveled south. He liked the fact that it was a bit like going backwards into Egyptian history. After Nasser, you pull into a station named after his successor, Anwar Sadat, assassinated in 1981 by a Brotherhood sympathizer as he was reviewing troops during a military parade. Next, you encounter a record of resistance to the British (Saad Zaghloul Station), the Islamic invasion of Egypt (Sayyeda Zeinab Station, named after the prophet's granddaughter) and even a nod to Egypt's pre-Islamic Coptic past (Mar Girgis, St. George, Station). The station list is right up to date. For many years there was a station named after former president Hosni Mubarak (overthrown in 2011 during the Arab Spring), but it was renamed for the 'martyrs' who died in ousting him (Al-Shohaada Station). So, if nothing else, it had to be admitted that (at least in the station names) the Cairo Metro is on the cutting edge.

At first, the stations were very close to each other. Then, journey times lengthened towards leafy Maadi, the haunt of expats and cashed-up locals across generations. These days the fact that the whole suburb was initially laid out as a model village by Jewish financiers is rarely mentioned. Yet, it is still hard to step into the neatly laid out grid of Maadi's streets, and not feel that you've somehow left the 'real' Egypt behind. Perhaps because of this, Maadi has been both a hotbed of resistance to foreign influence (Osama Bin Laden's right-hand man Dr. Aiman al Zahariwi grew up here) and a place where global ideas and trends are celebrated.

Emad hardly managed to stifle a chuckle as he observed Yusuf bristling as a group of giggling unveiled teenagers got into their carriage. Thankfully, he did not upbraid them for their 'un-Islamic' behavior there and then. Instead, he turned to Emad: "Where are their fathers and brothers? How can they allow this?" he spat. Not wishing to cause a scene, Emad merely shrugged his shoulders. This only increased Yusuf's irritation at not being backed up in what he regarded as a fundamental Islamic value. At least it had the benefit of sending him into a sulk which meant, to Emad's relief, that they spent the rest of the journey in silence.

It was in some ways entirely appropriate that they had started their journey at Nasser station. Helwan began life as a French-inspired, and funded, spa town: *Helwan les Bains*. However, all of its carefully cultivated gentility was swept away as part of Nasser's dream of establishing a uniquely Arab form of socialism. Part of this push was the creation of an Egyptian industrial sector. In lockstep with the Soviet Union and China, the emphasis was on heavy industry, and Helwan was the place to build it. Large parts of the upmarket riverside village had been swallowed up by steelworks, cement factories, and automotive industries. With jobs came people. New apartment buildings, often very shoddily constructed, marched into the desert at a staggering rate. Industrialization also made Helwan one of the most polluted spots on the African continent.

Nowadays, with most of the jobs long gone, Helwan was in many ways typical of how bad post-industrial decay can be. The upshot is that it is one of the few places in the greater Cairo area where young couples still have a chance of obtaining a moderately priced apartment (even if this comes at the cost of a marathon commute). As the train trundled towards Helwan Central station, Emad grimaced at the prospect of perhaps having to do this every day. He got off the train with a sigh: "The things we do for love."

As soon as the three of them stepped outside the station, they were caught up in a crush of humanity, all seemingly heading in the same direction. Emad did not have to wonder long about what was going on: "Good," Yusuf said, "We are just in time for Friday prayers." Emad's heart sank. Most of the five daily prayers are over relatively quickly because people pray and leave. Fridays are different, however. A sermon always accompanies the Friday midday prayer. A sermon that can, in Emad's experience, go on for far too long. He had hopes of getting this trip over as soon as possible so that he could go home and read up a bit on Coptic responses to the Islamic invasion. He was about to suggest that they skip the mosque and go straight to the apartment but quickly realized that this would give Yusuf one more reason to think that his soon-to-be brother-in-law was a less than properly observant Muslim. He reluctantly began to follow in the footsteps of the Helwan faithful as they headed to the Al-Farouk mosque, a block or so from the station.

Yusuf also quickened his pace but suddenly checked himself. He turned to his sister "Where will you pray?" he asked. Some Egyptian mosques have screened-off sections for women, but many do not. If this one did not have a women's section, Maryam would have to find a quiet spot to pray on her own. Maryam turned her face away: "I'm not praying," she said. Her response finally broke Yusuf's patience with all the laxity he observed around him so far that morning: "Why not!?", he snapped at her. Maryam stared at him for a moment, her cheeks reddening: "It's the wrong time of the month" she whispered. For a moment it looked like someone punched Yusuf in the stomach. In his anger, he had deeply embarrassed his sister. Of course, she could not pray in this state. Even the prophet himself said that there were more women than men in hell because they are 'deficient in religion.' The reason for this deficiency? They cannot pray while menstruating as they are considered to be ritually impure.

Yusuf would rather not have known that Maryam was having her period, but he chose not to apologize. In his embarrassment, he merely said "Fine!" and quickened his pace towards the mosque. "I'll explore a bit, call me when you're done," Maryam said softly, as she turned away from the ever-thickening mosque traffic.

While most Muslim men will pray at their local mosque whenever possible, some mosques get higher numbers on a Friday. These so-called 'Friday mosques' are often the largest in a locality and are more likely to host better preachers, which may be one reason why they are heavily patronized. They also usually have access to robust amplification systems from which they broadcast their Friday sermons. Few visitors to Cairo will ever be able to forget the resulting cacophony, a wall of sound that sweeps across the city early Friday afternoons.

Yusuf and Emad started their visit to the mosque by going through the purification ritual that precedes Islamic prayer. Emad relished the refreshing impact of the water splashing over his face, arms, and legs. As they took their place inside the mosque, he reflected on how quickly he was able to slip into 'autopilot.' Even though he was not very regular in his prayers, it would be tough to undo the impact of having done this, hundreds, if not thousands, of times during his boyhood in Upper Egypt. As he touched his forehead to the ground, it felt like slipping on a wellworn, but still comfortable jacket. He also noticed, from the corner of his eye, that Yusuf prayed in a very different way from himself. While his own movements could be described as languid, even somewhat lazy, Yusuf prayed with an intensity that seemed to strain every muscle. He pressed his forehead into the carpet with such force that it almost looked painful. "Not long before he gets his own 'prayer scar'" Emad thought. "Maybe this is exactly what he is aiming at," he chuckled inwardly.

At the end of the prayer ritual, the worshippers sat down on the carpet to listen to the sermon. In the earliest years of Islam, the prophet would often deliver his speeches standing on a short flight of steps. He liked this arrangement so much that he had a slave build some steps from wood that he could use as a kind of mobile pulpit. Mosque pulpits still follow this example. "Except," Emad smiled to himself as the preacher mounted the platform "Muhammad did not have a microphone." Perhaps it was for the best. At least back then most mosque sermons did not begin with a tapping sound and "Is this thing on?"

Emad was prepared to doze off a bit during the sermon, but as the imam got into his stride, he suddenly pricked up his ears because the chosen topic seemed to be history, his 'home turf' as it were. "Allah blessed us richly," the imam intoned, "all of the events that we base our faith on is firmly grounded in history. We can point to specific dates and places where different parts of the Qur'an were revealed. Even our prayers, a few moments ago, were directed at a place steeped in history. Other religions have myths and legends. We have the solid witness of history." Emad noted the enthusiastic nods of those around him and was even inclined to nod in unison. He may not be the most observant Muslim, but he had always appreciated this aspect of his faith. The sermon also reminded him that he would shortly, in chasing up the meaning of the strange poem in the Coptic clay jar, have to dig a little deeper into the history of the coming of Islam to his own country.

Leaving the mosque, Emad called Maryam. She had found the spot from where buses to the eastern part of the city departed. "Meet me in front of the Mikail Church on Gafaar Basha Street," she said. As they walked to the church, Emad could, once more, sense a rising irritation in Yusuf. As the large cross on top of the church loomed into view, the dam burst. "Sons of dogs, cross worshippers, may Allah curse them!" he spat. His rant was overheard by a middle-aged Coptic man exiting the church. He quickly looked away and crossed to the other side of the street. His reaction was completely understandable. Not too long-ago, Brotherhood aligned shooters stormed into the Mar Mina church, a few blocks away, and killed nine worshippers.

Emad had bitten his tongue far too often during this trip. He thought of Hana, his intern, and of many other Coptic friends and acquaintances. Were they "Sons and daughters of dogs?" He fixed his gaze on Yusuf and slowly recited the phrase with which each chapter of the Qur'an begins *"Bismillah ar Rahman ar Rahim"* (In the Name of Allah the Merciful and Compassionate) as a means of reminding Yusuf of the values he believed should be at the heart of Islam.

He should have known better than to try and play 'Qur'an ping-pong' with someone as devout as Yusuf. With a contemptuous look on his face, he immediately responded with a verse from the only chapter in the Qur'an, Sura 9, that does not begin with the 'In the Name of Allah. The Merciful and Compassionate' formula:

> *"Fight those who do not believe in Allah or in the Last Day and who do not consider unlawful what Allah and His Messenger have made unlawful and who do not adopt the religion of truth from those who were given the Scripture - [fight] until they give the poll tax willingly while they are humbled."*

After the reciting this, Yusuf said: "Allah's mercy is only for the believers, never forget that." Just at that moment, a microbus pulled up with the guard shouting the number 15 at the top of his voice. It was their signal, as they were heading to 15 May City, a suburb of Helwan.

Every few years some high government official looks at the chaos, congestion, and gridlock of Cairo and decides that the best solution would be to corral people into planned cities. 15 May City was such a place. Its name comes from the abortive attempt by the Egyptian army to invade Israel in 1948 to forestall its declaration of independence. As this attempt was unsuccessful the date is seen as a time of mourning, and perhaps as a spur to try again. The mournful aspect was reflected in the suburb. 'New cities' do not have an excellent track record in Egypt. It turns out that people still prefer Cairo with its erratic but lively heartbeat. In contrast, a carefully planned community in the middle of nowhere, away from friends and family, will always be a hard sell. So, it is very often the case that 'new cities' become refuges for the desperate or fail to fill up with people.

As they pulled into 15 May City Emad grimaced inwardly. Hastily constructed, and seemingly never since maintained, apartment buildings stretched in every direction. Some buildings were clearly beyond repair and unoccupied. Strangest of all, small children were grazing sheep in the once neatly laid out parks, now reduced to pastures. The overwhelming sense was one of decay and isolation. For people used to living cheek by jowl with millions of other Cairenes, this must seem like being in a permanent state of limbo. "And we might be moving here soon," he realized with a sigh. Once they got to the building containing the apartment they came to view, they had to step over the family of the *Bawab* (doorman) to gain entry.

Almost every apartment building in Egypt has a doorman who occupies a room near the entrance and controls access to the building, in exchange for whatever tips the residents are willing to pass on to him. They act as porters, guards and, often, as moral enforcers by taking careful note of who comes into the building with whom. "Life must truly have knocked you about if you end up as a doorman in a place like this," Emad thought.

A moment later the *bawab* appeared with the key. He was dressed in a flowing *galabia*, a kind of full-length robe favored by many men from Upper Egypt, and he spoke with the accent of the south. So far, so stereotypical. Most Egyptian *bawabs* hail from Upper Egypt. His next action confirmed that he was not new to this profession. As he handed over the key to the apartment they came to inspect, he held on to it instead of immediately releasing it. Emad sighed and slipped him a note. Not a very promising start at all.

The building's lift had long since given up the ghost, so they had to haul themselves up to the 6th floor via a dingy and dimly lit staircase. Naked light bulbs and dangling wires provided mute testimony to the fact that the light fittings had been 'liberated.' Once inside the apartment, it became clear why it was so reasonably priced. "Needs a bit of work," said Emad optimistically. Maryam tried to put on a brave face and half-whispered: "I suppose we have to start somewhere". Yusuf, confronted with the reality that he was not even remotely close getting married let alone to checking out apartments, no matter how dilapidated, went to the window to stare out across the desert.

They said very little in the microbus on the way back to the Metro Station. Like the others, Emad was deep in thought. Earlier that day, in the mosque, the Imam referred to the period before the coming of Islam as the 'Time of *Jahiliyah*' (Ignorance). He was suddenly keenly aware that just across the Nile from where they were, the pharaohs had built their ancient capital: Memphis. It was confronting to recall the splendor and sophistication of their great city alongside the desolation and decay around them. "Have we made that much progress?" he thought.

As they stepped onto the platform at the Metro station, it happened. A tall, friendly man spotted Yusuf, and his face lit up in delighted recognition. Yusuf saw him coming and tried desperately to swerve away, but with the station wall on the one side and the tracks on the other, there was nowhere to go. He knew Ashraf from their early years in the Brotherhood. Ashraf was deeply in love with the idea of glorious exploits for Allah, not so much with the discipline of keeping such feats to himself for the good of the organization. After being overheard in a coffee shop, boasting that the Brotherhood relies on his 'special surveillance skills,' he was given a severe beating and kicked out of the organization. Before Ashraf's expulsion Yusuf had been in a Brotherhood cell with him. He had always been uneasy with his 'loose lips' so he sincerely hoped that it would be last he would see of him.

As they neared each other, Yusuf braced himself, knowing that anything could happen. In the end, it was possibly even worse than he expected. With Emad and Maryam looking on, Ashraf embraced Yusuf and bellowed,

"Abdullah! What are you doing down here? Are you on an operation? So good to see a fellow soldier of Allah!"

"Wrong person," Yusuf growled and forcefully shoved him aside. The look of hurt and shock on the Ashraf's face instantly gave way to an admiring smile.

"I see," he nodded sagely, "Secret Operation. I'll be off then."

For a moment the three of them stood in stunned silence, watching Ashraf's head bobbing away into the crowd.

The silence did not last. With panic rising inside her like a high-pressure fountain, Maryam turned on Yusuf. The questions poured out,

"Why did that man call you Abdullah? 'An operation' to do what? 'Soldier? Why did he call you that? Who are you fighting?"

Emad looked on bemusedly. It seemed the trip back was going to feel even longer than he anticipated.

CHAPTER 11

Walking out of Mar Girgis (St. George) metro station, Magdy Botros reflected, as he almost always did when ending his morning commute, on how entering this part of the city, known as Coptic Cairo, was like a journey into the past. A past in which his people, the Copts, proud descendants of the pharaohs and their subjects, had controlled the destiny of Egypt. A short distance to the north was the mosque of Amr ibn Al-As, at the center of Islamic Fustat, but the heart of this part of the old city beat to a different drum.

Right in front of him was the ruins of the Babylon Fortress, built when Egypt was the breadbasket of the Roman Empire. It stood at the very point that marked the boundary between Upper and Lower Egypt. As such, it controlled, for centuries, trade and military movements on the Nile. It also played a starring role in the defense of Egypt during the Islamic invasion, as its occupants withstood the onslaughts of Amr ibn Al-As for almost a year before finally succumbing. In the end, however, it was not military conquest that destroyed the fortress. It was the Nile itself. It changed course, thus leaving the great fortress that towered over it high and dry.

Next to the fortress is the splendid Church of St. George, the seat of a Greek Orthodox Bishop who bears the evocative title of 'Bishop of Babylon.' Then on to Magdy's workplace: The Coptic Museum. These three buildings barely scratch the surface of what's on offer in this part of Cairo. It has the largest concentration of ancient churches anywhere in Egypt, all of them powerfully testifying to a long-distant past when the Copts were masters of their own destiny.

Magdy worked as a document curator at the museum and enjoyed his job immensely as it allowed him to indulge his passion for preserving the history of his people and get paid for it to boot. The Coptic Museum holds the world's most important collection of Coptic documents and artifacts. As such, it stands as a proud testament to the vibrant Christian culture that had flourished in Egypt before the coming of Islam. However, Magdy often thought that its presence here in Coptic Cairo was both a blessing and a curse. A blessing because it provides a dedicated space where Egypt's Christian heritage is celebrated. A curse in the sense that it meant that this heritage could be conveniently ignored in other places.

The sprawling Egyptian Museum on Tahrir Square in the center of Cairo is, of course, on the must-see list of any visitor to the city because of its vast collection of items from ancient Egypt, including the famous death mask of Tutankhamun. Visitors will see almost nothing about the history of the Copts inside the cavernous halls of the Egyptian Museum, however. In 1939 all the Christian antiquities hosted there were transferred to the Coptic Museum. On one level this was a wonderful gift. However, it also means that international tourists, most of whom are unlikely ever to set foot in the Coptic Museum, could be forgiven for thinking that there are only two parts to the history of Egypt: Pharaonic and Islamic.

Still, Magdy was grateful that they could exhibit aspects of the history of the Copts at all. Under the Morsi government, there was serious talk of closing the museum down, ostensibly because it could be seen as a 'target.' However, everyone knew that the real objective was silencing a powerful voice against the narrative that Egypt existed in a time of profound backwardness and ignorance before the coming of Islam.

Thankfully, the overthrow of the Brotherhood government put an end to this threat, but the challenge of running the museum on a fraction of what is lavished on its much larger cousin in downtown Cairo remains.

As he walked across the peaceful courtyard, one of the few open spaces in this densely developed part of the city, Magdy's eyes lingered for a moment on the cross above the main entrance to the museum. By stepping inside, visitors can immerse themselves in the story of those who sought to follow the message of the cross, here on the banks of the Nile. With pride rising in him he imagined the stunning collection behind that door, which even includes possibly the first painting of Christ and his disciples. The Egyptian church, his church, was founded in the 1st century by St Mark. It had been here for a long time and, if the Almighty permits, would be for a long time still. Even if the presence of the church continued to be accompanied by many tears, as had been the case since Islam arrived in their homeland.

There was no time to enter the central part of the museum to, once again, linger among objects he knew so well. He was already late for a Skype meeting with a potential donor in the US. Private donations, especially from overseas Copts, is one of the ways in which the museum manages to run a world-class facility despite receiving only a pittance from the Egyptian government.

As he entered the administration wing, he scanned what he came to think of as the 'organized chaos' of the reception area. The domain of Mrs. Salib, mistress of all she surveyed. "You're late for your Skype call," she said before handing him a few envelopes and a message slip. After this, his morning took on a life of its own; the Skype conversation, emails and a team meeting. It was lunchtime before he finally had the chance to look at the message slip that Mrs. Salib gave him. It read: *"Call Hana Tadros. She says it is very urgent"*, and then the number.

Magdy stared at the paper for a moment. It was a classically Coptic name (just like his own in fact), but he could not for the life of him place its owner. He pulled the phone closer and dialed the number. A young woman answered. After Magdy identified himself a long silence ensued. Then, as if she was afraid of hanging up before her courage deserted her, it all poured out: "My name is Hana Tadros, I'm a graduate student in archeology at Cairo University. I'm currently doing an internship at the Ministry for Antiquities, and I urgently need to come and see you!"

Magdy's heart sank. For many students from a Coptic background working at the museum is a cherished dream, but they did not have any openings. "How do they keep getting my number?" he wondered. He was about to tactfully get rid of Hana when her next sentence stopped him cold. "I could lose everything I've worked for by telling you this, but I think I've seen evidence of the existence of the Micah Order!"

Magdy's mind was instantly tipped into a swirl of emotions: Incredulity, excitement, fear, bafflement all vying for domination. To buy time he slowly said,

> "Say that again please."
> Hana, having found her courage, told him about assisting Emad in opening the clay jar and what they found inside.
> "You're sure that it is ancient and not someone's sick idea of a joke?" he asked.
> "Absolutely, it was unearthed in a layer that can be dated to before the 1168 fire."

Excitement slowly began to elbow aside all the other contenders for Magdy's attention.

"I think you'd better come and see me. Can you come straightaway?" Magdy asked.

Hana was obviously very anxious to get this off her chest because she immediately agreed. As he waited for her to arrive, the tug of war inside Magdy's mind resumed: "Surely this cannot be? I'm being gullible and wasting my time. Still, she said that it was undeniably ancient?"

Involuntarily his mind reached back to when he was a boy, growing up in Heliopolis, not too far from where he was sitting. The area has a vibrant Coptic community life. On the fringes of this community urban legends abounded, none more potent than the myth of the 'Micah Order.' Details varied, but Coptic kids would tell stories, in hushed tones, of a shadowy group formed in the wake of the Islamic invasion. The members of this 'order,' so it was claimed, waged a relentless underground insurgency against their new rulers. It was hounded out of existence during a brutal campaign of suppression that included the immediate beheading of all family members of men suspected of being members. And yet, and this is where the urban legends came into their own, rumors persisted that the Micah Order survived by going ever deeper underground. Tales claiming to cite 'evidence' of the order's survival, told long after midnight by wide-eyed teenage boys, had long been a staple of Coptic church camps. The fact that such camps were often held in the eerie silence of desert monasteries only added to the delicious sense of mystery tinged with hope.

As he waited for Hana to arrive, a sense of dread gradually replaced Magdy's excitement. Key to the survival of the Copts for so many centuries was their acceptance of their status as *dhimmis*. Dhimmitude refers to the system, supposedly going back to the time of Muhammad, under which Christians and Jews ('People of the Book' according to the Qur'an) were allowed to carry on their community life within an Islamic society. This 'privilege' was granted on the understanding that dhimmis should always understand that they are inferior to Muslims or that they *'should feel themselves subdued'* as the Qur'an has it. This sense of subjection was reinforced through the payment of a special tax, the *jizya* (also commanded in the Qur'an) and a host of petty humiliations. These ranged from unique clothes that dhimmis were supposed to wear to restrictions on worship and church building. Of these, it is the last that most grate modern Copts. Previous Egyptian governments had sometimes required official permission for even the smallest repairs to churches. Consent was often withheld for years, as a means of reminding the Copts of precisely who held the whip-hand.

It is but a small step from thinking that your Christian neighbor is an inferior dhimmi to supporting government measures (or even vigilante action) when you believe that they 'forgot their place.' For many Copts, the Morsi years were a rude shock as they saw Muslim people whom they regarded as friends agitating for ever-stronger measures against them. "We are only now beginning to heal from the hatred," Magdy thought. "The last thing we need is for something to inflame community tensions...", he glanced at the note with Hana's number, "like a discovery proving the existence of an ancient Coptic order dedicated to wiping Islam from the face of the earth perhaps?" He allowed himself a half-smile. At least he could still chuckle at his own jokes.

 Magdy put the message slip in his pocket and stepped out into the courtyard to meet Hana. He could see her walking towards the museum from the metro station. In these days of religious conservatism, the fact that a woman is unveiled is often a dead giveaway that she is a Copt. Also, Copts pride themselves on the fact that they are the descendants of the original inhabitants of Egypt. Looking at Hana as she approached him Magdy could not help but seeing something of the past in her. She could easily have been one of the thousands of pre-Islamic Egyptians whose eerily lifelike images were painted on their funerary urns, thousands of which were discovered in mausoleums at the oasis of Fayoum. Olive skin, wavy black hair, penetrating brown eyes.

On a whim, he decided to greet her in Coptic and not in Arabic. Most Copts do not speak more than a few words of their ancient language, but surely as a graduate student, she'd be different? So, turning towards Hana, he shouted, *"Ash Pe Pe-Reety?"* (How are you) across the courtyard. Hana was initially stunned by this but was able to get out a quick *'Nane shepehmot'* (Fine thanks) through her blushes. Magdy was immensely pleased by this. On some impossible to articulate level this exchange of greetings in a supposedly dead language, spoken by generations of their ancestors, confirmed a bond between them, even though they were total strangers to each other.

After ordering some tea from the kitchen, Magdy ushered Hana into his office. Following the usual pleasantries and working out how many relations they have in common, a perennial Coptic pastime, he addressed the question that brought them together:

> "Do you think this discovery is for real?"
> "I believe it is," she said
> "It was found just a stone's throw from here in old Fustat, underneath the mosque of Amr ibn Al-As. My boss oversaw the process of removing the jars from there."

Hana continued by recounting the process of opening the jar and her involvement in it.

Magdy was suddenly struck by a thought: "The archeologist. I assume he is a Muslim? Does he suspect anything?" Hana bit her lip: "When I saw the inscription on the jar, I had to do everything in my power to keep a poker face. I think I succeeded. He let me translate the Coptic words and did not ask many more questions."

"What will he do when he finds out what impact this discovery could have? Do you think he will let the find 'disappear' in the interest of not inflaming tensions?" Hana thought for a moment: "I think he is genuinely interested in history for history's sake. He's a professional and very skilled. I believe he even studied overseas for a few years. So, he will probably let the investigation run its course, wherever it may lead."

Magdy was mildly reassured by this and hopefully asked his next question: "Please tell me you took a photo?" Hana blushed: "I would have if I could, but it is strictly against the rules, and I was never alone with it." Magdy expected this answer but struggled to hide his disappointment. Hana continued: "After we were done, he sent us to get dressed, and I was alone in the ladies' room. I immediately wrote down the inscription from the parchment. I think I have it word perfect." She handed Magdy a piece of paper with a smile: "Who knew all those years of rote memorization in Coptic class at the cathedral would come in handy someday?"

Magdy read the words aloud:

In the blessed land
In the White Valley
From which many sought immortality
Where devotion was tested by sleep

At the place of the resurrection
She that walks will finally soar
The Saracens will be pulled apart
As the sons of Micah awaken

The Qibla of the Arabs
Will betray them
The Holy City of Islam
Shall be its downfall

"Do you have any idea what this means?", he asked Hana. She sadly shrugged her shoulders, "I was hoping *you* might be able to help!"

"Touché," Magdy thought before reassuring her that he would do his best to decipher it. Perhaps it would help to know a bit about the jar itself. So, he asked Hana to describe it in detail. When she recounted the image of a scale weighted to the left Magdy suddenly stopped, his head spinning: "You're sure the scale was weighted to the left and not merely badly drawn?" Hana looked somewhat surprised: "Definitely," she responded, "The bowl on the left looked like it would touch the ground if placed on a level surface." By now Magdy had jumped to his feet: "Follow me!" he said briskly.

Hana struggled to keep up as Magdy left the building, and the museum compound, to turn into a narrow passageway. She barely had time to take in the many souvenir shops, catering both to Copts and the occasional tourist, that line the narrow alley. You could get anything Coptic here, from bargain-basement knick-knacks to exquisitely executed icons that sell for thousands of dollars. Magdy paid little attention to the hustle and bustle around him and pushed determinedly on, with Hana desperately trying to keep up. They finally turned a corner, coming face-to-face with one of the crowning glories of Coptic Cairo: The Hanging Church.

Officially known as the 'Virgin Mary Coptic Orthodox Church', the church was built in the 3rd century, right above the main gate of the Roman Babylon Fortress. This meant that those coming in from the Nile could see the church 'hanging' above the entrance to the fortress that guarded the meeting place of Upper and Lower Egypt. Visitors to the fort would have walked right below the nave of the church as they entered the most important expression of Roman power on the Nile. It sent a clear and unambiguous message to the Coptic faithful. Yes, the Romans may be in political control here, but Christ was King even over earthly powers as they came and went.

The ground level in this part of Cairo is about 12 feet higher than it would have been in Roman times, so the visual impact of the church suspended over the fortress entrance has been lost. However, it is still an imposing symbol of the enduring power of the Coptic church to withstand the winds of fortune. In the aftermath of the Islamic conquest, the 'Hanging Church' for a while became the focus of the tenacious survival of the Copts. Coptic Popes (officially Patriarchs of Alexandria, 140 miles to the north) based themselves here for several centuries to better represent their community at the seat of Arab power.

The role of the church as a sanctuary against those who would seek to destroy the faithful was perhaps best exemplified in its high vaulted ceilings, made from sturdy wooden beams. Generations of Copts have taken comfort in the thought that this resembles the inside of the ark that carried Noah and his family to safety, despite everything that a 40-day storm could throw at them.

It was into this sanctuary that Magdy and Hana now stepped. Despite Magdy's evident hurry, they slowed right down. For a devout Copt, this was a space somewhere between heaven and earth. Not only was it a place for the faithful to gather, but it also housed the icons of more than a hundred saints who victoriously fought the fight in previous generations. Small groups of devotees gathered in front of different icons, and the air was thick with the smell of incense and candle smoke. They both made a slight bow in the direction of the altar. It was hidden from view by a tall wooden screen, known as the *iconostasis* that reached almost to the roof. The *iconostasis* serves the dual function of housing the most important icons in the church and shielding the altar from the congregation. In its center, there were two red velvet curtains, behind which only the priest and servers could enter when the Eucharist was celebrated.

Gazing down at them from the top of the screen were colorful and almost life-sized images of saints, silent reminders that theirs is an ancient faith. Closer to the ground, the screen was decorated with intricate geometric patterns carved into the wood and inlaid with mother-of-pearl. As he approached the *iconostasis,* Magdy reflected on how grateful he was that this magnificent work of art was not in a museum but that it is the liturgical focus of a vibrant community of faith. When he reached it, he got down on his knees. Hana initially thought that it was rather odd that he came here in such a hurry to pray, until he beckoned her to come closer. "Come and look at this," he said. As she focused in on the area where Magdy was pointing Hana did a double-take.

Where the *iconostasis* met the ground, the artisans placed a skirting to help keep the structure in place. The decorative motif on the skirting deviated significantly from the geometric patterns above it. On it were a series of scales. All of them heavily weighted to the left.

Hana immediately understood why Magdy was in such a hurry to get here. "I can't tell you how many times I've puzzled over these," he said, "When you look at the patterns above, the focus is on perfection. Down here we have scales that are out-of-balance in the most literal sense possible."

This could not be a coincidence. The jar that Hana had worked on confirmed that much at least. The 'weighted scales' in the Hanging Church were not produced by a bored craftsman who ran out of ideas. Whoever carved them had a message to deliver. But what?

Magdy stepped back from the *iconostasis* and sat down in one of the pews, deep in thought. He looked up at Hana: "Please describe the jar again. In as much detail as you can."

Hana cleared her throat: "Well, it is a high-quality jar. Must have been glazed at some stage. The scales are right in the middle of the jar, with the word 'Micah' above it."

She was about to go on to list the dimensions of the jar when Magdy suddenly jumped up: "Micah that must be it!"

Hana shot him a perplexed look: "What do you mean?"

Magdy did not answer but was already halfway to the main entrance of the church. Next to the door was a collection of bibles and hymn books. He picked up a bible. By now, Hana knew better than to think that this was an act of sudden devotion. Magdy leafed through the book until he found what he was looking for. He then shut the world out and began to read. Hana shifted her weight from leg to leg, not quite sure what the correct protocol was in this kind of situation.

After several minutes she could see Magdy clench his jaw and lean closer to the sacred text. A few seconds later, he handed the book to her with a look of triumph in his eyes. "Here it is! Look." Magdy's finger rested on the Book of Micah, chapter six:

> *"Can I forget any longer the treasures of wickedness in the house of the wicked, and the scant measure that is accursed? Shall I acquit the man with wicked scales and with a bag of deceitful weights?"*

Hana gulped, this was confirmation, as if any was needed. The Order of Micah existed and took its name and its imagery from this passage. Magdy, who was as white as a sheet, echoed her thoughts. He waved his hand towards the scales at the bottom of the iconostasis: "There are still many questions to be answered, but we can rest assured that the scales are more than an artistic motif. It is a symbol of resistance!"

CHAPTER 12

To say that things were tense in the Abbas household barely scratched the surface of the suspicion, anger, and fear that had taken over the lives of those inside their small apartment at the heart of Imbaba. Ever since Yusuf's fateful encounter with Ashraf at the Helwan metro station, Maryam had been trying to get him to tell her exactly what was going on. More than that, she positively required a total renunciation of violence from him. 'Soldier' indeed! She could still just about abide his support for the Brotherhood when this meant working on slum projects and as a government engineer. This, however, was a bridge too far. He could get them all imprisoned.

So, in many ways, things came full circle. Yusuf turned from being Maryam's persecutor to being the target of her furious attentions. What made matters worse from Yusuf's perspective was that she had the full support of their parents. They had seen far too many promising young men choose the path of *jihad,* only to end up blown to pieces or tossed into a shallow grave somewhere in Syria. Up to this point Yusuf had been ducking and weaving, always falling back on the line that Ashraf was 'a loony,' but he was failing to convince anyone.

Yusuf was genuinely torn by his family's reaction. Despite the harsh words they often exchanged, he truly cared for his sister and wanted the best for her. If only she could see that the 'best' was scrupulous adherence to Allah's laws. Yes, this may look like a prison to those looking in from the outside, but as a believer, he had tasted something of the joy of knowing that you are squarely in the middle of God's will for your life. If only she could experience this for herself. Sadly, Yusuf thought: "The joy destined for the devout, *'those who prevent vice and promote virtue'* according to the Qur'an, is unlikely to be her lot with Emad.

Yusuf had hardened in his opposition to their proposed marriage since the day they spent together in Helwan. He was ever more convinced that Emad was part of what was wrong with Islam in Egypt. There were far too many people professing to be believers but showing no evidence of this in their words and actions. He clenched his jaws. Getting Maryam to break off the engagement would undoubtedly be a stain on family honor, but allowing her to go into a life that would pull her ever further from Allah must surely be worse? He decided, therefore, even though the odds were stacked against him, to attempt to bring Maryam back from the brink.

When he made his first attempt, the house was quiet. Their parents had gone to bed, but Yusuf knew Maryam would be awake. In happier times they had often joked about belonging to the 'Night Owl Society.' Yusuf got up and knocked on Maryam's door. When she opened the door, he softly, almost gently, said: "We need to talk." Maryam looked at him quizzically. When she realized that it was Yusuf at the door, she was ready to resume her lectures, but there was something in his tone that surprised and unsettled her. She resolved to hear him out: "Talk away," she said.

Yusuf cleared his throat: "What I'm about to say will probably not come as a surprise after what that idiot Ashraf did at Helwan station but, here goes: I am more than merely a political supporter of the Brotherhood. I have, for years, been part of a corps of Brotherhood members who were being prepared for military action. I'm a trained operative if you will."

Maryam looked at him, her breathing coming thick and fast. Of course, she would have had to be beyond gullible not to suspect this after the Helwan exchange but hearing him say it out loud was like a kick in the guts. Her brother, the gentle, smart boy she grew up with, may have blood on his hands. She blurted out the first question that popped into her head: "Have you ever killed anyone?" Yusuf looked at her with a mixture of relief and embarrassment: "Honestly, no. Up to now, the higher-ups felt that I would be more valuable as an engineer than as a soldier." Maryam felt a wave of relief wash over her. *"Alhamdulilah* (Praise God), so this is all in the past then?" she exclaimed.

Yusuf knew that his next sentence would break her heart, but he had to say it anyway. "I'm afraid it has only begun" he half-whispered. Maryam looked up at him, tears welling up in her eyes. She stepped away and sat down on the edge of her bed, her back turned to him. Yusuf walked over to her: "You have to understand, those on the side of Allah are more needed than ever to strive in His cause with their wealth and their bodies?" Maryam looked up plaintively. She recognized this phrase from the Qur'an but had never thought that she would hear it used as a manifesto that would tear their family apart.

Yusuf sat down next to her. In muted tones, he calmly, almost apologetically, explained to her that desperate times call for desperate measures. So much of the front-line fighting strength of the Brotherhood were either dead or rotting in prison, that his moment had come. He did not know where he would go or what would be required of him, but his meeting with the Sheik made it clear to him that he would be an (unemployed) engineer no more. Instead, he was destined to be one of those marching in the front ranks to see the achievement of Allah's purposes.

Looking back later, Yusuf realized just how bold, if not foolhardy, his next words were. Still, he had to try. "When I am deployed I want you to come with me!" Her stunned silence at least allowed him to finish another sentence or two: "This is the most glorious thing that any follower of our *deen* (faith) can ever do! Besides, there is bound to be some *mujahid* who would love to have you as his wife!"

Maryam's eyes narrowed, and she all but spat out her next words: "I am engaged to a wonderful man and will not be spending my last few days on earth looking after some toy soldier, thank you! Have you completely lost your mind? Have you forgotten about the fact that the prophet commanded men like you to look after their families? How will you do that if you're rotting in a grave or sitting in a stinking prison cell, your best years slipping away like sand in an hourglass?"

Her last question stung Yusuf more than he cared to admit. One of the principal obligations of a Muslim man was to make sure that his family was cared for and that its honor was protected. His father would not be around forever, and he realized that he would soon have to step into the shoes of the head of the family. Something that would be rather hard to do if he was away fighting somewhere. Still, only the spiritually deaf could ignore the fact that Allah made it clear in His word that there is one obligation that trumps all others: To strive with everything for the victory of Islam.

Instead of answering Maryam he merely closed his eyes and softly recited the holy text to let it speak for itself:

> *"O you who have believed, what is the matter with you that, when you are told to go forth in the cause of Allah, you adhere heavily to the earth? Are you satisfied with the life of this world rather than the Hereafter? But what is the enjoyment of worldly life compared to the Hereafter except very little."*

Maryam looked up at him, her tears now flowing freely: "It is not a matter of 'enjoyment' Yusuf! I know that we've had our disagreements, but you're still my brother and I love you. If you go through with this, you are very likely to plunge those who care most for you into mourning. And for what? The approval of some Brotherhood head-honcho for whom you're just another piece on the chessboard?" Yusuf shook his head sadly: "You will never understand, Allah calls me to do this!"

Maryam's grief finally morphed into righteous anger: "You go ahead and follow your 'calling.' Just remember as you chase your dreams of glory that there are people back here who may reap a bitter harvest because of your rashness."

There was nothing more to be said. With her words still ringing in his ears, Yusuf turned around and walked to his room. It would have been so good if he could be sent away, as he is sure other Brothers were, with the encouragement of his people. Yet, even if that was absent, he knew what he had to do, and it was sometimes necessary to be strengthened in your resolve. He opened his laptop, and after connecting to a VPN to make sure that he could not be traced, typed in the address for *Dabiq* the online magazine produced by ISIS. He was just about to start reading an article describing life in Raqa, capital of the ISIS caliphate, when his cell phone pinged into action.

Yusuf reached over. It looked like an overseas number. Yet, the sender was right here in Egypt. How did he do that? The message on the screen said: "*The Mosque of Sayyeda Zeinab. Tomorrow Night. 8 pm*" He smiled to himself: "The Sheik always has a few surprises up his sleeve. Fancy meeting there of all places." Still, he was very thankful that things were moving ahead. He was not sure how much more of the tension at home he would be able to endure.

The next evening found Yusuf making his way through the crowds outside Sayyeda Zeinab's mosque. Perhaps the Sheik had some didactic purpose in bringing him there. He would generally avoid this place like the plague, and he could feel his pulse quickening and irritation rising in him the moment he stepped off the metro. For an orthodox Muslim, the area outside the mosque could just as well be an object lesson in what happens when Islam is unmoored from the Qur'an and the pure example of the prophet. Sure, those who frequent this area see themselves as proud *Sufis*, those who follow a mystical approach to Islam, but to Yusuf, they were little better than unbelievers.

The Zeinab who gave her name to the mosque was the granddaughter of the prophet, who had died in Cairo. The mosque was supposed to remind the pious of her life and faith, but far too many people go way beyond merely remembering. Over the centuries Zeinab's legacy had been embroidered and embellished to the point that many ordinary Cairenes came to regard her as a great saint. Yusuf shuddered at the thought that some people would even pray to her to ask her to intercede on their behalf with Allah. This was not a minority concern. The *mawlid* (festival) of Zeinab is probably Cairo's largest annual festival. A wall of silence is mostly maintained to conceal all the goings-on at this festival, but it is fair to say that piety is not high on the agenda of many attendees. It is, for example, common knowledge that the festival represents by far the best time of the year for Cairo's ladies of the night. "How perverse that vice flourishes right next to a house of prayer!", Yusuf scoffed.

That night was just an ordinary evening, with the festival a few months away, but the courtyard area outside the mosque was still a sea of humanity. Tables of merchandise looked like they were floating in the circles of light created by hissing gas lamps. Some tables contained fruit, vegetables or items of clothing. Others, however, were piled high with books detailing the lives of Islamic saints and their 'areas of specialization.' These were supposedly very beneficial in helping devotees to know whom to address in their prayers. Even worse, were the charms and amulets that could supposedly channel Zeinab's power into any situation or illness.

As he observed all this, Yusuf felt like he was going to be physically sick. Within Islam, the greatest possible sin is *shirk*, or the act of associating anything or anyone with God.

"God has no partners," Yusuf muttered this phrase like a mantra as he passed yet another huckster loudly promising the saint's blessing if only people would buy tiny bottles of oil, that he claimed was stored overnight next to her grave. "How could these people so blatantly ignore Allah's clear words?", Yusuf mumbled in exasperation.

Shirk cannot be allowed to flourish! In those places where the devout gained control in recent years, they struck a mighty blow against it by destroying the graves of so-called saints and by clapping chains on the fraudsters who made their money by leading the faithful astray. Yusuf did not doubt that the Morsi government would eventually have acted against Zeinab's *mawlid* (festival) and against all the naked expressions of *shirk* that he saw around him. Time had run out. Egypt was, once again, under the control of a government that looked the other way when faced with such blatant deviations from the teachings of the Qur'an and the example of the prophet.

As he approached the mosque, Yusuf's path was blocked by a woman wearing a blue *abaya* and a pink headscarf. A small crowd was gathered around her as her body swayed this way and that. Then he saw it; she was swaying because she was playing with a snake, guiding it to sail across her face and torso, all the while invoking the name of Zeinab. This was too much! Yusuf elbowed his way into the group around her and spat at her feet: "Shame on you, filthy *kufar* (unbeliever)!" She must have heard it all before as she merely laughed and called out: "Welcome *habibi* (my dear)! Tell me, for how long have you been playing God?" Many other mocking voices joined her smirking laugh as Yusuf headed into the mosque. "Just you wait," he thought in his anger "True religion will yet be established in Egypt!"

Entering the mosque was like swimming free from a whirlpool. Zeinab's shrine was off to the right in a dedicated space and not part of the main prayer hall. The clinging and cloying of shirk was left behind, and an utterly familiar scene presented itself: Thick carpets, chandeliers, a staircase pulpit and a niche in the wall facing Mecca. At the front, some people were praying, but most devotees had finished their prayers, so the mosque was pleasantly empty. Here and there, little groups of men sat chatting quietly. Yusuf breathed a sigh of relief and started looking for the Sheik. It was a little strange that he would want to meet in such a public place, but his record in avoiding the tender mercies of the *mukhabarat* (secret police) was at least somewhat reassuring.

Over to Yusuf's left a group of *fellaheen* (Upper Egyptian peasants), all *galabias* and turbans, were having an animated discussion. Yusuf looked at them with a strange mix of irritation and admiration. These 'sons of the soil' had lived and toiled next to the Nile for generations and formed the backbone of Egypt, 'the true Egyptians.' Still, their rustic ways and credulity mean that they became somewhat dangerous once they left their farms and paddies behind. Cairo is far too full of ex-country bumpkins who brought their small-town superstitions and shirk with them. The goings-on outside the mosque was a case in point. Many native Cairenes would see devotion to Zeinab as more than a little unsophisticated and uncouth. But for many of the fellaheen the city's festivals represent the very things they dreamed of when they were still slaving away on their farms: Excitement, color, wild-eyed emotion and just a whiff of scandal.

Yusuf was mortified when one of the fellaheen got up and walked towards him with outstretched arms. The man greeted him in a thick Upper Egyptian accent and with the fellaheen's trademark mixture of deference and mockery: "*Ya Bey!* (O Governor!) Your presence with us is like the morning star in a dark sky!" Yusuf was mentally prepared to send him on his way without acceding to the request for a contribution to some worthy, though no-doubt un-Islamic, cause that was sure to follow, when he noticed that this particular *fellah* was wearing a pair of expensive rimless glasses.

The Sheik embraced Yusuf with a glint in his eye, his rough turban brushing against his cheek. "Follow me!" he whispered.

As they walked out of the mosque, the Sheik turned to Yusuf: "I brought you here for a reason, as you probably guessed. Look around you! These people are devoted; they are passionate!" He waved his hand across a scene that could just as well have been conceived to give an orthodox Muslim an immediate headache. As the Sheik stepped around a wild-eyed young man claiming to have pieces of Zeinab's coffin for sale, he continued: "They believe. They want the best for their country. It is just that their beliefs are misdirected. I think our mistake when we were in government was not to take them with us. Yes, we lectured and harangued the fellaheen to let go of shirk. But we did not show them an alternative. If we are to succeed this time, we must get them to flock to our standard!"

Yusuf struggled to keep up, both with the Sheik's words and his pace, as they crossed a traffic-clogged street towards a row of restaurants. Not for the first time this evening Yusuf had to shake his head at how blatantly the teachings of the prophet were flouted. Many tables, even tables occupied by people who were obviously Muslim, sported bright green bottles of 'Stella Lager.' Yusuf winced at the logos on the bottles, proudly proclaiming this to be *Authentic Egyptian Lager Beer.* That a Muslim country should have its own 'authentic beer,' given the Qur'an's clear stance on alcohol, was almost too much for him to bear. He held his nerve. He certainly did not want to make a scene while trailing the Sheik.

A few moments later, Yusuf spotted the sheik's flowing galabia as it disappeared into a narrow side street. He rushed to catch up and stepped into a nondescript alley. It was like thousands of others in Cairo: part shopping mall, part social space, and part workshop. This particular alley seemed to specialize in vehicle repairs, and they had to duck and weave their way through engines, tires and goodness knew what else. Cairo's trades people are notorious for regarding the sidewalks as essential parts of their workshops, and this narrow street was a case in point.

Halfway down the alley, the Sheik stepped into one of the workshops. The scene that greeted them could have been anywhere on the planet. It was dominated by cars in various stages of disassembly and engines hanging from hoists. A five-year-old calendar provided local color, still featuring a haughty Hosni Mubarak. As they went deeper towards the back, the scene began to change. A burly guard stood impassively next to some heavy shutters at the end of the room. Upon seeing the Sheik, he gave the tiniest of nods and pressed a button to raise a shutter. This revealed a boardroom that would not have been out of place in one of the high-rises that crowd the Nile not far from there.

The Sheik was very much at home in this space. As the shutters closed behind them, he went over to a fridge, took out two bottles of water and placed one before Yusuf. He sat down at the end of the table and looked intently at Yusuf before speaking. When he finally spoke, Yusuf was somewhat stunned by the question: "What was Amr Ibn al-As' greatest mistake while conquering Egypt?" Yusuf was floundering a bit as he struggled to come up with an answer. He was accustomed to thinking of the great Islamic conqueror in the most respectful of terms. A sentiment clearly, and surprisingly, not shared by the Sheik.

"He left a cancer in the heart of Egypt," the Sheik finally said. "Did you notice those bottles of beer," he asked rhetorically. Who could miss it? The Sheik went on: "Why does Egypt produce beer? Why do we have liquor stores? You know the answer! Because the Christians are not forbidden these things." Yusuf was very familiar with this dilemma. The pious explanation for why alcohol is so freely available in Egypt was that it was not for Muslims at all, but for the Coptic minority. Yet, when you look at production numbers, it becomes clear that either every single Copt must be a hopeless alcoholic many times over, or that much of the accursed stuff was disappearing down Muslim throats.

"The corrupting influence of alcohol is a perfect metaphor," the Sheik was on a roll, the theme very close to his heart. "I believe we would still have been in power if it were not for the fact that at least 10% of the population is permanently immune to our message due to being non-Muslims. Also, the Copts were in the frontline of the counter-revolution and missed no opportunity to undermine our international reputation through their overseas networks!"

The implication of his words was utterly shocking but clear. The Sheik believed that an Islamic Egypt should be genuinely that: An Egypt made up solely out of Muslims.

As if to confirm this conviction, the Sheik picked up a remote. A television at the far side of the room flickered into life. Immediately a familiar scene greeted them. Two lines of men walking along a deserted beach. One line dressed in orange jumpsuits. The other all in black. A caption identified the men in orange as *Followers of the Cross. Members of the Hostile Egyptian Church.* Yusuf had seen this video so often that he could recite the words and recount the events almost perfectly. After denouncing the 'Crusaders', the leader of the group in black declared: "The sea you've hidden Sheikh Osama bin Laden's body in, we swear to Allah we will mix it with your blood." A few moments later twenty beheaded corpses lay on the beach. The men, Coptic 'guest workers' from Upper Egypt, all worked in the Libyan town of Sirte where they were captured.

The death of those Egyptian Christians, in February 2015, on a Libyan beach, provoked several days of national mourning. This was followed by Egyptian airstrikes on ISIS positions in Libya and a flowering of nationalism, with even Muslim leaders repeatedly stating that it was an attack on 'all of Egypt,' not just the Copts. The Coptic Church eventually declared all those who died to be saints and martyrs and dedicated a cathedral to them in Minya (the Upper Egyptian city most of them were from). Yusuf was, however, sure that the courage of the Copts was not the main message that the Sheik wished him to take from the video.

"What will get the fellaheen on our side, Yusuf?" he asked. "I'll tell you what. Many of them are desperate for more land. The Copts have plenty of land. If they were not here anymore...," he let the sentence trail off.

Eventually he continued: "What will take care of many temptations and deal with the core of resistance to our revolution? Again, the removal of the Copts. Our brothers in ISIS could clearly see that they were a danger in Libya. Why can't we see it here in Egypt?"

Yusuf scanned the Sheik's face to see if he was being serious: "Was he advocating the removal of as much as 10% of the Egyptian population?" The look of grim determination on his face suggested that this was precisely what he meant. Yusuf found an objection forming in his mind: "What about the *dhimma* (pact of protection)? The Qur'an tells us that we are supposed to let them live as 'People of the Book' as long as they pay the *jizya* and accept a state of subjugation."

When the Sheik finally spoke, it was clear from his thoughtful and measured tone that it was not the first time that he had considered this question. "Yes, Christians and Jews can indeed live under the protection of the *ummah* (Muslim community) but only if they accept their subjugation. The Copts are not doing that! They continue to declare that they are the 'true Egyptians.' Also, their constant campaigns under Morsi to undermine our government by using their international contacts mark them out as a hostile force." Yusuf thought about this for a moment, on one level, what the Sheik is saying was making a great deal of sense. However, it did steer dangerously close to ignoring an explicit command given in sacred scripture.

Almost as if he was anticipating Yusuf's objection the Sheik leaned in a bit closer and produced his trump card: "Can you remember what the Prophet said about the People of the Book in his *Last Will and Testament?*" he asked. Yusuf had to think hard for a moment, but then it struck him, "He said that the Arabian Peninsula should be cleansed of Jews and Christians!"

The Sheik shot Yusuf a triumphant look. "Can't you see?" he asked. "Even Muhammad, *Peace Be Upon Him*, believed that there are some circumstances under which the protection offered by the *dhimma* contract becomes null and void. In the case of Arabia after his death, he feared that the presence of the People of the Book would dilute the faith of the Muslims. So, for the sake of the establishment of true faith, he made sure that his community lived in circumstances where there was not even a hint of *shirk*. Is this not the need of the hour here in Egypt? Is it not the case that our people are in much more danger of falling into idolatry, with Christians egging them on, than the companions of the Prophet ever were?"

Yusuf could not help but agree. A simple walk across the courtyard outside the Sayyeda Zeinab mosque would confirm the truth of what the Sheikh just said.

The Sheik continued: "So I want you to know Yusuf, that you are not being deployed to engage in some pointless martyrdom operation. You are stepping up to become part of what will long be remembered as one of the most glorious campaigns ever waged by the *Mujahideen!*"

The Sheik leaned forward, "You will wage war against the People of the Cross. You will help us drive them from this land."

CHAPTER 13

'*The Qibla of the Arabs will betray them!*' Emad could not quite work out why, but it was this particular phrase from the piece of parchment that he kept turning over in his mind. "What a strange statement. How can one be betrayed by the direction in which you are praying (*qibla*)?" he wondered. He continued to think of these words as he walked to work on the next Monday morning.

Around him, Gezira Island was shaking itself free from its morning grogginess. Rickety white taxis were buzzing across the 15th of May bridge, hoping for some early fares. Fruit and vegetable sellers were setting off on their morning routes. Each one was melodically calling out the name of the product they were selling. They were joined by the rhythmic clanging produced by the cymbals of an enterprising *erk sous* seller. This licorice drink is sold from huge glass containers slung across the backs of the vendors. The sound of their little cymbals is as much part of Cairo as the pyramids.

Through all of this flowed the Nile. Patiently heading into the Delta, and from there into the Mediterranean. These days the Nile flowed at a steady pace and level. The final taming of the river was achieved with the Soviet-funded completion of the Aswan High Dam in 1970. Emad was very aware that his relationship with the river was very different from that of his ancestors. For him, the river was 'just there.' Earlier generations of Egyptians watched the Nile like hawks, as their fortunes were intimately bound up with it. Every year the river would burst its banks, depositing water and fertile silt across the Nile Valley like a great benefactor. This process made agriculture, and indeed life, possible. Egypt is the gift of the Nile. Except, that the gift did not always materialize. On, Roda, the next island down from Gezira, just across the river from old Fustat a unique building was constructed to measure the level of the river between July and November. This 'Nilometer,' now merely a relic of a vanished past, had marks that indicated whether the next year would be one of famine, feast or flood. If the river was too low, harvests would be terrible. If too high, there would be a destructive flood. If just enough water, soil and silt were pushed across the Egyptian plains, the people would eat well and be content. No wonder that stories abounded, of dark sacrifices, even human ones, being made at the Nilometer to ensure that the people of Fustat and Qahira would have bountiful years.

As he gazed out across the river, Emad could not help but wonder about the lives of those who placed the clay jar under the mosque of Amr ibn Al-As. They would have been part of a teeming city, made up of many cultures and languages. The Arab conquerors initially probably seemed like just one more addition. Except, the Arabs did not come to be part of the melting pot but rather to dominate.

Later in the day, Emad would have to give an initial report to his immediate superior about the significance of the find. He would also be expected to make a recommendation about whether further investigations would be merited. He needed to get some reading done about the Old City before then. Fortunately, it was not that hard to conjure up an image of life in old Fustat. The source of this knowledge came from an unlikely direction. The intimate picture that can be constructed of life in Medieval Cairo is thanks not to Muslims or Christians, but Jews.

Given current political sensitivities, the Ministry for Antiquities tends not to emphasize the role of the Jewish people in the history of Egypt. It is, however, a fact that Jews had been living in the area now occupied by Cairo from long before the coming of Islam. The Jewish presence in the city, furthermore, only effectively came to an end when Jewish people were made to feel decidedly unwelcome after the establishment of the State of Israel in 1948, and especially, after the disastrous (for the Arabs) Six-Day War of 1967.

A key focus of Jewish life in Fustat was the synagogue of Ben Ezra, almost on the doorstep of the Hanging Church. The Jewish people of Cairo believed that this synagogue was built next to the spot where pharaoh's daughter pulled baby Moses from the Nile. It was, therefore, a place of extraordinary sanctity. Still, this is not the main thing for which Ben Ezra is famous. The synagogue included a *genizah* (storeroom) in an attic, and it was here where, for almost a millennium, the members of the community deposited unwanted paper. Having such a space was necessary because Jewish law prohibited the careless discarding of paper which might contain the name of Yahweh. Most Jewish communities would, therefore, bury unwanted paper. Often close to the grave of a respected scholar. The Ben Ezra synagogue was quite some distance from the nearest Jewish cemetery, however, so all unwanted paper was thrown into the *genizah*.

The genizah of the Ben Ezra synagogue would eventually contain a staggering number of individual pieces of writing. Some just fragments, others whole books. The randomness of it all was entirely baffling. A 15th-century marriage contract may have spent centuries next to a letter written by the greatest of all Jewish philosophers Moses Maimonides, who died in Fustat in 1204. The 400,000 or so documents found in the *genizah*, in 1897, enabled scholars to draw an incredibly detailed picture of life in medieval Cairo.

The portrait of Fustat that emerges from the genizah documents is of a vibrant society linked through trade, pilgrimage, and scholarship with the four corners of the world. Perhaps one of the most significant fault lines within this community was the gradual repositioning of the society of Fustat away from its orientation towards the Mediterranean in the direction Arabia and the religion of the prophet. If pre-Islamic citizens of Roman Egypt had any occasion to direct their gaze across the Red Sea, it would have been to laugh at the backwardness of the residents of Central Arabia. Many would also probably have suppressed a few chuckles at the foolhardiness of some Arabs in conducting trade across the burning deserts of Arabia when a perfectly good sea route lay within easy reach.

It must have been something of a shock when the Arabs arrived with a message that proclaimed that their region, the object of Roman and Egyptian scorn, was home to the most important city on the entire planet. Mecca, situated in the middle of an empty desert, so the Arabs told the no-doubt incredulous cosmopolitan citizens of Egypt, was the 'mother of all cities.'

It was more than civic pride and disdain towards the wild beliefs of upstart provincials that caused many Egyptians to sniff at the boasts of the Arabs. The claims that they were making were not merely political but also decidedly religious. By the time the Arabs came along, Egypt viewed itself as a proud bastion of Christian orthodoxy. It was here that St. Mark planted one of the very first churches in the world, where St. Athanasius of Alexandria struggled heroically for the faith against those who would pervert it and where St. Anthony founded the very first monasteries of Christendom. Accepting what the Arab conquerors said about Mecca and its prophet would mean repudiating this glorious heritage. This was something that many of Egypt's Christians were patently not ready to do.

Most Christians and Jews tried to keep their heads down and survive as best as they could. If they did try to stem the Arab tide, it was mostly through preaching and teaching, but were these the only options? As he closed the book on old Fustat that he was reading, Emad wondered aloud: "Could it be that some Christians believed that active resistance was the best course of action? Did I stumble across a record of that resistance?"

Whatever the actual importance of the clay jar, Emad knew that he would have his work cut out to convince his superiors to devote significant resources to investigating it further. The first reason was financial. The ministry was a major recipient of government cash, but this could not be said to come without strings attached. Its work of research and preservation was supposed to produce a significant return on investment in the form of increased tourist arrivals. Tourism was, after all, consistently among the top foreign currency earners for Egypt.

Most visitors to Egypt have an excellent idea of what they want to see: Pharaohs, temples, pyramids, and mummies. To put it bluntly, Pharaonic Egypt is what fills planes. Coptic Egypt? Not so much. In fact, not at all. Many Westerners would probably not even be aware that Egypt has a rich Christian history and that it is still home to a vibrant Christian community that can be counted in the millions. So, research money for Coptic studies comes mainly from donations by overseas Copts to the Coptic Museum, with the ministry very much taking a backseat.

The second reason for the official lack of interest in Coptic artifacts is the fact that successive Egyptian governments have always found it somewhat problematic to emphasize Egypt's Christian heritage. Any reminder that the coming of Islam had forcibly displaced Coptic Christianity could perhaps inflame community tensions. It also served as a direct challenge to the idea that the arrival of Islam somehow rescued Egypt from ignorance and backwardness. It was, therefore, regarded as a safe and convenient option to 'quarantine' Coptic history in the Coptic Museum, mostly out of sight of those within Egypt's Muslim community who might otherwise object to what they see as a celebration of the achievements of a vanquished foe.

So, while Emad had a real sense that he had stumbled across something very significant, he still despaired of convincing anyone at the ministry to devote any time, money, or energy to further investigations. As he left his office and headed up the stairs for a meeting with the ministry's Director of Exploration, he was prepared to argue his case vigorously, but he was also ready to be disappointed.

Stepping into the office of Dr. Tariq Awad was a bit like entering an Egyptological wonderland, albeit a very disorganized and jumbled one. Dr. Awad had spent many years on digs and was proud of the fact that he learned his archeological skills, not primarily through academic study, but through getting his hands dirty. Emad had immense respect for his achievements. Several display cases at the Egyptian Museum were filled with objects that were excavated by Dr. Awad at Deir el-Medina, near the Valley of the Kings. He could spend hours regaling listeners with stories from the lives of the workers who built the splendid tombs that made the Valley of the Kings perhaps the most magnificent necropolis on earth.

Deir el-Medina, was a high-security workers village in pharaonic times. Its occupants were tomb-workers, sworn to absolute secrecy. They nevertheless left copious written records, and these had always been a focus of Dr. Awad's career. Many objects and documents associated with the village were strewn across the room. Emad could not help wondering how this aligned with the ministry's security protocols, but he also realized that one of Egypt's most celebrated archaeologists could probably get away with having a personal stash of antiquities on which to work.

As he entered the office, Emad could hardly see Dr. Awad's head above the pile of books and papers on his desk. Dr. Awad greeted him with a warm smile. He genuinely liked Emad and wanted to see more native Egyptian archaeologists succeed in a field that had for so long been dominated by foreigners. As a result, he had been following and promoting Emad's career with great interest. "Come in my friend, take a seat!" As soon as Emad sat down, Dr. Awad launched into an entertaining account of how the villagers of Deir el-Medina organized the first recorded strike in world history. He chuckled at how these lowly workers held all the cards. They knew the secret locations of some of the most richly endowed tombs in the world and used this as the ultimate bargaining chip. That caused even the pharaohs, semi-divine as they were, to cave in to the worker's demands. No telling what would happen to them in the afterlife if they did not! Dr. Awad was still smiling at how the willingness to go toe-to-toe with those with delusions of grandeur was still very much part of the Egyptian psyche, when he remembered that this was not a social visit.

Dr. Awad pulled himself up in his chair and, as he did, Emad thought that he saw a distressed look flash across his face. "Now, that jar" Dr. Awad sighed. Emad was mentally preparing himself to be told that there was no scope for him to devote time and resources to studying the jar, so Dr. Awad's next sentence came as quite a shock: "I want you to make it your exclusive focus for the next couple of weeks!" A host of questions rushed through Emad's head, but in the end, it was the most basic one that he blurted out: "Why?"

He almost immediately regretted asking, as he saw that it caused significant discomfort to his friend and mentor. Dr. Awad made all the right noises about the ministry having to follow all leads. Emad could see, however, that his boss' heart was not in it. His explanation was accompanied by far too much shifting in his seat and refusing to look Emad in the eye.

There was something else going on, but what? Dr. Awad was not slow in supplying the answer, he sighed and said, "Might as well be honest with you Emad, some very influential people would like to see this investigated further. I would rather you were doing useful things, but there are times when it is tough to say no." Emad's mind raced. Which of the ministry's contacts would be interested in Coptic clay jars to such an extent that they wanted the investigation expedited? Also, how on earth did they get to know about its existence?

Dr. Awad almost immediately provided a clue to the last question: "I want you to offer your intern Abu Bakr a part-time paid position to help you in the investigation." So, it was Abu Bakr, who was so deeply upset by the words on the parchment, who had gone against regulations and let word of the find get out to some influential outsiders. This was more than enough to get him terminated; instead he was being made a regular part of the investigation. This was beyond strange. Emad barely managed to keep up with all the interns passing through the ministry, even those assigned to him. Why would Dr. Awad not only know the name of one of his current interns but also order Emad to offer him a job? He was about to vehemently protest when a stern look from Dr. Awad made him think better of it.

In the end, he decided to at least ask who the shadowy 'they' were. This way, he would have some idea of the agendas at play. Dr. Awad gave him a sad look, acknowledging without words that it was not always possible to do their work without outside interference, "To be precise it is not a 'they' it is a 'him'. A 'him', that can make life impossible for us if we do not cooperate. He said he would be in touch." With a tiny nod, Dr. Awad indicated that their interview was over. As Emad walked back to his office, he found it impossible to make sense of what just happened.

"Please let this not be anything to do with illicit antiquities trading," he repeated to himself. The looting of Egypt's treasures over the centuries was like an open wound for the Egyptian archeological community. The Rosetta Stone in the British Museum, the massive Ramses II obelisk from the temple at Thebes on the Place de la Concord in Paris, countless mummies gracing small museums across the American midwest. The list goes on and on. Objects that, by rights, should be in the Egyptian Museum, had been carted off to enrich other cities and countries. "But who would want a simple clay jar with an obscure inscription?" Emad mused. "Besides, Dr. Awad had a reputation as a tireless and fearless campaigner against the illegal trade in antiquities. He would never become involved in the under-the-table sale of anything. So that can't be it."

Emad did not have to wait too long for the next piece of the puzzle to fall into place. As he sat down in front of his computer, his phone rang. A voice speaking in very formal Arabic greeted him: "Dr. Almasry. My name is Shafiq Ramadan. I am very interested in the clay jar on which you are working. Would you be able to come and see me at the Nile Hilton at 4 o'clock?" Emad could not help thinking that, polite as it was, this was not a request, but an order.

I'll be there," he replied.
"I am very grateful. May Allah bless your efforts and increase your fame", came the elegant response.

Emad sat back in his seat, at least he now had a name. He opened Google and typed in 'Shafiq Ramadan.' The results flashed into view: A fading pop star, a football player with Al-Ahly, a former governor of Minya province. None of these seemed to be promising. Then he saw it on Page 6 of the search results: A link to the website of the Arab League with a profile of its Director for External Affairs, Mr. Shafiq Ramadan. It had to be him. He was dressed in a Western suit, rimless glasses, clearly well-heeled and educated. Even the location made sense. The headquarters of the Arab League is right next to the Nile Hilton. "So, what would a senior Arab League official, with a distinctly Muslim name, want to do with a Coptic clay jar?" Emad wondered.

The Arab League was founded in 1945 and today has twenty-two member states. Its purpose was to keep peace and foster cooperation between the Arab nations. Its record in this area is sketchy as the only thing that most Arab countries seem to agree on is their opposition to Israel. Still, it is a matter of great pride for many Egyptians that the 'Arab UN' maintains its headquarters right there in the most populous city in the Arab world. As he passed the Arab League Building, Emad took in the scene before him. The building sits on Cairo's grand square, known as 'Tahrir' (Liberation). This square had been thrust into prominence in 2011 when it acted as ground-zero for the revolution that toppled Egypt's strongman leader Hosni Mubarak. However, even before it entered international consciousness, Tahrir Square had long served as the beating heart of Cairo. Before Egyptian independence, it hosted barracks for the British Army and Cairo's Anglican cathedral. These had been torn down to make space for the massive square, the Arab League headquarters and Cairo's first Western chain hotel, the Hilton.

Next to the Hilton stands one of Cairo's most celebrated landmarks, the Egyptian Museum. Its dome and neoclassical architecture boldly make the statement that this should be reckoned among the greatest museums in the world. And why not? It housed perhaps the most significant collection of antiquities on the planet. At the other end of the square is the *Mogamma*, the largest government office block in Egypt, built in brutalist 1950's concrete. Most Egyptians will probably at some stage of their lives enter through its doors to apply for ID papers or to get some government documents stamped. Many feel that the classical phrase 'Abandon all hope, ye who enter here' might as well be over the door, especially if you are visiting the dreaded Ministry of the Interior.

The buildings surrounding Tahrir Square marked it out as a place of power and influence, but it is at night that the square comes into its own. Its flashing neon lights, including a massive illuminated glass of Coca Cola, are iconic symbols of Cairo and have appeared in countless Egyptian movies.

By the time Emad was walking towards the Hilton, dodging crowds of people as they emerged from the metro station under the square, the Tahrir lights were still some hours from being lit. Tour buses were disgorging groups of tired tourists, back from the pyramids or one of the other sights of Cairo. It was easy to scoff at so many people feeling very special after having had the same experience as millions before them. Yet, Emad knew better than most how utterly essential tourists were for the economic survival of his country.

Entering the Nile Hilton was like stepping into another world, as well as another age. It is fair to say that Cairo's first Hilton (built in the 1950's) was beginning to show its age. In fact, it was slated to close and come back to life as a Ritz-Carlton, once again making a pitch for being the place to be seen for the A-listers of the Arab world.

As Emad walked through the metal detectors, a stark reminder that in Egypt tourists have sometimes been targets, the old-fashioned hospitality of a few decades ago, although fraying at the edges, came alive. The tea room was all silver service, dainty sandwiches, and starched napkins. Next to it, three levels of shops were entirely focused on overseas tourists, down to the tinned Muzak piped through the air-conditioned hallways. The lower level unsuccessfully tried to simulate an authentic Arabic *souk* (market), presumably aimed at those who were not quite brave enough to visit the real thing, just a short taxi ride away.

Emad was conscious of being sized up by a head-waiter in a tuxedo that had seen a few too many dry cleans. Before he could state his business, he was waved over by a man in an immaculate suit ending a call on his cell phone. Mr. Ramadan looked exactly like the picture of him on the Arab League's website. He stood up and gave Emad's hand a firm shake. "Apologies that it had to be here," he said, as he cast a rather sad eye across the Hilton's tea room "But I'm right next door and have only half an hour or so." Emad was about to say "I know" before he checked himself. It was probably not wise to let on that he had Googled his host before walking across the bridge from Gezira. "Still," Mr. Ramadan said "After all these years they still probably make the best vanilla slices in all of Cairo. Shall I order some for us?"

As the coffee and pastries arrived, Mr. Ramadan gave Emad a long hard look. After what seemed like an eternity, he finally said, in his formal, clipped, tones: "Congratulations on your work with the clay jar. My contact tells me that you are a consummate professional."

"His contact?" This all but confirmed it for Emad. There was more to young Abu Bakr than what met the eye. "Can you please describe exactly what you saw?" Mr. Ramadan continued, studiously ignoring Emad's look of dismay. Emad weighed his options for a moment. He finally figured that he would not be sitting there if it was not with the knowledge, and possibly grudging support, of his superiors. So, even though he felt very uncomfortable doing so, he swallowed hard and slowly recounted the discovery up to Hana's deciphering of the Coptic words on the parchment. As he did so, Emad could not help noticing the briefest flash of irritation shooting across Mr. Ramadan's eyes.

He sat thinking for a moment, and when he finally addressed Emad again, it was in a deliberate tone. "You have probably figured out that I'm not here representing the Arab League. I am here as part of a group of loyal Egyptians. That's all you need to know for the moment." Emad could take some guesses at what that last statement meant, but he kept his silence. Mr. Ramadan continued: "We are very concerned at the centuries-old treachery of the Coptic people and would like to open our people's eyes to this."

Things were beginning to fall in place. Some shadowy group wanted to use the clay jar to inflame tensions towards the Coptic community. Emad's heart sank. As if to confirm this line of thinking, Mr. Ramadan spoke up again: "The scales weighted to the left. Do you have any idea what that means?" Emad shook his head. He was still hoping to get to that, but it seemed that he would be presented with a theory whether he'd like it or not.

"Listen to this," Mr. Ramadan said. Emad jerked his head upwards at the incongruous sight of someone in a business suit reciting the Qur'an with the cadence of a professional reciter:

"Then as for him whose balance (of good deeds) will be heavy, He will live a pleasant life (in Paradise). But as for him whose balance (of good deeds) will be light, He will have his home in Hell."

After he finished his recitation, Mr. Ramadan looked at Emad: "Do you know which side of Allah's scales contain good deeds?" Emad could at least remember this much from his Upper Egyptian Qur'an lessons: "Good deeds go on the right," he said, wondering at this sudden investigation of his Islamic knowledge. "So, what would a scale weighted to the left mean?" Mr. Ramadan asked, a knowing look in his eyes. Emad could kick himself. How could he not see this? Perhaps it was because he did not expect Muslim imagery on a Coptic jar. "See," Mr. Ramadan continued, "The weighted scale represents a coded insult directed at Islam. The Copts could use this as unobtrusive shorthand to declare our beloved *deen* (faith) evil and contemptible before Allah! Like scales weighted to the left."

Mr. Ramadan was warming to his theme: "This symbol is found in Coptic churches up and down Egypt. When asked, Copts always say that it means nothing, that it is the equivalent of a doodle. You now know better. The Cross Worshippers are laughing in our faces." Emad was a little stunned. He did not want to accept Mr. Ramadan's theory, but he had to confess that it made sense. "How do you know this?" he finally asked. Mr. Ramadan looked at him hopefully, at least Emad was not rejecting his interpretation out of hand. "Because," he said slowly, lowering his voice, "Throughout history this symbol has consistently turned up in places where Muslims were reminding the Copts of their place."

"You see," he continued, "The weighted scale is a symbol of the Copts' rejection of Islam. Of their continued mischief-making against us. They are merchants of *fitna* (mischief or corruption) and, therefore, do not deserve our protection."

"You do know what the punishment for those who spread *fitna* is don't you?" Emad groaned, he had heard enough would-be *jihadis* recite this verse to know the answer. Before he could respond, however, Mr. Ramadan lapsed into Qur'an recitation mode again:

> *"Indeed, the penalty for those who wage war against Allah and His Messenger and strive upon earth [to cause] corruption is none but that they be killed or crucified or that their hands and feet be cut off from opposite sides or that they be exiled from the land. That is for them a disgrace in this world; and for them in the Hereafter is a great punishment."*

"That's the Copts," Mr. Ramadan said, "And your find is proof that they have been doing this for centuries and have never been worthy of our protection!"

Emad could feel his blood run cold. Was this man seriously proposing that the jar should be added to the rhetorical arsenal of those Egyptian Muslims who believed that the Copts should be treated with the utmost ferocity? The look in Mr. Ramadan's eyes made it clear that he knew that Emad understood. He did not have to wait long for Emad's response.

"If you think that I will help you to use archeology to inflame hatred against fellow Egyptians you have another thing coming!", as he said this Emad was surprised to notice that his voice had been raised to an urgent pitch. He became vaguely aware of people at adjoining tables staring at them. The next moment he was standing in the air-conditioned mall outside the tea room. The frothy piped music formed a perfect counterpoint to the emotions raging inside him.

Back in the tea room, Mr. Ramadan watched him leave. A smile was playing at the corners of his mouth.

CHAPTER 14

At the Coptic Museum in Old Cairo, Magdy Botros' index finger hovered over the keypad of his phone. "This is ridiculous," he thought to himself, "the guy is not quite right in the head! Still, recent events seem to have vindicated him." After seeing the weighted scales on the *iconostasis* of the Hanging Church, Magdy and Hana had rushed to two other ancient churches in Coptic Cairo. Sure enough. At St. Barbara, the scales could be found above a stone doorway. At St. Sergius, regarded as one of the holiest churches in the country as it was reputedly built on the site where Jesus had stayed with his family during their time in Egypt, it could be seen carved into the foot of the altar.

"So, does Samuel Mounir know something that I do not?" the thought irritated Magdy, but he went ahead and dialed the number anyway.

It was fair to say that Magdy and Samuel did not move in the same circles. If Samuel had a 'circle', it orbited the outer fringes of Coptic life. Most Copts try to draw as little attention as possible to their differences with the Islamic majority in Egypt. The official line from the church seems to be 'Don't Rock the Boat!' This approach goes right to the top, with the Coptic Pope regularly sending messages of congratulations and solidarity to Islamic leaders during major Muslim festivals.

Samuel Mounir, however, belonged to the small minority of Copts who insisted that the Muslims of Egypt should continuously be reminded of the fact that Islam was the Johnny-come-lately and that the Copts were the ones keeping the traditions of ancient Egypt alive. Even more than this, he believed that any transgression of the rights of the Copts should be met, not with deference, but with militant zeal. Magdy, and most other Copts, firmly believed that this was a hazardous course of action for a beleaguered and vulnerable minority to take.

Magdy knew Samuel through his regular attendance at events put on by the Coptic Museum. No matter whether it was a lecture, dinner, or new exhibition, Samuel almost always caused trouble through his loud assertions that their glorious heritage should cause Copts to be much more assertive. There had even been talk of barring him from the premises. And now Magdy was about to call him for advice. In his agitation in being asked to 'cool it' Samuel had often hinted at being part of an organized group fighting for Coptic rights. When he became especially worked up, he even let slip the name of the ultimate Coptic urban legend: The Micah Order.

Previously Magdy had dismissed this kind of talk as the ravings of someone with severe delusions of grandeur. And now, with the discovery of a jar possibly belonging to the order? Could there be substance to all the stories? It still seemed implausible, but Magdy realized that he had to pursue all possible leads, no matter how personally distasteful he may find the process.

After a few rings on the other side of the line a strong, confident, voice said, "Samuel Mounir here," Magdy took a deep breath: "Mr. Mounir it is Dr. Magdy Botros from the Coptic Museum." There was a long silence at the other end. Finally, Samuel spoke, the confidence had gone from his voice, "Dr. Botros, if this is about my argument with the speaker at the lecture on early Coptic monasticism..." his voice trailed off. Magdy swallowed hard before saying "It is not. I wanted to talk with you about the Micah Order." This time there was silence at the other end for several seconds. "Who is this? What kind of sick joke are you trying to play?" Samuel seemed genuinely angry.

Magdy had not quite expected the conversation to play out this way. He sighed and finally said, "This is not a joke. It really is Dr. Botros. If you want, you can Google the number I'm calling from to verify that it belongs to the museum. Shall I wait?"

"No need," Samuel said, the confidence slowly returning to his voice, "Would you mind giving me some time to think and talk to some people? I'll get back to you as soon as I can." With that, there was a click, and the call was over. Magdy sat back in his chair and replayed the conversation in his head. Years of being ridiculed and attacked for talking about a mysterious 'Order' had clearly left its mark on Samuel Mounir.

Samuel apparently did not need too much time to do his thinking and make his inquiries. Magdy was about to resume work on catalog descriptions for an upcoming exhibition on Athanasius of Alexandria when his phone rang. "I don't know what brought this about," Samuel said, but I think it is best if we do not meet at the museum. Can you meet me at 8 pm tonight at the *Palais Hindou*?"

Magdy could hardly believe his ears. Samuel was taking a cloak-and-dagger approach to all of this. The 'palace' in question, had been built between 1907 and 1911 by the Belgian nobleman Baron Edouard Louis Joseph Empain. He was a wealthy industrialist who was instrumental in setting up the '*Cairo Electric Tramways and Heliopolis Oasis Company*'. His vision was for an entirely new Western-style planned community a few kilometers from Cairo. This new suburb, Heliopolis, quickly became a very desirable address and remained so to this day. In fact, the Egyptian Presidential Palace started its life as one of Baron Empain's showcase projects, the Heliopolis Hotel.

For his own home Baron Empain pulled out all the stops, and in the most unusual way possible. Many in Egypt see the physical representation of the divine as the most grievous of all sins, this did not stop Empain from building a house that was modeled on the magnificent Hindu Temple at Angkor Wat. This means that one of the first landmarks that international visitors encounter on the way into the city from Cairo International Airport would not have looked out of place in the middle of a temple courtyard in Delhi or Mumbai.

It is perhaps its very incongruity at the entrance to a city dominated by Islam that gave the 'Hindu Palace' such a dark and sinister reputation. Both the Baron's wife and daughter died mysterious deaths here, and a series of owners had come and gone, all complaining of strange happenings and stranger noises before selling up for ever-lower prices.

Today the palace is still one of the most recognizable landmarks in Heliopolis. Although it has taken its place amongst Cairo's ruins, the gardens have long since ceased to exist, the rooms were crumbling into dust, and many of the Hindu gods on the outside had been vandalized. This was perhaps done by super-devout Muslims who saw no reason for putting up with such a blatant expression of *shirk* (idolatry) defiling a city conquered by the blood of the faithful. For the most part, however, the palace stands in splendid isolation in the middle of a barren expanse where its perfectly manicured grounds used to be. It serves as a sanctuary for owls, rats, stray dogs and (if some of the wilder stories are to be believed) the occasional *jinn* (evil spirit).

All of this meant that there was a strong belief that anyone who went into the ruins of the palace must be up to no good. This perception was reinforced when in the 1990s, a group of teenagers were arrested there and accused of being Satanists involved in dark rituals. Most educated Cairenes eventually came to believe that they were merely heavy metal fans looking for a place to have a party. However, this was not the line taken by the authorities who, for some years, posted guards around the building to make sure that there were no more secret goings-on. "And now Samuel wants to meet there of all places!" Magdy sighed as he pulled the phone closer to tell his wife that he would not be home for dinner.

Some of the busiest roads in Cairo pass through Heliopolis, and for a city that contains millions more cars than it can cope with, that is saying something. So, Magdy gave himself plenty of time to get there. As he approached the palace, in the midst of what in most other cities would be regarded as the mother of all traffic jams, the road passed military base after military base. After the army-led coup, it would not be too far-fetched to suggest that the real center of power and authority in Egypt could be found behind these walls.

When he finally reached Baron Empain's dream home, after spending what seemed like an eternity trying to find a parking space, Magdy could not help but reflect on the fact that in Egypt so many dreams of glory had ended up in ruins. And this particular ruin was not in great shape. As he walked through the former gardens, pieces of broken glass, cigarette butts and assorted bits of detritus crunched under his feet. When he entered the ruin itself, things looked even worse. The remains of several fires blackened the corners of many rooms and the walls contained decades worth of graffiti. The historian in him perked up at the realization that this might provide a neat summary of Egypt's recent political turmoil to some future archeologist, but in the here-and-now, it added an extra layer of menace to the place.

Magdy was just getting into trying to decipher some of the scratches, evidently left by the unfortunate heavy metal junkies, when Samuel entered. He seemed almost apologetic, "I'm sorry it had to be here," he said, "But it is one of the few places in the city that you can count on being deserted. So, thank God for superstition!" Magdy looked at him quizzically; he had always thought of Samuel as merely a troublemaker and did not expect him to arrive on the scene cracking jokes. "Anyway," Samuel continued "We can speak freely here. Even if someone did come, they are sure to leave when they hear that we beat them to it." Magdy could not help but feel that this emphasis on secrecy was a bit over the top, but he decided to humor Samuel. He said, "Yes, that's good" before sitting down on an upturned crate that had already previously doubled as a chair for someone else.

Samuel remained standing and gave Magdy a questioning look: "So to what do I owe this honor?" he finally said. Magdy decided to be as forthcoming as he could be. He took a deep breath and recounted what he knew about the finding of the clay jar, the establishing of a link with the Old Testament prophet Micah and their discovery of 'weighted scales' in all three of the holiest and oldest churches of Coptic Cairo. As he was talking, Samuel gave him the occasional excited look, but for the most part, he just sat and listened. When Magdy finished, he could have sworn that he saw the beginnings of a tear forming in the corner of Samuel's left eye.

When Samuel finally spoke, his voice was thick with emotion, "We are few. We are despised. But we always knew that we are carrying on the work of centuries!" Magdy did not quite know what to make of this: "Who are the 'we' that you're referring to?" Samuel leaned in closer, "The Micah Order, of course," he said. "So, it still exists?" Magdy asked softly.

"Yes," Samuel responded as if that was all that needed to be said. Magdy paused for a moment. He realized that much more work would have to be done to link whatever Samuel was doing with the shadowy ancient group that had buried a clay jar in Fustat, but this was not the time for quibbling. After a while, he said, "Okay then, tell me about the Micah Order, please."

It was now Samuel's turn to have the floor. Hesitantly at first, but with mounting passion, he began to relate a story of a group of Copts spread out across Egypt who formed an informal network dedicated to protecting Coptic interests. "These days," he said, "We work mainly on the kidnapping issue." He did not have to explain. Magdy knew exactly what he was talking about. Few issues cause so much inter-communal tension in Egypt as the persistent belief among Copts that Christian girls were snatched from the bosom of their families and forcibly converted to Islam before being 'married off' to Muslim boys. Such tales had very often led to violence when Coptic communities tried to 'recover' one of their daughters - a daughter now regarded by the Muslim majority as one of their own. There are undoubtedly cases where Coptic girls follow their hearts into marriage with Muslim men. However, most human rights groups working in Egypt recognize that the Copts have a legitimate grievance in this area.

"We need to act fast and quietly," Samuel continued, "Once we become aware of a case, we get to work at trying to find where she is, and then we whisk her away as soon as her 'guardians' relax their vigilance. Sometimes, this leads to an uproar, but once a girl is in our hands, the kidnappers generally know that the game is up. The key is not to make too much of a fuss, but to get in there and do what we need to do." Magdy listened in silence, wondering at the new side of Samuel that was emerging. He was, of course, aware of the kidnappings, but he had no idea that there was an organized group of Copts 'fighting back'. He decided that he wanted to hear more, "What do you do with the girl once you have her? Presumably, you cannot simply take her back to her family. There would be hell to pay."

Samuel nodded, "Yes, once she had said the *shahada* (the Muslim confession of faith), even under duress, they will always try and bring her back into the Islamic fold. Sadly, she has to disappear."

"Disappear?" Magdy shot Samuel a quizzical look. Samuel pulled his shoulders back. He was proud of the work he was doing: "We have people up and down the Nile. We help girls to get new identities. A girl from Cairo might be settled in Aswan under a different name. Someone from Luxor may be taken to Alexandria. This way, she can start a new life. We even use this network for Muslims who convert to the way of Christ, but only once we are certain of their sincerity. If we do not help them, the rest of their earthly lives could be rather short!"

Magdy sat back, deep in thought. He was slightly ashamed of thinking that Samuel was all bluster. Sure, he could get carried away and was too free with his opinions in public. However, if what he was saying was true, he was also putting his safety on the line for the sake of some of the most vulnerable members of the Coptic church. Maybe all this talk of a 'Micah Order' was more than just one of the most persistent Coptic urban legends and had real substance to it.

Their thoughts were suddenly interrupted by an unearthly noise. They had somehow forgotten that their conversation was taking place in a building that many Cairenes would refuse to set foot in. Fortunately for them, they did not come face-to-face with final proof of resident evil spirits in the heart of the Baron's palace. Instead, a frantic cat, clearly the loser in some epic struggle with a rival, flashed passed them. Once their heart rates returned to normal Magdy asked Samuel to elaborate on what he knew about the order.

Samuel thought for a moment: "All that I know are the tales that are passed around the dinner table when we gather. People say that we had our origins in Fustat when the church began to feel pressure from the Arabs to convert or conform. It then grew hand-over-hand during the time of the crazy khalif." Magdy assumed this referred to Al-Hakim bi-Amr Allah (AD 996-1021), a caliph who abandoned the relative tolerance of his predecessors and attempted to turn Egypt to Islam by force. The Nile ran red with the blood of Christians and Jews during his reign. "That would make sense," he said, "That level of persecution cannot but generate resistance." Samuel nodded and continued, "I think the order finally went underground during the Crusades. Between AD 1163 to 1169 Crusader armies repeatedly attempted to capture Egypt and there were great fears among the Muslim rulers that we Copts could act as a kind of fifth column, providing easy entry to an enemy army made up of fellow Christians. This led to relentless efforts to disarm the Copts and to snuff out any possible form of resistance. So, I believe the order went underground back then and has remained hidden ever since. Much was lost in the process. To be honest, modern members know little more than the name, but it is one we wear with pride."

Madgy thought hard for a moment, "The timing would be about right," he said, "That jar was buried before 1186 when Fustat was burned with the move of the capital to Qahira, as it was found below the resulting layer of charred earth." Samuel smiled, still getting used to his references to the Micah Order being taken seriously, he finally said, "It would be the happiest day of my life if you can somehow manage to confirm that we are part of a movement that had been protecting our people for more than a millennium." Magdy winced a little, he usually dealt more in theories than in proofs, but he understood Samuel's excitement. It was at that moment that he decided to share something that he left out of his earlier description of the find.

He leaned in closer and slowly said some words. Words which, like Hana, he had also by then memorized. "Does this mean anything to you Samuel?" he asked:

In the blessed land
In the White Valley
From which many sought immortality
Where devotion was tested by sleep

At the place of the resurrection
She that walks will finally soar
The Saracens will be pulled apart
As the sons of Micah awaken

The Qibla of the Arabs
Will betray them
The Holy City of Islam
Shall be its downfall

Samuel looked like someone who had been kicked in the gut. He stared at Magdy, his mouth agape: "Where did you get that?" he finally asked. Magdy, somewhat perplexed by Samuel's reaction, said, "It was in the jar." Like a punch-drunk boxer, Samuel came forward and stood right before Magdy, their noses almost touching. "My friend," he said slowly, "I believe that you have found the 'Blessed Land' prophecy!"

"The what?" Magdy responded. "Sit down," Samuel half-ordered. Magdy obediently sank onto the upturned crate which he had vacated when the cat bounded past. Samuel, still clearly in shock, finally spoke: "There is a legend passed around in the order. A legend about a prophecy that will give us a secret weapon. I have never met anyone who really believed in it. We all assumed that it was simply something that was thought up in a particularly dark time to help us to hope against hope." He looked at Magdy: "Do you understand how big this is?" then not waiting for an answer he added excitedly, "This must be the 'Blessed Land Prophecy'. Repeat the first line. Listen to it. This is it!"

Magdy had so many questions popping into his head at that moment, but he began by asking what to him was the most baffling one: "This 'secret weapon,' what is it supposed to do?" Samuel stared at him, a mysterious look on his face. When he spoke, there was steel in his voice: "It will achieve the final defeat of Islam."

The words seemed to hang in mid-air as a crescent moon appeared through a hole in the palace's roof.

CHAPTER 15

At the Abbas house in Imbaba, Yusuf and Maryam were still hard at it. They had had the same argument so often that they could just as well have given numbers to each phrase that they uttered to get it over with quicker. Their running battle was intensified by the fact that their parents had gone to visit family in the Delta and were, therefore, not around to douse the flames like they usually did. So, it seemed as if their days were filled with unrelenting verbal sparring with not much else on the menu.

Yusuf never ceased to extol the virtues of following his faith in Islam to wherever it led, even if that road led to a battlefield. For her part, Maryam always reminded him of the responsibilities of a Muslim man towards his family. In truth, Yusuf did not want to be there anymore. When the Sheik called him to the meeting near the Sayyeda Zeinab mosque, he believed that it would be some time before he would see his family again. Yet, for some reason, the Sheik ended their meeting by giving him explicit instructions to return home. He said he would be in touch in due course.

It was dusk, and Yusuf stood on the balcony of their apartment building and looked out over their suburb. On the roofs of countless other buildings, he could see pigeon-coops, lines of washing swaying in the breeze and hundreds of white satellite dishes. Cairo from above sometimes resembled a giant mushroom farm. Yusuf knew that wholesome Islamic sermons were traveling through some of those dishes, while others acted as conduits for Western filth and, Allah-forbid, even Christian preaching. There was so much work to be done.

The fact that his city was not what it should be, was further confirmed by the religious buildings dotted between the apartment complexes. True, many minarets were reaching heavenward, towering above the mosques where Allah's final revelation was preached. However, here and there, there were also the smooth, perfectly circular, domes of Coptic churches, each one topped with that accursed symbol: The cross. It did not seem to matter that regulations stipulated that no church spire was allowed to be taller than the minarets of the mosques in the vicinity. After his conversation with the Sheik, Yusuf was ever more convinced that the crosses should not be there in the first place. He took comfort in the fact that there was a *hadith* (tradition) that stated that *Nabi Isa* (Prophet Jesus) would one day return to break all crosses and turn the world to Islam. In the meantime, it was up to him and his fellow warriors to speed up that process.

Yusuf was still turning this thought around in his mind when he felt the vibration of his phone in his back pocket. It was an unknown number, but a familiar voice came through the speaker when he answered. Without so much as a greeting, the voice said: "This is a burner SIM card. Don't call this number; the phone will be discarded after our call. Be ready to deploy at 11 pm. Don't bring anything but a few changes of clothes. Leave your mobile phone and computer at home. They can be traced. Also, bring your sister." Yusuf was utterly stunned by that last demand. He knew, of course, that the Brotherhood would have checked out his background, but he had never discussed his family with the Sheik, they did not have that kind of relationship.

He gulped hard before he told the Sheik that Maryam would never in a million years agree to going along. There was steel in his voice when he answered, "It is not a matter of 'agreeing.' She is vital to this mission. See to it that she is ready." With that, the phone went dead. Yusuf stared at the screen for the longest time, totally bewildered. How on earth would he ever be able to persuade Maryam to accompany him? And why would she be 'vital'? Were the rumors correct that the Brotherhood was training female suicide bombers, who were more likely to be waved through checkpoints?" He tried to string his thoughts together, but there were far too many of them, and they all marched off in different directions.

What he had said to the Sheik was correct - he knew beyond a shadow of a doubt that there was no way that Maryam would go with him. Still, he decided to try one last time, if only to assure the Sheik that he had done so. On reaching her room he softly knocked on the door. She looked up from the novel she was reading and said: "Get out, I don't have time for this!" He turned to leave; there was nothing for it, he was going to have to tell the Brothers that whatever the plan was that involved Maryam, it was dead in the water.

Yusuf went to his room to throw some clothes into a bag, his mind in turmoil. He would not dream of defying his commanders, but surely this request was a bridge too far? He knew that he would have to explain this to the Sheik, whatever the consequences would be. He sighed; this deployment had undoubtedly taken a bewildering turn. Then again, whoever expected participation in a war to be straightforward? Yusuf was still turning these thoughts around in his head when there was a sharp knock on the door. He looked at his watch, 11 pm.

He slung his bag over his shoulder and went to the door. At last, he was embarking on his own 'struggle in the path of Allah'. He thought about saying goodbye to Maryam but checked himself. It would be far better if she found out that he had gone in the morning; that way, the inevitable bust-up could be avoided. He opened the door; two men stood there. Both looked like their area of expertise was the skilled application of violence rather than engaging in rarified theological debates. In short, they were the kind of men that Yusuf was about to become. Yasser, the taller of the two, after the proper Islamic greetings and introductions, said, "The Sheik sent us. Are the two of you ready?" Yusuf knew this was coming and he believed that he was prepared for it.

He took a deep breath and stated with as much conviction as he could muster, "I am ready. But my sister is not coming." Yasser stiffened: "What do you mean 'is not coming'? Is your father here at the moment?" Yusuf did not know what to make of this question, "No, my parents are away for a few weeks" he responded.

"Well, that means that you're her guardian at present, does it not?" Yasser asked with a triumphant look in his eyes. Under strict Islamic law, every woman is always under the protection and authority of a male relative. Yusuf was not sure that he liked where this was going. "Yes, I suppose that is the case," he eventually said, knowing very well what the response would be. And, sure enough, it swiftly came, "So why didn't you order her to come with you?"

On hearing this, Yusuf wanted to respond by saying that she would throw his 'order' right back in his face, but he thought better of it. He knew that he would at least have to make a show of trying to persuade Maryam to accompany him. "This way," he said, leading the way to Maryam's room. As he did so, she came towards them in the hallway, wondering what the commotion was all about. She stiffened as Yusuf pointed to the two men and said, "Maryam this is Yasser and Rafiq, they are fellow *mujahideen*."

Maryam's surprise instantly turned into white-hot rage. She rounded on Yusuf, "Really brother, what the hell do you think you are doing? What will we say if the *mukhabarat* (secret police) knew that they were here? Do you want us all to be arrested?" Yusuf was still trying to think up an answer when Yasser, clearly out of patience, interjected. In an almost painfully formal, yet at the same time slightly menacing, tone he said, "Sister, I need you to pack a bag. You are coming with us. You have five minutes!"

Maryam stared at him for a moment. Her mouth agape. When she spoke, her voice was dripping with sarcasm, "I'm coming with you? Is that so?

Well, 'Mr. Soldier,' here's the thing. I'd rather have all my teeth pulled without Novocaine than go anywhere with you!" Yasser looked at her, a smile playing at the corners of his mouth. He continued with the utmost formality, "Sister, your brother is your guardian, and he desires that you grace us with your presence. Isn't that right Yusuf?" Yusuf was deeply embarrassed by how this was turning out, but he did his best to muster up some authority in his voice, before saying, "Yes, Maryam, you need to come with us!"

Maryam all but spat out her response, "Really, brother? You're a fine 'protector' with the way you are placing your entire family in peril. Besides, what are you going to do if I disobey your so-called 'order'?" Yasser, stepped in, clearly unimpressed with how Yusuf was handling the situation. Looking intently at Maryam he shifted his jacket to reveal the butt of a revolver, "I really wished that it would not come to this sister, but perhaps this will help you make up your mind?"

Both Yusuf and Maryam took several steps back in shocked disbelief. Once, they regained their composure Maryam shot Yusuf a withering look and said: "Some charming friends you've brought into our lives brother. What great warriors of Allah they are, harassing defenseless women!" Yusuf looked at the ground. He certainly did not expect this turn of events. What on earth was the Sheik playing at? He shot Maryam a pleading look that seemed to say, "Please cooperate, or we're dead."

Yasser interrupted their inner turmoil by walking over and unplugging the phone, handing it to Rafiq. The latter had, by then, taken out his revolver and stood with it in his right hand. Not entirely aiming it at anyone but certainly making it clear that he knew how to use it. Yasser, still apparently with deep sincerity and civility, said, "Now if you could please hand all phones, tablets, and computers to brother Rafiq here, it would be very much appreciated. Also, sister, I will have to come with you as you pack. I sincerely apologize for the intrusion, but you will have to understand that it is to prevent you from doing anything that could place you in danger!"

The next few minutes passed in a haze as they got ready to leave. Yusuf tried to protest a few times, but the contemptuous looks he received in return quickly stopped him in his tracks. Once they were ready, they walked down the stairs in silence. Outside their apartment building, a Land Cruiser was waiting, its engine running. As they got in, Yasser said, "We are embarking on an important and historic mission. Please do not jeopardize it by trying to attract attention or, even worse, attempting to leave the vehicle." Yusuf could see that Maryam was seething, he could not blame her, but sensibly, she merely nodded.

As the sights of late-night Cairo passed by the window, Yusuf could not help but reflect on how suddenly this mission had transformed from a long-cherished dream to less-than-dreamlike reality. From what he knew about the Sheik, he was confident that there would be some rational explanation for this. Whatever it was, it had better be good. On the other side of the vehicle, Maryam might as well have been on another planet. She refused to look at him and seemed to scrunch herself up as close to the door as she could so as to put as much distance between them as possible.

Defiance had given way to fear. From the movement of her shoulders, he could see that she was softly crying. He tried very hard to think of something to say to her but realized that there were no words that would make the situation better.

When the twin-minarets of *Bab Zuweila*, one of the ancient city gates of Qahira, came into view, Yusuf realized that they were passing by the area commonly known as 'Islamic Cairo.' Its narrow streets, many mosques, and markets, all seemingly unchanged from medieval times, made it clear that this was a very different Cairo from the Western-inspired city that grew up around the great squares closer to the Nile. Its name indicated precisely what this part of the city represents. If not, in the personal Islamic piety of its residents, certainly in its architecture. This had been the beating heart of Islamic rule in Cairo for centuries. In a sense, it still retained that role. Al-Azhar University dominates part of the neighborhood. It is regarded as the pre-eminent institution of higher learning in Sunni Islam, and its Sheik as the foremost theological authority in the Islamic world.

For a moment Yusuf thought that they might be heading to the University. Then he remembered that the Al-Azhar theologians had consistently condemned the Brotherhood during the presidency of Hosni Mubarak. When Muhammad Morsi came to power, they praised him and the Brothers to the sky, only to revert to being stern critics when the Brotherhood was toppled. In short, they could not be trusted. As Yusuf turned this over in his mind, the thought promptly dashed off in an unwelcome direction, "Given the events of the night, can the Brotherhood itself be trusted?"

They gradually left the domes and minarets, the very epitome of an Islamic city, behind and headed north. Eventually, Yasser steered the Land Cruiser off the main road down a side street. They were now surrounded by what looked like row upon row of small houses. It was a very different face of Cairo. No apartment buildings were reaching to the sky here. It was only as they penetrated deeper into the warren of 'houses' that Yusuf realized where they were: 'The City of the Dead.'

It seems that the desire to be splendidly commemorated in death becomes part of the psyche of anyone who spends a significant amount of time in Egypt. It eventually even infected Egypt's Muslim conquerors, despite the prophet's prohibition of lavish graves. True, they did not go about claiming to be living gods like the pharaohs, but the tombs of the Islamic rulers of Egypt became ever more elaborate over time. The result was that some of the most impressive minarets towering over the Cairo skyline do not stand above mosques, but as silent way-markers to magnificent mausoleums. As with the rulers, so with the people. Just north of 'Islamic Cairo' a vast necropolis, stuffed to the gills with the graves of the pious, grew over time. Most of the tombs were housed in single room structures, but they did their best to add a bit of posthumous exuberance to the memories of the deceased. Except, it was not just the dead who could be found here.

Over time it became clear to many of those struggling on Cairo's margins that these sturdy buildings, within hailing distance of downtown Cairo, could be used for more than just housing bones. So, people started moving in. At first, it was only the caretakers of the largest tombs and their families. Then more and more people, desperate for a roof over their heads, followed. Today the 'Northern Cemetery' (the official name of the 'City of the Dead') is home to a community that numbers in the hundreds of thousands. Whole families live their lives inside the tombs of the departed. This did not mean, however, that the neighborhood was exactly family-friendly.

The narrow warren-like streets, the superstition that keeps everyone but the bravest at bay, and the solidarity created by living in genuinely desperate circumstances all combined to make the City of the Dead a haven for those who preferred that their activities were not apparent to the whole world. So, if you needed drugs, prostitutes or even weapons, this was your place. Rumour has it that there are some alleyways in the cemetery that have not seen a policeman since the time of King Farouk.

A place tailor-made for the hiding of contraband will do just as well when it comes to hiding people. Yusuf realized with a sinking feeling that they were not passing through the City of the Dead, it was probably their final destination. This suspicion was confirmed by the fact that they wove ever deeper into the warren of alleyways. Here and there some of the tomb-dwellers looked up from their cooking fires as they passed, only to quickly lower their gaze. Minding your own business was a particularly valuable survival skill for the tomb dwellers.

Eventually, the passages through the tombs became too small for them to continue in the vehicle. Yasser stopped the Land Cruiser and got out, his weapon in his right hand. He made a slight motion for Yusuf and Maryam to get out. As soon as they did this, Rafiq got into the driver's seat and reversed the vehicle back up the lane. As its headlights retreated, Yusuf gave it a rueful look. They would never find their way out of this maze unaided. Yasser started walking away from the spot where they had stopped; and they had no alternative but to follow.

The next few minutes had a surreal quality to them. Then again, what else would you expect in an inhabited cemetery? Dirty kitchen utensils stacked on a tomb. A faded picture of a distinguished-looking business-man over the entrance of an imposing doorway. A small child sleeping, her hand almost touching a vase filled with dull plastic flowers. A piece of black velvet tacked next to a name written on a wall-mounted marble slab — muffled sobs, coming from who knows where.

Yasser finally stopped in front of a tomb with a wooden door inlaid with intricate geometrical patterns. At its center, Yusuf could make out the Islamic confession of faith. He became aware that Maryam was softly crying beside him. He reached for her hand, but she quickly withdrew it.

Yasser got out his phone, dialed a number, and said: "We're here!" The door swung open. An old *bawab,* whom Yusuf assumed was the guard-ian of the tomb, waved them inside before quickly closing the door. As soon as their eyes adjusted to the bright lights that greeted them, they were confronted with the most bizarre sight. Inside it was all clean lines and minimalist *chic* as if the room somehow teleported from a Swedish furniture catalog. The sheik obviously had a penchant for creating mod-ern spaces in the most unlikely places.

He could not help it. The engineer in Yusuf immediately set to work, trying to figure out how they got all the materials through the narrow alleyways. He was, however, quickly yanked back to reality and the peril of their situation when the Sheik himself walked into the room.

The Sheik smiled, but there was no warmth in his face when he did so. *"Ahlan*!" (Welcome!), he said, without much enthusiasm. He turned to Maryam: "I'm sorry it had to be like this. I was confident that your brother would do a better job in explaining the will of Al-lah to you". He cast a reproachful look towards Yusuf. "Still," he con-tinued, "You're here now. I guess that's all that matters." The Sheik's words finally spurred Yusuf into action, "But what do you want with her?", he blurted out.

The Sheik gave Yusuf another cold, calculating, look. He was clearly weighing up his answer. He finally said with stark finality, "All shall be revealed in due course brother Yusuf. In the meantime, I suggest that you and your sister make yourselves at home. You might be here for a while."

As if to signal that the conversation was at an end, he reached into his pocket and got out an iPhone. His face showed intense concentration as he dialed a number and waited for an answer. When it came, he said in a soft and measured tone, "Dr. Almasry. Mr. Ramadan here, I was wondering if you'd be so kind as to reconsider your reluctance to assist me? You see, I have something, or rather someone, rather precious to you with me."

CHAPTER 16

For an absurd moment, Emad felt like he had been dropped in the middle of a colony of ants as a scientific observer. As he joined the crush of humanity ascending the steps out of the Metro station into the bright sunlight of Tahrir Square, he could not quite shake the feeling that he was somehow not one of them. The call he'd just received made sure of that. These people were thinking about meeting a friend at the *Carl's Jr* on the other side of the square or readying themselves to do battle with Egyptian bureaucracy at the hulking government office building dominating the southern end of the square. And him? In a flash, he went from being just another archeologist at the Ministry for Antiquities to the fiancé of a hostage.

They had Maryam. Nothing else mattered, or registered, at that moment. This is what brought him back to the square again to see Mr. Ramadan. Only, this time, it would probably not be for vanilla slices at the Nile Hilton.

He was suddenly aware of someone in a suit standing next to him. "Thank you for coming," said a voice. He was instantly pulled out of being an observer into cold hard reality. He heard himself say, "As if I had a choice in the matter."

"Fair enough," said Mr. Ramadan, "Oh, and I'm sure you would not be foolish enough to do anything silly. However, if you are thinking of trying, this is the cradle of revolutions, which makes it probably the most intensely surveilled spot in the entire country. If you so much as lift a finger against me, you'll be tackled to the ground before you can say *Mubarak*! Sometimes even the enemy's muscle has its uses."

Emad was barely listening. He had only one priority, "Never mind that, where's Maryam, what have you done with her?" he blurted out.

"Patience, my friend. Let's go for a walk," Mr. Ramadan said and started towards the southern end of the square without waiting for an answer. They passed the Mosque of Omar Makram, scene of the last farewell of generations of the great and the good, to the extent that many Cairenes refer to it as the 'funeral mosque'. From here they mounted the pavement to walk alongside the edge of the mammoth *Mogamma*, the largest government building in Egypt. At its back, El-Sheik Rihan street used to separate the building from Kasr Dobara Evangelical Church. The road was now totally cordoned off however and housed what amounted to a military encampment.

They kept going until they encountered what looked like giant versions of carelessly strewn Lego bricks, piled high against a formidable wall. The purpose of the enormous blocks of concrete was to ensure that no one could get anywhere close to the wall.

They came to a stop opposite a statue, incongruously camped out on a traffic roundabout in front of the Semiramis Intercontinental Hotel. It represented the icon of South American liberation, Simon Bolivar. Emad rushed to catch up to Mr. Ramadan, "Again, where's Maryam!" he half-screamed at him. Mr. Ramadan had other things on his mind. "This is one of the places where what has become of Egypt can be most clearly seen," he said, half to himself. "You know as well as I do that those concrete blocks protect the American Embassy. You also saw the armored personnel carriers in the street behind the *Mogamma*. What you did not see is that the entire bottom floor of the building was cleared out and that there are hundreds of troops in there, ready to rush onto Tahrir Square at the merest hint of trouble. No repeat revolution will be allowed. In the shadow of it all, there shelters a church. The largest Protestant church in the entire Arab world, and quite possibly the best protected. This is what has become of our revolution. The might of the state employed to guard foreign imperialists," he motioned towards the American Embassy and then to the church, "and Christians."

Emad was hardly in the mood for a lecture on politics. He faced Mr. Ramadan and said through gritted teeth, "This is all very interesting, but where is Maryam!?"

Mr. Ramadan gave him a half-annoyed look, almost as if he resented this intrusion into his musings on the realities of modern Egypt. Finally, he said, in his most formal tone of voice, "Dr. Almasry, if we are to work together, you need to understand why I do what I do. I, at least, owe you that."

"We are not 'working together,' and all that you 'owe' me is to release Maryam," Emad growled at him. They were beginning to make a scene, and several people gave them curious looks as they walked by. Cairenes seem to have a special fondness for eavesdropping on, or even participating in if the occasion allows, public arguments.

Mr. Ramadan said slowly and emphatically, "Your cooperation is the only thing that will make any release possible Dr. Almasry. So, may I suggest that you hear me out?" Emad realized that he had little choice but to back down, "Make it quick," he muttered. Mr. Ramadan nodded and walked towards the river. When they reached the Corniche after a few minutes, he leaned over one of the railings and motioned to Emad to join him. Below them the Nile was, as ever, calmly making its way to the sea, forming a perfect counterpoint to the churn of emotions swirling inside Emad.

"Maybe I should begin by telling you about my grandfather," Mr. Ramadan said. Emad rolled his eyes. What could this have to do with anything? He stopped short; however, when Mr. Ramadan said, "His name was Hassan al-Banna."

Emad was suddenly very interested, in spite of himself. "*The* Hassan al-Banna?" he asked. "The same," Mr. Ramadan said softly. Most Egyptians know the basic outlines of Hassan al-Banna's life. How he, the son of an Islamic scholar, moved to Cairo from the Delta in 1932, already the leader of a tiny group known as the 'Muslim Brothers'. He led this group until 1949 when he was assassinated, at age 42, by the Egyptian Secret Police. Little did he know that his little band of followers would eventually turn into a movement that would rule all of Egypt after the ousting of Hosni Mubarak, only for the dream to come crashing down when the Muslim Brotherhood government under Muhammad Morsi was toppled in 2013.

Emad looked at Mr. Ramadan with new eyes, "So you're Brotherhood Royalty?" he asked in an ironic tone of voice. Mr. Ramadan looked at him sharply, "There is only one who is 'royal,' and that is Allah, we are merely Brothers struggling in his cause!" he said. "But you are half-right, my family has worked hard and suffered much for the cause." He continued, "Perhaps you have heard of my father and my brothers?"

Emad thought for a moment, and then it came to him. Hassan al-Banna's daughter was married to Said Ramadan, who became a senior Brotherhood leader from the 1950s. Nasser's Egypt was, however, not a welcoming place as far as the Brothers were concerned, and so Said Ramadan made his home in Geneva, Switzerland from where he played a significant role as a leader-in-exile. Two of his sons Tariq and Hani became Islamic scholars, with Tariq, in particular, working very hard to forge a path for Brotherhood ideology (under the guise of a supposedly benign 'European Islam') in the West. That is until he came under the scrutiny of the #MeToo movement, with allegations of sexual misconduct effectively ending his career. Apparently, there was a third son who managed to live his life outside of the limelight, and he was gazing out over the Nile, right there next to Emad.

As if reading Emad's thoughts, Mr. Ramadan continued, "You're probably wondering why I did not follow the same path as Hani and Tariq?" Emad noticed a slight twitch of discomfort as he said the last name. The disgrace of the family's brightest star, the darling of Western academic elites, but now languishing in a French jail on rape charges clearly still had the power to cause pain. "Well," he continued, "I always thought that my struggle should be here in Egypt. It is all good to try and carve out a place for our ideas in the West, but unless we take the masses right here in the House of Islam with us, we might as well not get out of bed."

"Of course, with my family connections, it would have been suicide to turn up at Cairo airport. But my father had a plan. Through his connections in Saudi Arabia, he got me a job at the Arab League. I filled several low-level positions across the region and was eventually appointed to a senior role at headquarters here in Cairo. This meant that I could come back to my ancestral home under what amounted to diplomatic immunity. There would be hell to pay if an Arab League official 'disappeared,' even if he was an Egyptian citizen." He half-smiled as if the ingenuity of his father's plan to get him back into Egypt still pleased him. "Besides," he continued, "We let it be known that as a key official in the 'External Affairs' department I had tons of dirt on what just about every senior Egyptian official got up to on overseas visits. It always helps to have some extra insurance in place", he chuckled.

Emad looked at Mr. Ramadan with new eyes. He had been waging his grandfather's struggle in his own way and, unlike many of his compatriots, he was still standing tall due to being on the payroll of the Arab League. Yet, for him to survive this long must have required an extraordinary degree of tenacity and ruthlessness. Mr. Ramadan gave him a knowing look, "You will appreciate that I need to complete the work I embarked on. Yes, we suffered a setback, but we are not beaten. There is something that we need to do to achieve victory. That 'something' is intimately tied to the fate of your fiancé. Naturally, I have no wish to hurt her, but she is, if you will, another insurance policy. If you cooperate, she will be restored to you..." He let the sentence trail off. There was no need to spell out the unpleasant alternative.

Emad swallowed hard, "What do you want from me?" He finally asked. Mr. Ramadan gave him a smile that seemed to say: 'I knew you'd see sense'.

"It is not difficult," he said, "I want you to continue your research into the clay jar and to appear on television to discuss it when you're ready. I will arrange a suitable channel and interviewer. All that I need you to do is to lay bare the centuries-old treachery of the Copts for the entire nation to hear. You're an archeologist with the Ministry for Antiquities, people will listen!" Then, with a mysterious look on his face, he added, "And, once they have listened, we'll take it from there!"

Emad turned around, barely noticing the people walking past, enjoying the cooler air next to the river. So, it seemed that he would be used by the Brotherhood to inflame tensions against the Copts even if everything inside him recoiled at the idea. Maryam's life depended on it.

Mr. Ramadan reached into his pocket and pulled out a phone, handing it to Emad. "This has a Swiss SIM card with roaming enabled," he said. "Makes it harder to trace the call. Get to work on your research and give me a ring on this phone once you are ready for the interview. My number is pre-programmed on it." With that, he turned and disappeared back across the street in the direction of the Arab League building.

Emad stared hard at the phone for a few moments, resisting a powerful urge to throw it into the river. That would not do. Rash actions would not get him anywhere. He needed some way to connect with the Coptic community to try and avert disaster and save Maryam in the process.

He paced up and down for a few moments. Finally, drawing upon a deep inner resolve, he placed the Sheik's 'foreign' phone in his pocket, drew out his own and dialed a number.

He hesitated for a moment upon hearing the voice of a young woman on the other side, then he took a deep breath and said, "Hana, can we meet in my office in half an hour?"

On the walk back across the Nile, the enormity of what he was about to do suddenly struck him. He was about to place himself at cross-purposes with the person who held the power of life and death over his fiancé.

CHAPTER 17

What must only have been a few days felt like months, as the hours dragged by in the City of the Dead. Yusuf was still struggling to come to terms with the fact that his 'deployment' consisted of nothing more than providing the means through which the Sheik could get at Maryam. For her part, Maryam spent her days worrying about what would happen with Emad. Mr. Ramadan told them all about his plans as a means of explaining why they were being held. They knew that she was 'leverage.'

Maryam did not know what to think. On the one hand, she wanted Emad to do what was asked so that this nightmare could be over. She also realized, however, that if he did this, it would only be the start of a nightmare for many others. It horrified her to think that the words of her fiancé could be the spark that would inflame a religious war.

At least they were relatively safe. The Brothers would not do anything to Maryam while their demands were still unmet. Also, they may have been ruthless in pursuit of their goals, but they always acted according to what they believed were proper Islamic principles. It would, therefore, not do to detain Maryam without an acceptable 'guardian,' in the form of a close male family member, in the vicinity. As her brother, Yusuf could fulfill this role, and the Sheik never ceased to remind him that this was his most significant contribution to the struggle at that moment.

Yusuf would much rather have contributed with a gun in his hand, but he knew that it was futile to protest, so he kept his peace. Of course, he resented being misled and cooped up like that, but he could just about convince himself that he was part of the process of reestablishing godly rule in Egypt. Still, he could not help but feel that his connection with Maryam was perhaps the only thing of value that he brought to the table in this great struggle.

So, ironically, her passionately expressed wish that he would step back from becoming a soldier was being fulfilled, albeit in a rather strange way. This was, however, not the first time that she had managed to pull him back from the frontline. There were so many deep and conflicting emotions associated with the previous time this happened that Yusuf still did not quite know what to make of it. At the very least he could commend his sister for her ingenuity.

It happened during the so-called Rabaa Uprising during which the members of the Muslim Brotherhood desperately tried to hang onto power after the ousting of Muhammad Morsi on 3 July 2013. Tens of thousands of them massed in two Cairo squares, called Al-Nahda, and Rabaa al-Awadiya, refusing to budge. The new military government under General Abdel Fattah al-Sissi did everything it could to get them to move on, but to no avail. The protesters vowed to stay put until Morsi was reinstated.

On 14 August 2013, the authorities finally moved against the Brotherhood die-hards, who by then had occupied the squares for more than a month. The protestors vowed not to leave without a fight. The result was a massacre in the most literal sense of the word. About 900 Brotherhood supporters were killed and close to 4,000 were seriously injured. For a while it looked like Egypt would erupt into yet another bout of widespread revolutionary violence. Churches and government installations were attacked up and down the country. International condemnation rolled in like a flood.

In the end, however, the Brothers had to acknowledge defeat. They had lost the support of the people through moving too harshly and too quickly in attempting to turn the country to 'pure Islam.' For a while, a symbol known as the *'Rabia'* (a hand holding up four fingers) proliferated across Egypt as a means of reminding the population that the Brotherhood was still around, but eventually even this disappeared.

In the lead-up to the massacre, Yusuf got a call from Fatima asking for an interview. Fatima Shoukry was a journalist with the Capital Broadcasting Center, one of a slew of television stations that emerged after the Arab Spring that had toppled Hosni Mubarak. It was generally pro-military and anti-Brotherhood, which meant that the Morsi years were tough. Its star act, Bassem Youssef (known as 'the Jon Stewart of the Arab world'), was arrested for insulting President Morsi and disturbing public order. The station itself was, however, allowed to continue broadcasting. Fatima Shoukry was one of its rising stars. She also happened to be a childhood friend of Maryam.

Over the years, Yusuf had watched her blossom from an awkward teenager into a very confident, and far too 'modern' to his tastes, young woman: All high-heels, sharp suits and sassy attitude. She was, in short, the very antithesis of the Muslim Brotherhood's ideal of pure femininity. Still, Yusuf could not help but feel flattered when she called. Her pitch was simple and effective. She acknowledged that her station had a reputation of being on the other side of the political divide; however she said that it would be good, in the interest of balance, to hear the perspectives of a Brotherhood supporter as the sit-ins at Rabaa and Al-Nahdaa unfolded. She had heard through Maryam of his turn to religion and proposed that they sit down for an interview to enable him to relay the views of a grassroots Brotherhood supporter.

'Sitting down' turned out to be a bit of a misnomer since the interview that she recorded with him stretched over several sessions. The fact that his words would be used to put the Brotherhood's views across to a skeptical audience brought him much joy. The whole experience was also slightly disconcerting, however. He could, of course, not help but notice her feminine presence. Her perfume, her hair, her slight smiles at his answers. He wondered several times if the whole thing was not *haram* (forbidden), but he rationalized it by convincing himself that it was a roundabout way of striving for the cause that he so sincerely believed in.

On the day of the massacre, they were, once again, sitting down to go over the subtler points of his responses, when his phone rang. One of his friends told him that the army was moving in, and he could hear gunshots in the background. He walked over to Fatima in a daze and said to her that he had to go. What happened next was still seared in his memory for the unexpectedness of it all. She rushed over to him and held on to him. He held her for the briefest moment and then recovered his senses. He tried to push her away; this was totally out of line. "Please don't go!" she pleaded. "I have to!" he said and managed to extract himself from her arms. He can still see her defeated look and hear her muted, "Be careful please," as he walked away.

The one thing that will always stay with him about what happened next, was how many people ran towards the protest rather than away from it. Thousands of Brotherhood supporters rushed to Rabaa Square to defend their brothers in the faith. They were, of course, not allowed to get anywhere near the scene and Yusuf eventually slinked off into a side street to avoid arrest. He was, at least, wise enough to see that those who got too close were merely rushing into the waiting arms of the Secret Police. Still, he was close enough to hear the shots and the shouts. They were all there: Fadl, Harun, Mahmoud, Khaleel, Umar. His friends, his brothers. All dead now. He should have been among them.

A few days after the events, he had another call from Fatima. "I heard from Maryam, you're okay, I'm so thankful!" she said. She was silent for the longest time: "I have something to tell you," she eventually half-whispered.

It turned out that the whole interview process was a hoax. It was a way of keeping him away from Rabaa Square. It would not be broadcast, not then, not ever. Maryam, in her desperation to keep her brother safe, had turned to Fatima for help. This was why she never seemed ready to declare the project at an end. Yusuf did not quite know what to say. Finally, a bitter, "How could you?" was the only thing that escaped his lips. Her next words were so unexpected that he almost recoiled from them. He waited for scorn and ridicule at backing the wrong horse. Instead, she hesitantly said, "We can still see each other, right?" Yusuf was silent for a moment, then he was jerked back to reality and the enormity of what she had done. "Of course not!" he snapped and slammed the phone down.

The row with Maryam that followed these events was of such epic proportions that their father threatened to call the police on them. He accused her of robbing him of his chance at martyrdom. She countered that she did all that she did out of love for him, and out of a desire to save their parents from heartache. In the end, the whole thing simmered down. Of course, he was still plagued by survivor's guilt, but at least he could see that she acted in line with her convictions. He resolved to change those convictions to be more attuned to Allah's will, with somewhat limited success it should be noted. This was also the reason that he tried so hard to get her to accompany him on his 'deployment.' If she was on board, there would be little risk of a repetition of the kind of stunt that she pulled with Fatima.

He watched her as she listlessly flicked through a Brotherhood magazine, he could not help reminding himself again that Maryam was probably the only reason he was still alive. Sometimes he did not know if this was something to be thankful for, but he had to acknowledge that she really did love him. They had come to a strange truce, cooped up as they were, there at the heart of the City of the Dead. They both knew that one almighty row lay somewhere in the future, but for the moment they knew that they had to cooperate to make the situation as tolerable as possible.

True, they were not suffering in any real sense. There was plenty of food, and how the tomb was transformed into an ultra-modern apartment was a wonder to behold. Still, they were under no illusions about their lack of freedom of movement. The *bawab* was the only person who opened the door and would not allow them within a few feet of it. He was also the only person, along with Mr. Ramadan, they ever saw. So, they spent their time reading and watching television. No phone or internet access was allowed. Many people, including their parents, must have been frantic with worry about them. However, given Yusuf's history, they most probably assumed that they were somewhere in Syria with ISIS. They may have shaken their heads at the apparent strangeness of Maryam going along. Still, "Who would have thought?" was an all too common theme when it came to people throwing in their lots with the *jihadis.*

They found it interesting that the Sheik came for regular visits. He had better things to do than to check on the welfare of his hostages. Yusuf could not help but wonder whether he did not feel at least a little bit guilty at the way things had turned out. This was borne out by the pep-talks that he gave them about just how significant their contribution to the struggle was. Initially, Maryam contested almost every statement he made, but she quickly realized that she was wasting her breath. So, eventually, she learned to merely sit stony-faced and wait for him to finish.

The Sheik seemed to delight in his ability to harness Western ideas and history for his purposes, as if this would add further legitimacy to his arguments. During his last visit, he asked them: "Have you ever heard of the St Bartholomew's Day Massacre?" When they both professed ignorance, he gave a half-condescending smile and continued: "I grew up in Geneva, where there are many people whose ancestors fled to Switzerland from France after that event. So, it still looms large in local history."

He continued, "In 16th century France many people, known as the Huguenots, were breaking away from the Catholic Church and forming Protestant communities. The authorities were at a loss when it came to how to deal with them. They tried talks, they tried debates, but nothing worked. More and more people turned Protestant, even among the nobility. Then on August 24th, St. Bartholomew's Day, in 1572, a large group of Protestant and Catholic nobles had gathered in Paris for a wedding. Making the most of the opportunity, the king gave a signal that the key Protestant leaders should be killed. This signal was heard loudly and clearly, and not only in Paris. All over France, it was open-season on Protestants. Tens of thousands of them were slaughtered throughout the country. People were waiting for a spark to put to the gunpowder of their resentments. Some Catholics believe that it saved France from becoming Protestant. The pope even ordered a special celebratory mass!"

Yusuf and Maryam both gave Mr. Ramadan a bemused look. What did any of this have to do with Egypt? He soon supplied the answer, "Our country is also just waiting for the 'spark' to show them that it is okay to act against the cross-worshippers. Dr. Almasry will supply it. Only this time, it will not just be a few words whispered into a few ears. It will be nationally televised!"

Yusuf was bracing himself for an angry response from Maryam and was astonished that none came. He was even more perplexed at her eventual reply, "You're right. This could help our cause no end. I think you should approach the Capital Broadcast Center to host the interview."

The Sheik looked at her in surprise, while she shyly lowered her gaze. A delighted smile spread across his face. "Good thinking sister!" he said, "With some stations, we will probably be preaching to the converted, but with CBC we will be able to reach a broad and impressionable audience!"

Yusuf's mouth was wide open, and he was about to blurt out something along the lines of 'What the hell?', when a look from Maryam stopped him dead in his tracks. He, therefore, muttered a sheepish, "Good idea!" before getting up to fetch a glass of water.

The Sheik did not seem to notice anything of what passed between Yusuf and Maryam. He got up and walked towards the door. "Splendid," he said with his hand on the door handle, "I'll get right onto it!"

CHAPTER 18

Hana Tadros' heart pounded in her chest as she walked towards Emad Almasry's office. Why did he want to see her? What could be so urgent that he called her on her private number? Had he somehow found out that she had discussed the clay jar with someone who was not part of the investigation?

She had not seen Magdy since that day when they went from church to church in Old Cairo to look for the sign of the *weighted scale.* Still, she was sure that he would have continued his investigations. Had word of this reached her boss, who must have figured out where the 'leak' came from? Could it be that her career as an archeologist was over even before it properly began?

As she sat down opposite Emad, she could not help noticing that he did not look totally at ease. Dismissing indiscreet employees must be a new experience for him. Her heart sank; this was not going to end well. She gave a feeble smile and waited for him to begin.

Emad spoke softly, so she had to strain to hear him: "Hana, do you remember that Coptic clay jar that we worked on?" Hanna nodded, hoping that he would not notice that her heart was racing. "Well," he continued, "I need to tell you something about it, and when I'm done, we need to talk about how we can prevent a catastrophe." Hana stared at Emad; this was not unfolding as she had expected it would.

"I'm going out on a limb here," Emad continued, "Still, here goes." Dread rose in Hana as he told her about the Sheik, about Maryam, about the TV interview, and about the real prospect of violence being unleashed against her people as the masses learned about what would be perceived as the ancient 'treachery' of the Copts.

"If only we could make people see that the jar was just the work of some lone crank. Every community has them," Emad said, as he ended his retelling of the events of the past few days.

Hana shifted in her seat. Emad had placed a great deal of trust in her by telling her all of this. He could have thrown his lot in with 'The Sheik' and hoped for the best. Instead, he wanted to do all that he could to prevent a hammer from falling on the Coptic people. She felt that she had no choice but to repay his trust. She shifted in her seat, blushed and blurted out, "I'm afraid it was not just a lone crank, sir!"

"What? How do you know this? What do you mean?" Emad demanded. Hana looked down at the floor, "Because I discussed the case with Dr. Magdy Botros from the Coptic Museum, and we made an important discovery connected to the symbol on the jar."

Emad looked at her in amazement. Apparently, Abu Bakr was not the only intern who did not keep the details of the investigation secret. For the briefest moment, a look of irritation flashed across his face, only to be replaced by an amused smile a moment later. The discovery of this rather special clay jar must be the worst kept secret in modern Egyptian archeology.

He sat back in his chair, "You'd better tell me what you found then..."

Hanna told him everything about her meeting with Magdy. How Magdy traced the scales to a passage in the Biblical book of Micah and how they found the same symbol in three different churches in Old Cairo. "And, I'm sure you will find it in many other ancient Coptic churches across Egypt, if you went looking. It is a resistance symbol!" she concluded.

Emad looked gravely concerned. If this was true, every single church where the scales were found could be viewed as a legitimate target, and who knew where else violence directed at these churches would spread. He sat silently for a moment and then suddenly remembered the Sheik's response upon hearing of the scales, "It is, of course, not only the words in the book of Micah. There will no doubt be many who would be livid at how a Qur'anic image was used to insult Islam!"

Hana was not entirely sure that she followed, "What do you mean?" she asked. Emad got up, opened a copy of the Qur'an and showed her the passage that the Sheik had so masterfully recited during their first meeting at the Nile Hilton:

> *"Then as for him whose balance (of good deeds) will be heavy, He will live a pleasant life (in Paradise). But as for him whose balance (of good deeds) will be light, He will have his home in Hell."*

Hana's eyes were riveted to the page. The meaning of the fact that the scales were weighted to the left, the side of evil, could not be more apparent. It stood as an utter repudiation of Islam as a path to paradise. They were silent for the longest time. Muslim man and Christian woman, both contemplating the present-day implications of this ancient symbol of defiance. Emad finally broke the silence, "You're right, if word gets out and this is found all over Egypt, the 'lone crank' defense goes out of the window!" The task of somehow ensuring that present vengeance justified by past resistance did not fall on modern Copts suddenly became even more daunting.

Hana looked at Emad with new eyes, comforted that he seemed to find the possible fallout from the contents of the jar just as horrifying as she did. "Isn't there something we can do?" she finally asked, hoping against hope.

Emad had been racking his brain for an answer to this very question ever since his first meeting with the Sheik. He was no closer to a solution, but at least his conversation with Hana had convinced him that there would be allies in his quest. So, far from getting the sack, Hana found herself being confirmed in her role as an intermediary when Emad asked her, "So when can I meet this Dr. Botros of yours?"

CHAPTER 19

In his office at the Coptic Museum, Magdy Botros' eyes flitted between a picture of his wife and their two daughters and the website of the Canadian Immigration Department. Over the past few decades, many Copts have responded to the relentless pressure associated with living as a minority in an overwhelmingly Islamic society by leaving to seek greener pastures. This is how it has come to be that many cities across the Western world now contain thriving Coptic communities.

Magdy had so far resisted the urge to join the exodus, but the events of the past few days had shaken him up. What would happen if word got out that there was an organized Coptic resistance group out there, dedicated to the downfall of Islam itself? Still, his life was in Egypt. He would not be able to bear being away from the museum, the repository of the achievements of his people. He sighed as he closed the browser and tried to concentrate on his inbox. It was no use, the details of his conversation about the Micah Order at the Baron's Palace held his thought processes hostage.

His phone rang. It was a number he did not recognize. He initially resolved to ignore it, but something made him pick up. He barely had time for a greeting when a voice on the other side said, "Dr. Botros, this is Emad Almasry. We need to talk. Urgently! Can I come straight over?"

So, it was Emad, Hana's boss, the archeologist from the ministry. Magdy tried to slow Emad down a bit. What could be so urgent, and why did it involve him? He did not get the impression from Hana that the ministry had any intention of engaging the Coptic Museum in the further investigation of the find. Still, it was clear that this archeologist must have some other reason for reaching out to him. "Okay," he finally said "Come to the main entrance of the museum. I'll meet you there." Magdy was conscious that some of his co-workers may by then have been aware of some strange arrivals at his office door. It would be better if he could pretend that he was a guide for an hour or so.

Magdy sometimes gave personal tours to visitors to the museum. This only occurred when some particularly deep-pocketed donor or sufficiently important government official turned up. Still, it happened often enough that the sight of him walking someone through the museum displays would not be viewed as particularly noteworthy. Meeting Emad like this would mean that he would not have to pass through the office reception area where his visit might cause his colleagues, some of whom may perhaps recognize Emad, to wonder what was going on. On some level, Magdy felt that this was a silly precaution to take. However, after his conversation with Samuel, and the confirmation of the continuing existence of the Micah Order, he felt that it was better that way.

Magdy went outside to wait for Emad. For a moment, he lost himself in imagining how the scene before him had looked 1500 years ago when he would have stood at the heart of the Babylon fortress. Back then this must have been a self-consciously Christian place, to the extent that a church towered over the main gate. He glanced in the direction of the Hanging Church. If only these walls could talk, what glories would they relate? His musings were interrupted when he saw Emad striding towards him across the marble courtyard. He got there in record time and was sweating profusely. Magdy shook his hand and said softly, "Let's go inside."

As they entered the museum, Magdy was indeed very glad that he did not let Emad come to his office. His guest's obvious state of nervous excitement was bound to attract attention in a busy workplace, while the museum itself was deserted that early in the morning. When Emad finally spoke, it was with an air of desperation, "Thank you for seeing me. Hana told me all about your deciphering of the symbol on the jar. You have to help me. You have to help your people." Magdy was entirely taken aback by all of this. Why was he not angry at an employee of the Coptic Museum's interference with his case? Why did 'his people' need help?

He finally said, "I'll hear you out, Dr. Almasry. Every last word. But first, you need to slow down! Walk with me." The next few minutes was slightly surreal as Magdy instinctively took up the role of tour guide as he waited for Emad's breathing to resume a regular pattern. He walked him through rooms filled with the remains of pillars and decorative carvings that came from churches up and down the country. The most impressive items were displayed in a large courtyard where several surviving pillars showed something of the splendor of the buildings they came from. Magdy could sense how the professional archeologist in Emad was pushing his agitated self to the background. He started to calm down and listened with interest to what Magdy had to say.

After a while, they ascended some stairs and stepped into a room that was markedly cooler than the others they came through. Its center was occupied by a large glass case stretching almost halfway to the ceiling. Inside it, there were four glass tables and two wooden pedestals. On each of them, there were parchments that were darkened with age, with some of them very close to pure black. Magdy gave a proud smile: "The Nag Hammadi Gospels" he said. Emad gave a start.

When he first heard that the clay jars had Coptic writing on them, these gospels, written by Gnostic Christians, were the first thing that he thought of. They were discovered in an Upper Egyptian village in 1945 and revolutionized the study of early Christianity. He supposed that he must have known that they would be in the Coptic Museum, but to his shame, he had never given their current location much thought.

And there they were, beautifully preserved in a temperature-controlled room. Despite the urgency of his present predicament, he felt that there was a certain symmetry associated with discussing what he had come to regard as 'his find' in their presence.

There were some chairs against one of the walls, for those who wanted to spend some 'alone time' with the precious manuscripts. Magdy sat down on one of these, motioning for Emad to do the same. The room was wonderfully cool and quiet, and they had it all to themselves. "Okay," said Magdy finally, "Let it all out!" He was surprised when Emad gave him a melancholy look, almost as if he felt sorry for him, before he started speaking. "I am sorry to burden you with this. I'm probably putting you in danger by telling you what I'm about to say. I honestly don't know where to turn." Magdy gave a small nod to encourage him to continue.

It took only a few minutes for it all to pour out. Maryam, the Sheik, the upcoming television interview. The imminent danger that was hanging like a sword over the head of every Copt in Egypt. When Emad had finished, Magdy had his worst fears confirmed. What had previously been a private concern had now widened to an awareness that the jar could change the destiny of his people and that there were enemies out there who were determined to ensure that this change would decidedly not be for the better. The broken and damaged nature of many of the objects around them in the museum silently testified to the fact that this would not be the first time that the Copts would have to suffer through an attempt to eradicate them. Still, they could all do with a breather. Was merely being left alone to worship and to raise their families in peace too much to ask?

Magdy finally spoke, "This Sheik of yours is determined to go ahead. He has enough to go on. Go ahead, give the interview, and get your fiancé back. If you don't, he will just find another mouthpiece to call the masses to arms against us."

Emad stood staring at the darkened gospels in front of them for the longest time as if he somehow imagined they would magically provide some answer. When he finally spoke, it was with the determined air of someone who passed an invisible point of no return, "There is one option. We need to try and solve the riddle contained on the piece of parchment. Perhaps it will lead to an even greater find that will push the mere existence of the jar into the background." Magdy had not seen this coming. He looked at Emad, half in wonder and half in shock, "There's no guarantee that we will find anything, and even if we do, it could inflame the situation even more. Remember, the claim that it makes is dynamite:

The Qibla of the Arabs/Will betray them/The Holy City of Islam/ Shall be its downfall."

Emad understood Magdy's concern, but he was convinced that looking closer at the problem posed by the statement inside the jar represented the tiniest presence of an option for taking some action instead of being swept along by events. He fully realized that they could be heading off on a wild goose chase or that what they might find could be profoundly disruptive to his faith (lukewarm though it may be) and those of millions of others. Still, the desire to do what he could to help Maryam, to not merely be a victim, and more than a bit of professional interest, combined in him to suggest this seemingly crazy course of action.

Magdy did not quite know what to make of Emad's suggestion. It sounded too much like the clutching at straws of a desperate man. He was staking everything on some ancient Coptic riddle that they may not even be able to solve. Still, like Emad, he could not see any alternative other than waiting for the storm to engulf his people. He also felt a frisson of excitement at the possibility of unearthing something that would illuminate a previously hidden part of Coptic history. He finally gave a resigned shrug and with an ironic grin said, "Okay partner, let's give it a shot!"

Emad could still not shake the feeling that his life had now taken a direction that was leading to a very uncertain future, but none of this registered on his face as he returned Magdy's smile with, "So where do we start!"

Magdy thought for a moment, "I suppose the first thing that we need to do is to buy some time. Tell the Sheik that you need to do some more work on dating the jars, and that you need permission from the ministry to talk about it on television. Say anything! Do whatever you can to make him back off a bit. That will give us time to tease out some of the threads of the puzzle in front of us. Whatever you do, don't alienate him. He may decide to plow ahead without you, and then there's no telling what would happen to your Maryam."

Emad hesitated a bit before answering. Then he felt a steely determination rising within him, the source of which he did not know. He took out the 'Swiss phone' that Mr. Ramadan gave him and tapped on his name. It took only a few seconds for a familiar voice, that he would rather not have been familiar with, to greet him, "Ah, Dr. Almasry, I knew you would see sense. I presume you're calling to discuss your television interview?"

Emad took a deep breath before responding. He knew that he must be seen to be cooperating, but how do you sound affable when talking with someone you deeply loathe, about something that goes against the core of your being? Still, he had to push on: "Yes," he said, "but I have two conditions. If they are not met: 'No Deal'!"

A note of hesitation crept into Mr. Ramadan's voice, but he tried to keep up his gracious and reasonable persona: "If you name them, I can consider them," he said after a moment's silence.

Emad continued: "Firstly, I need more time. If you want a good case to be made about the so-called betrayal of the Copts, you'd want that to rest on the best possible archeological research. Also, I have my reputation to protect. I don't want to go on national television and waffle on about something that I do not know enough about. So, you will have to give me some more time for research." There was silence on the other end. After what seemed like minutes, the answer finally came. It was clear that Mr. Ramadan did not like this compromise, but that he could also see that it was a reasonable one. "Fine," he said "We'll hold back a little. Call me when you are ready, but make sure that you do not go beyond two weeks from today."

Emad inwardly sighed with relief; this would indeed buy them some valuable time. "Thank you," he said softly. Before he could continue Mr. Ramadan said, "You mentioned two conditions, what is the other one?" Emad steeled himself, he did not discuss this with Magdy, but it is something that he had to do. When he finally spoke, it was with the voice of a man who should not be trifled with, "There is one reason that I am doing this, and her name is Maryam. I need to speak with her to confirm that she is okay before I can continue."

Emad could almost feel the Sheik's hesitation reaching towards him from the other end of the line. Still, after a moment's consideration, he relented, "I suppose that is a reasonable request. I'll go and see them tonight. You can have five minutes on the phone with her then." Emad bristled at the absurdity of his contact with his fiancé being rationed by a stranger, but he kept his composure and even managed a muffled "Thank You," before ending the call.

Emad spent the next few hours working out what he'd say to Maryam. He was in uncharted waters. How, after all, do you address someone who is being held hostage? He need not have worried. When the phone finally rang that evening, he answered immediately and without so much as a 'hello' Maryam's voice sounded in his ear. She was very determined and in a great hurry! "Listen Emad," she said, "he is outside, so I don't think he can hear me, but he can come in any time to have a listen, so I need to make this quick! Here goes, you should agree to the interview, but you must, I repeat must, insist that I be present as well. Do you understand?"

Emad was still thinking about his reply when Maryam's voice abruptly changed from steely to sugary. He could barely believe the transformation as she suddenly said softly and with great feeling: "Oh, I miss you so Emad, what are we going to do?" Emad could only guess that the Sheik came within earshot. He was right, within a minute or so, he heard him quietly telling her that it was almost time to hang up.

Emad had no idea what to make of Maryam's urgent plea at the beginning of the call, but he had always trusted her judgment. He dialed Mr.

Ramadan's number after his call with Maryam ended. The latter said, "Well?" Emad paused for a moment, realizing once again that he was playing a dangerous game, "I'll do it. But only if Maryam is in the audience as well. You made it clear that my participation is the condition for her release, and I want it to happen there and then. When I've said my piece, you can do what you must do, but I am leaving with her and will have nothing whatsoever to do with you after that."

In the end, Emad was surprised at how easy it was. The Sheik agreed to his request almost straightaway. He strongly suspected that Maryam must have been playing a kind of double game to earn his trust. This was all but confirmed when the Sheik said, "Yes, it will be good if Sister Maryam can hear it from your lips!"

After the call ended, Emad sat down, his head in his hands. How had it all come to this? He was in the middle of a hostage situation in which the hostage was making her own mysterious plans. As if this was not enough, he was about to try to double-cross the Muslim Brotherhood, with a Coptic Christian he'd only just met as his key ally. The icing on the cake was that he could only succeed in his mission by solving an ancient riddle as impenetrable as a London fog.

He was still pondering this when his thoughts suddenly flitted to the Indiana Jones figurine above his desk. Despite the mess he was in, he could not help but chuckle. "Life imitating art", he thought. His recent experiences, and no doubt those to come, seemed worthy of the Spielberg treatment. But why on earth did it have to be him?

Chapter 20

The multi-lane Cairo to Alexandria highway is perhaps where Egypt is least like its ancient self. True, the tollbooth at the Cairo end does unconvincing homage to the pharaonic past with its faux Luxor pillars, but the road soon leaves the Nile, the wellspring of Egypt, behind, and rushes through the desert to the 'second city.' For the next two hours the highway is dominated by massive advertising billboards selling the 'good life,' here and now, to the descendants of a people fixated on the afterlife.

Still, reality intrudes. The outer fence of one of Egypt's most notorious prisons stretches for miles along the highway, causing motorists zipping past to reflect with a shudder at what life must be like on the inside. At that moment it was, again, full of Brotherhood supporters who had been caught up in the post-Morsi crackdown, but who was to say where the wheel of fortune would turn next?

Emad stared out of the window. They had left Cairo well and truly behind, and every now and then they would pass the gaudy gates of estates with grandiose names where people with too much money and too little sense were trying to build property empires in the desert. Straggly olive trees, scrawny looking ostriches and broken irrigation pipes all testified to the brutal realities behind why owning land next to the country's premium highway confers much in bragging rights and very little in terms of return on investment. Still, it was not to one of these estates that they were heading.

Emad looked over at Magdy and reflected on the process that had brought them here. They had spent days holed up in his office, looking at the words on the parchment from every angle. Ideas were floated and just as quickly shot down against a backdrop of endless cups of coffee and mounting frustration. Their first order of business was obviously to find the '*White Valley*' that was somehow associated with a search for immortality.

An obvious place to start was the Valley of the Kings near Luxor where Egypt's pharaohs supposedly began their journey to immortality between the 16th and 11th centuries before Christ. Still, there was no record of it ever having been called the White Valley, and ancient Copts would have known little of it since full excavations, eventually leading to the spectacular discovery of Tutankhamen's tomb, had only started about 140 years ago.

Another candidate was the so-called 'White Desert', a depression housing some oases in the middle of Egypt's barren Western desert. It had a long association with the Bedouin, who still roam the tracks across the Sahara in this very remote part of the country. Both Emad and Magdy were somewhat unconvinced that this would be the place, due to its isolation and the lack of any documented link to Coptic Christianity. Yet, it was the only place that looked even remotely promising. So, Emad listlessly started to enquire about accommodation options in Farafra, the main town in the area, while mentally preparing himself for the eight-hour drive with nothing but empty desert to keep them company.

Thankfully, the solution (or what they sincerely hoped would be the solution) appeared from an entirely unexpected angle. A few months previously, Emad had made an appointment with a reporter for an American travel magazine who was writing an article on pharaonic sites in Egypt.

She thought it would be good to get a few quotes from someone working at the Ministry for Antiquities, and somehow the request landed on his desk. It was the last thing that he wanted to do at that stage, given that he had quite enough on his plate. Still, she had traveled from America for her article, and it would only take an hour or so of his time. In the end, he decided to go ahead.

Alicia Daniels, the reporter, was nothing if not enthusiastic. Every response was met with 'How Interesting!', or a long-drawn-out 'Awesome'. She even thought that his Indiana Jones figurine was the funniest thing that she had ever seen. Emad could not help but wonder what her reactions would have been like if he had been a bit more engaged. As it was, he merely tried to get through her questions as quickly as possible so that he could get back to trying to tease some meaning from the parchment. Then the crucial question came, "Thank you so much Dr. Almasry. This is so fascinating. It really is! Now, can you please tell me a bit more about how the ancient Egyptians embalmed mummies?"

Emad did not have to think about the answer. He explained, as if on autopilot, how a body would be laid out on a stone bench after some appropriate rituals. Then the internal organs were removed and replaced with Natron, now known as *sodium carbonate decahydrate* which would dry out the body cavity before the rest of the process (which would include removing the brain through the nose) could get underway. Inspiration hit in a flash: "Mummification, a quest for immortality. Natron… salt…white!"

The '*White Valley/From which many sought immortality*' must be the place from where the ancient Egyptians sourced their 'mummification salt.' Alicia Daniels was probably still wondering what on earth had come over Emad. He started speaking very fast, in order to get the interview over as soon as possible. More than that, for some strange reason, he thanked her profusely for coming. The moment she was out of the door, he called Magdy. Before the latter could even get a word in, Emad shouted: 'We need to get to Wadi Natrun!"

There was a moment's silence before he heard Magdy's soft: "But of course! You're absolutely right", coming back at him.

Wadi Natrun takes its name from the Natron that was harvested there in industrial quantities during pharaonic times. It is, however, far from the only thing for which it is famous. With the coming of the Christian church to Egypt, there were at least some Egyptian Christians who felt deeply uncomfortable with the fact that their church had become a mass movement. They believed that the Christian life should ideally be lived in isolation from the masses. Separation would leave them free to pursue lives of prayer and devotion, unencumbered by the mundane realities of daily life. Some of these spiritual athletes initially isolated themselves as hermits, living on the edges of towns and villages. It took the genius of a man, known to posterity as St. Anthony the Great to realize that the objective of more profound devotion to God could be better achieved through *both* isolation and community. But how to square such a difficult, if not paradoxical, circle?

Anthony's great innovation was to affirm the impulse towards isolation from society but to channel it into communities of people who all had the same desire to be separate from the world. The Greek word for someone living apart was *'monakos.'* This word lives on in 'monk.' The name is a bit of a misnomer since Anthony worked hard to bring these solitary individuals together in one place. To forge them into a community of brothers dedicated to a singular idea: Seeking the glory of God, in houses specifically built for the *monakoi*, monasteries.

Anthony's invention would, of course, eventually spread far beyond Egypt. Not least because the *'Life of St. Anthony,'* written by his friend and admirer St. Athanasius of Alexandria, was for a long time next only to the Bible in terms of its distribution throughout Christendom. Still, it must be remembered that it had all started in Egypt. Thus, monasteries around the world can look back to the so-called Desert Fathers, with Anthony at their head, as the fountainheads of Christian monasticism.

The monasteries established by the Desert Fathers were concentrated in the desert between Cairo and Alexandria. Many of them eventually succumbed to the combined pressures of Islamic encroachment and the sheer backbreaking effort of sustaining life in the desert. There is, however, still one place where a few of the oldest Christian monasteries in the world survive into the present day. These monasteries are concentrated in the very same valley from where the ancient Egyptians sourced their 'mummification salt': *Wadi Natrun* (Natron Valley)

All of this explained why Emad was so excited. Here was a 'White Valley' closely linked to a search for immortality. More than that, it was as intimately intertwined with Egyptian Christian history as it was possible to be. Scetis, the ancient Coptic name for the valley, is one of the deepest sources of Egyptian Christian pride. Magdy's immediate acceptance of this place as the 'White Valley' was just the icing on the cake in confirming to Emad that he was on the right track.

Magdy was, of course, very familiar with Wadi Natrun and had been there many times, unlike Emad for whom it was just another archeological site connected with pharaonic Egypt. For the Copts, Wadi Natrun was a living, breathing place - confirmation, in bricks and mortar, of their position at the very heart of Egyptian and worldwide Christian history.

Unfortunately, it was not merely a matter of driving into Wadi Natrun and finding what they were looking for. The valley plays host to four surviving monasteries. The largest of these is dedicated to St. Bishoy. Then there are also the monasteries of St. Macarius the Great, the Baromeos Monastery and the Syrian Monastery. Emad sighed in desperation when Magdy told him this. They did not have the time to go through four monastic complexes with a fine-toothed comb.

Still, they had to start somewhere. Turning off the Cairo-Alexandria highway, they entered the dusty streets of the town that clustered around two of the Wadi Natrun monasteries, St. Bishoy, and the Syrian Monastery. Magdy directed Emad towards the Syrian monastery. "Might as well start here," he said, "It does contain the most celebrated archeological artifact in the area after all."

Magdy had phoned ahead, so a guard at the gatehouse was waiting for them. Emad looked nervously at the standard-issue Maadi AK47 assault rifle slung at a jaunty angle across his shoulder. He knew, of course, that the Coptic community was under siege, but seeing this visual reminder of that fact was confirmation of just how dangerous the mission that they were engaged in was.

The monks were engaged in one of their daily rounds of prayer in a chapel somewhere in the bowels of the complex, so the courtyard near the entrance of the building was eerily quiet. Fortunately, Magdy did not need a guide. He knew exactly where he was going. The Syrian monastery is home to the fabled 'Door of Prophecies.' On the surface, it looked just like a thousand other doors, containing intricate patterns, adorning churches up and down Egypt. When you looked closer, however, you would see that in this case the door was made of ebony inlaid with ivory. This was no ordinary object. It had been there since the year 914 and is justly treasured by the monks as their pride and joy.

It was not merely the door's venerable age that brought Magdy to the Syrian Monastery. It was more the fact that this door was widely believed to provide a potted history of the Christian church, hence the name 'Door of Prophecies.' The door is divided into seven rows: Each with different panels of inlaid ivory patterns, arranged in intricate designs. These panels each portray a distinct epoch in the history of the church. Copts have been arguing for centuries about what each row means, but there is absolute unanimity about the fourth one. Its pattern consists of crosses surrounded by crescent moons.

It is a depiction, therefore, of the coming of Islam and how this enveloped the church in a sea of troubles. Magdy wanted to visit it, as it seemed directly relevant to the world from which the clay jar and its parchment sprung. However, standing in front of the door made him feel rather silly. It was just a door. A venerable one, yes, but nothing on it seemed to shout: "This is the end of the road!" Worse, as he walked around the room, he could not see any indication of the 'weighted scales.' It was almost ridiculously easy to find this symbol in Old Cairo, once he knew what he was looking for. And yet here, at the heart of what they believed to be the 'White Valley'. Nothing.

"Let's go around again," he said after they did a careful circuit of the interior of the church to look for something, anything, that could indicate that they were on the right track. In the end, it was Emad who asked the question that made Magdy realize that their quest might be futile: "Given that we are thousands of miles from Syria, why is this place called the 'Syrian Monastery'?"

"Of course," Magdy mentally smacked his forehead. This place was the haunt of Syrian monks, and had been funded by wealthy Syrian merchants in Cairo for centuries. Its purpose was to allow the Syrian monks to immerse themselves in the way of St. Anthony before going back to their homeland to set up similar monastic establishments. It was easy to forget this fact now that it was just another Coptic monastery, albeit an impossibly ancient one, with hardly a Syrian in sight. How could he overlook this? A monastery filled with foreigners during the coming of Islam would scarcely be the home base of a secret Coptic order. Sure, the Syrians must have seen Islam as a significant threat, given that their homeland was ravished earlier and worse than Egypt, but they had other ways to comment on this situation. The 'Door of Prophecy' was probably an example of such a response, but Magdy sadly concluded that it would not shed any light on the Coptic Order of Micah.

While they were standing around, at a loss what to do next, Magdy suddenly noted an information board next to the front door of the church. Wadi Natrun is a World Heritage Site. The board was placed there by UNESCO and explained in several languages why the monasteries in the area enjoy this status. Despite the pressure of their current situation, Magdy could feel his chest swell with pride at this symbol of the recognition of the contribution of his people to world civilization.

UNESCO's paragraph did not tell Magdy anything that he did not know already. Still, a section jumped out at him. It read:

"Daily Life in Scetis: One of the features of monastic life at Wadi Natrun was extreme asceticism. Monks often had to endure extended fasts, long prayer times, and hard physical labor. Many monks even went beyond formal requirements and strove to outdo one another in extreme acts of devotion. Some monks became famous across the valley for their ability to pray deep into the night."

The information board went on to list more actions of these spiritual supermen, but Magdy had stopped reading. Unbidden, but clear as day, a childhood memory shot up from his subconscious. Sitting in Sunday School, half-listening to an ancient priest as he told stories about the saints. The tales of daring and spiritual rectitude all morphed into one after a while. That was until the priest took out a picture of a man with an intense and wild look. Here was no ordinary saint. For starters, his hair seemed to reach his hips. Highly irregular for your standard Coptic holy man. Before Magdy could ask why this man was so different from the others, the priest, sensing a heightened level of interest in the room, proceeded to tell them about St. Bishoy.

Bishoy, who lived from 320 to 417, was very frustrated by the fact that he invariably fell asleep during what he fervently hoped would be all-night prayer sessions. He was even teased about this by his fellow monks. The plan that he came up with was nothing if not radical. Drawing inspiration from Samson he grew his hair to the point where he was able to tie it to a hook that he had installed on the roof of his cell. That way he would be jerked awake every time his sleepy head bobbed downwards. Problem solved!

"Where devotion was tested by sleep," Magdy muttered to himself. Surely this must refer to the monastery of St. Bishoy, neighbor to the Syrian Monastery. It is dedicated to the memory of this long-haired saint. It is even believed that his body remains entirely intact more than a millennium after it was interred near the site of his most significant spiritual

exploits. Magdy was suddenly very grateful that he happened to perk up when the priest told that story.

They would have to go next door. Magdy pulled out his phone, dialed a number and half-chuckled at the American accented Arabic that cheerfully greeted him at the other end, "Far out! You're here? Sure, come on over!"

Chapter 21

In later years Hana Tadros would often look back to that morning at Groppi as the calm before the storm. What genteel surroundings in which to spend a last few moments of peace.

In the latter part of the 19th century, downtown Cairo was transformed, with money from the Suez Canal, into what was sometimes called 'Paris by the Nile.' Until 1952, wide boulevards culminating in stately squares, an opera house, and plush department stores all combined to give the impression that Cairo was turning into a mainly European city at breakneck speed. Even back then, this notion could quickly be dispelled by walking past the Opera House towards *Bab Zuweila*, the ancient city gate. Beyond it, the medieval warren of streets, unchanged for centuries, still forcefully reminded those who navigated the alleys and byways that this was an oriental city.

Black Saturday, 27 January 1952, definitively marked the end of 'Paris by the Nile.' On this day large mobs, furious that British occupation forces had opened fire on Egyptian auxiliary police officers torched almost a thousand European-connected buildings across the city. It was the spark that would, by the end of that year, lead to the fall of the pro-Western

King Farouk and his eventual replacement by President Gamal Abdel Nasser. Downtown Cairo had suffered particularly badly. Hardly a building was left intact. Particular fury was reserved for the Opera House. Long resented as a symbol of Western decadence and profligate spending, it was left a smoldering ruin. Giuseppe Verdi wrote Aida for its opening in 1871, yet this jewel in Cairo's crown was never rebuilt. A massive government carpark now occupies the site.

Through it all, Groppi survived. Founded in the early 1900s as one of the very first Parisian style coffee shops in Egypt, it probably reached the height of its fame in the fevered atmosphere of WWII Cairo. With Rommel's *Afrika Korps* coming to within spitting distance of Egypt's major cities it was said that every second table contained a German spy and every other one an Allied intelligence officer keeping an eye on the city's Germans and Italians. Quickly reopened after being destroyed in 1952, Groppi continues to serve up European delicacies and red-hot political speculation.

Hana did not go to Groppi for its atmosphere of intrigue. Its chandeliers, overfilled display cases and the general air of faded charm allowed her to forget, just for a little while, that as both a woman and a Copt the decks were doubly stacked against her in this society. Still, she could not help but feel as if her presence stood in the long tradition of Groppi being a place where fates were decided, no matter how much she tried to push current events to the back of her mind.

Finally yielding, she took out her phone and flicked to a picture of the Fustat clay jar. Of course, she knew by then that Emad also had an inkling that the jar was special when they first opened it. What she did not realize until recently was that he went against all regulations to take a photo of it. The fact that she was now in possession of this photo somehow linked their fates together in an enterprise of which she still did not fully understand the contours. Yet, for Emad to send her concrete evidence of serious rule-breaking must mean that he was taking the potential impact of the jar very seriously indeed.

When the waiter came over to place her coffee and a slice of Black Forest cheesecake, artfully presented on a small silver tray, before her, she shifted her phone to one side. Next to it, she placed a little slip of paper. On it was a name, 'Samuel Mounir,' and a number.

For a few moments, she dwelled on the conversation at the Coptic Museum from the night before, during which Magdy had handed her the number. He asked her to come after closing time, and when she had arrived, she was surprised to see that Emad was there as well. Their conversations about the jar did not end with a single meeting. It was evident that a friendship or at least a deep appreciation for each other's talents had developed between the two men. Magdy seemed intensely agitated, with rapid-fire sentences always trailing off into many different directions.

Still, she did get the gist of it. Magdy and Emad were heading to Wadi Natrun in the hope of solving the mystery posed by the parchment they had found in the jar. She could sense that Magdy's restless energy was a mixture of wide-eyed excitement and fear. It was in this context that he insisted that Emad send the photo to her cell phone, so that 'there is evidence if something goes wrong.'

Just before she left, Magdy bent down to rapidly scribble Samuel Mounir's name and number on a piece of paper. His next words chilled her to the bone: "Hana, don't be alarmed, but I need you to do something for me. I will check in at least once a day while we are away. If you do not hear from me for three days running, please call this number. He knows. He'll be able to help." There were so many questions racing around in her head, but she very quickly realized that it would be virtually impossible to get a coherent explanation of where the investigation was going. Yet, it was somehow profoundly comforting that these two men were working together, not only to solve an ancient riddle but also to prevent a storm from descending on her people.

She looked around her. Groppi was full. There was a low murmur in the room as people compared their days or perhaps tried to solve the perennial question of whether the chocolate prepared on-site can be called 'Swiss' since a Swiss chocolatier had founded Groppi and it still followed the recipes laid down by him. All the while events were taking place outside that could rip apart the lives of many sitting there. Its apparent imperviousness to the struggles of the wider world was perhaps why Groppi continued to thrive and survive. In a society constantly buffeted by the winds of change, and even mortal threats to life and limb, it was good to have a place where it was possible to at least pretend that civilization was built on solid foundations and that it would last forever.

For a moment, Hana wondered if it would not have been better to just go home after taking part in the opening of the jar. The fact that she had memorized the words on the parchment, and then shared them with Magdy set in motion a chain of events that, at the very least, called the career path that she was carving out against all the odds into question. But what were the alternatives? She had always been a firm believer in following the evidence wherever it leads. She knew that she had thrown in her lot with two men who shared this fundamental conviction. Even so, it would have been good to have an assurance that everything would turn out fine, but that was a luxury that none of them had. In fact, given the recent travails of her people, chances were that this was not even the most likely outcome.

Hana's sense of uneasiness was not alleviated, as she hoped it would be, by her rarified surroundings. Yes, Groppi was a shelter from the storm, but she could not stay in there forever. As she got up to leave, she could not help but think that over the years many people left this place with the best-laid plans, perhaps made at the very table where she was sitting, that eventually ended in disaster.

If she could have observed a scene being played out, about a fifteen-minute walk from Groppi, Hana's vague feeling of anxiety would likely have morphed into full-blown dread.

In a spacious office in the Arab League building, a distinguished-looking gentleman was hunched over the screen of his laptop. His eyes firmly glued to a little blue dot moving across a map on the screen...

Chapter 22

Emad, who had never been to Wadi Natrun, was not quite sure what to expect next, but a large self-contained monastic town was probably not high on the list of possibilities. However, this was exactly what greeted them as they moved from the much smaller Syrian Monastery towards St. Bishoy. It stood in the center of extensive farmlands, and its cluster of buildings contained no fewer than five churches. The largest of these could provide seating for thousands of people and was often the focus of huge Coptic festivals. Even during non-festival times, the monastery played host to a constant stream of tour buses disgorging pilgrims, eager for a glimpse of the relics of some of the most celebrated saints in Egyptian Christian history.

Counted among the number of those the pilgrims came to venerate, was the person behind the revival of monasticism in Egypt during the 20th century. The St. Bishoy Monastery was at the heart of this project, and Pope Shenouda III (Coptic Pope from 1971 until his death in 2012) had expanded the lands and buildings of the monastery to make it the jewel in the crown of Egypt's monastic establishments. He also left explicit instructions that his body should be buried in the large church that he had constructed inside the monastic complex. This church quickly became a shrine to Shenouda himself. He is, in fact, well on his way to becoming one of the most popular saints of the modern Coptic church.

Besides energetically promoting the growth of monasticism, which he saw as one of the main bulwarks for ensuring the long-term survival of the church, Shenouda had also aggressively promoted international expansion. When he ascended the Coptic papal throne in 1971, there were two Coptic Churches in the USA. By the time of his death, there were more than 200. It was, in fact, with a member of this Coptic diaspora that Magdy spoke on the phone as they left the Syrian Monastery.

Brother Michael looked every inch the Coptic monk. It was all there: Long black robes, beard stretching down his chest, a stylized cross made of rolled-up strips of leather and a black hood with tiny white crosses embroidered on it. Yet, when he opened his mouth, it sounded like he had just emerged from the waves at some Southern Californian beach. Back in the days when he was known as 'Mike', this was indeed where he spent most of his time. All of that had changed when he was, to his great surprise, selected to be one of the hundreds of overseas Coptic-background young people brought to this very monastery for a week-long conference. This annual conference was another of Pope Shenouda's innovations, and it has been crucial in fostering an international Coptic identity.

Mike was absolutely smitten by his ancestral homeland and especially with St. Bishoy, a place positively pulsing with history. So, upon returning to the States, he started, to the great amazement of his surfing buddies, the process of being received into Coptic monastic life. Given that St. Bishoy was the place where this journey started, it was only natural that he would eventually contrive to be sent to live and work there.

Interestingly, the monastic authorities wanted to make use of the fact that he was much more comfortable in English than in Arabic (let alone Coptic). He was promptly given the job of welcoming international visitors to the monastery. This role suited him to a tee. It meant that he could share his love for this place, one of the oldest monasteries in the world, with wide-eyed visitors on an almost daily basis. The questions asked by visitors, and his natural curiosity eventually caused him to know as much about every nook and cranny of St. Bishoy as anyone alive.

Magdy had met Brother Michael during the few times when he brought overseas visitors up from the Coptic Museum and had always been impressed by his friendly 'can do' spirit and his comprehensive knowledge of the place he now called home.

Magdy agonized about how much to tell Michael. He did not know him well enough to be sure that he would keep everything he heard to himself. Just how sensitive the situation was, was brought home to Magdy when the monk gave Emad a puzzled look after being introduced to him. Emad did not act like someone who knew his way around a monastery and thus did not bow, genuflect, or pause at the appropriate places upon entering the church in which they met Brother Michael. When Magdy mentioned that Emad worked for the Ministry for Antiquities, Michael's eyes widened. They were used to visits from the Coptic Museum, but there had not been an official from the government there since he had joined the brothers at St. Bishoy.

Once the dust had settled after what he came to think of as the 'Dark Times,' Michael often reflected on how things could have been very different if Magdy came out and told him everything at that meeting in the St. George church, one of the churches inside the monastery. If nothing else, it would have caused him to see to it that the guards at the gatehouse were a bit more careful about who they allowed inside. Instead, he heard from Magdy just the merest outline of the story behind the discovery of the jars. Michael put Emad's interest in the jar down to professional curiosity and the chance to be part of a significant discovery, so he did not think much more of it.

Since it was already late afternoon, it was decided that Magdy and Emad would stay overnight. Michael made a quick call to arrange this and then took them to their rooms in the guest quarters. As he was about to leave Emad in his room to freshen up a bit, Michael's eye caught the large cross on the wall. This was slightly awkward; they were not used to house Muslims, who are taught by the Qur'an to despise the cross, in the guest house. He hesitated for a moment before pointing to the cross and saying to Emad, "Would you be more comfortable if I removed this?" Emad gave him a somewhat surprised look before shaking his head, "Of course not, leave it, this is your space after all." Michael was mildly reassured by this and gave a beaming smile before leaving the room with a cheery, "As you wish."

An hour or so later Michael led Magdy and Emad to the refectory where they joined the monks for dinner. They sat apart, and Emad was deeply conscious that he was the object of several long and searching looks from the other tables. One of the roles of this place was to keep outsiders out, to the extent that the monastery had a wall and a medieval keep that would allow it to withstand a siege lasting several months. And there he was, an outsider right in the heart of the building, being treated to a meal from the monastery kitchen. Emad tried to diffuse the tension by loudly asking Michael questions about St. Bishoy. This way, he could at least demonstrate that he was genuinely interested in the history of the monastery, which was on some level undoubtedly true.

Later that evening Michael came to fetch them to show them the new church, dedicated to St. Bishoy, the burial place of the recently deceased Pope Shenouda. Even at 9 pm, it was a hive of activity. People were milling about in the courtyard, buying 'holy bread' stamped with a series of Christian symbols or catching up with old friends who also traveled from across Egypt to this auspicious place. After proudly showing them some of the most important relics of the church, Michael asked them to sit down in one of the pews so that they could tell him more about why they believed St. Bishoy had something to do with the jars found in Fustat. Magdy recited the words from the parchment:

In the blessed land
In the White Valley
From which many sought immortality
Where devotion was tested by sleep

At the place of the resurrection
She that walks will finally soar
The Saracens will be pulled apart
As the sons of Micah awaken

The Qibla of the Arabs
Will betray them
The Holy City of Islam
Shall be its downfall

He continued on to explain why they were convinced that Wadi Natrun was the place *from which many sought immortality*. He also told Michael about how the story of St. Bishoy praying with his hair tied to a hook suddenly came to him as he reflected on the statement about 'devotion tested by sleep.' Brother Michael's face suddenly lit up, "Do you want to go and have a look?" He chuckled at Magdy's surprise, "Remember, it is my job to welcome visitors!" He patted a pocket somewhere deep in his robes, and they could hear the jingle of keys.

They got up and Michael took them towards the oldest part of the monastery. The ancient Church of St. Bishoy dominates it. Right next to it was a reminder of the fact that the faith of the Copts had been lived out in the teeth of fierce opposition since time immemorial. A sign pointed to the '*Well of the Martyrs*' where, according to Coptic tradition, Berber invaders had washed their swords after killing 49 residents of the monastic valley. They were, however, not heading for either the church or the well. Instead, Brother Michael led them in a wide arc around the church. Behind it, their minuscule domes glowing eerily in the moonlight, was a row of monk's cells.

Tradition has it that St. Bishoy himself occupied one of these cells. Michael stopped at a heavy wooden door and reached into his pocket for his master key. While the monk was fiddling with the lock, Emad looked around at the church where the former resident of the cell now lies buried. This was a rich Egyptian story that had known absolutely nothing about until that day.

When the door swung open, they were ushered into the tiny space where, if tradition can be trusted, St. Bishoy had fought his heroic battles against sleep. Even with only three people inside the small room, it felt impossibly full. Michael chuckled, "It's a good thing we came now. This place gets more crowded than the Cairo Metro during the day!"

An icon showing St. Bishoy kneeling at the feet of Christ adorned the wall where his bed would have been. Brother Michael's eyes traveled upwards, and as they followed his gaze, they saw it. Right above them, a massive metal hook protruded from the roof. This was, indeed, a place where 'devotion was tested by sleep'. Emad could picture the long-haired monk praying away in the wee hours of the morning, his head jerking back every time his hair was pulled taut by the hook. No wonder the Coptic faithful flocked to this place as one of extraordinary holiness.

After they stood around in the tiny cell for a few more moments, Magdy gave a little cough. They had to start investigating whether this space had any connection with the Micah Order. It made sense that the order would use a spot at the heart of Coptic spirituality, to announce their presence. But where? It was not as though there was heaps of space where something could be hidden. Still, they had to have a thorough look.

Almost as if someone gave a signal, they spread out, as far as it was possible, which was not very far at all. The icons were clearly from more recent times, but they had a look behind them anyway. No niches or other hiding places presented themselves. There were many little crevices in the rough stonework. These were filled to the brim with scribbled prayers on bits of paper. Interesting to be sure, but probably of much more recent vintage. Anticipating the question forming in Emad's mind, Michael said: "No use looking at these, they are cleared out every two months or so!"

After a few more minutes of fruitless searching, it gradually dawned on them that there may indeed be nothing to see. They were just about to give up and go to bed, it had been a very long day after all, when Emad's archeological training kicked in. In a way, this was an archeological site. A site must be examined methodically, with not an inch left uninvestigated.

He stopped for a moment. They may not have been totally methodical, but they had a good look around. What had they missed? Almost mechanically his eyes were drawn upwards to St. Bishoy's hook.

He turned to Brother Michael and tentatively asked, "Please understand that I'm not questioning your traditions, but would you know if that is the original hook?" Michael shot him a quizzical look before cracking a half-smile, "To be perfectly honest, we do not even know if this cell is the original one, let alone the hook. But we need a focus for our devotion, and we can be sure that this cell had been here for centuries. So we accept, by faith, that this is the place."

Emad noticed that Magdy was, by then, also staring intently at the hook. He finally spoke up, "Do you think it would be possible for us to have a closer look?" For the first time since they arrived at the monastery, Michael's enthusiasm seemed to flag, "Not sure how we can do that, it hangs from the ceiling after all!" Then, just as quickly as his spirits dropped, he perked up again, "What good is a master key if you're not going to use it?", he shouted over his shoulder as he rushed from the room.

A few moments later he emerged, huffing and puffing, carrying a step-ladder. "We use one of the cells as a storeroom, please don't tell UNESCO!" he said by way of explanation.

They all looked up at the hook for a few moments, before Emad gave Magdy a little nod. It somehow just felt right that it should be a Copt who investigated the hook, object of the pious admiration of so many over the years. Magdy gave a tiny smile to acknowledge Emad's gesture before gingerly mounting the ladder. As he did so, he wondered how long it was since anyone had a close look at the hook. Given its position high up on the ceiling and the emphasis on leaving the cell undisturbed, better to reflect its ancient sanctity, he would guess that it may have been decades or even centuries.

It was a strange and unique experience to have his face right next to an object that generations of the faithful had been restricted to observing from below. As he got closer, he was startled by how sturdy and solid the hook was. It measured at least two feet along its shaft, from where it emerged from the ceiling to its tip. The metal, he thought it might be copper, was darkened with age. He quickly noted, with rising excitement, that deep indentations were snaking around the outside of the shaft. They were probably carved into the hook, or perhaps pressed in when the metal was still hot.

Magdy did his best to make sense of the indentations, but it was no use. No matter how he bent his neck, they still looked like nothing more than a series of lines. "I would love to have a closer look in brighter light; I think there might be writing on here!", he called down to Emad and Michael, their expectant faces staring up at him.

"Maybe you should try to dislodge it" came the reply from the monk. Magdy was somewhat taken aback by this rather cavalier attitude towards his heritage from one of the guardians of the monastery. He realized, however, that Brother Michael was right. They would have a much better opportunity to properly investigate the hook if it was not immovable and way above their heads.

Michael sensed Magdy's hesitation. He chuckled, thinking what his brother monks would have done in this situation. Still, they were not adrenaline-addicted big-wave surfers in their former lives. He smiled up at Magdy and shrugged his shoulders, "In for a penny, in for a pound! Let's do it."

Magdy grabbed the hook with both hands and was surprised to feel it move slightly. He continued to wiggle it back and forth, a cloud of dust descending on Emad and Michael below as he did so. As he increased the force of his movements, he was thankful that this was not some delicate artifact but a solid piece of metal. He was elated as he felt the hook moving towards him but had to stop to cough and splutter as bits of masonry settled on his face; this was heavy work.

With a final heave, the hook was free. Magdy could not help but let out a little whoop of joy, before suddenly remembering that he had just disturbed one of Coptic Christianity's holiest sites. With a guilty grin, he handed the hook to Michael, who immediately began turning it around in his hands.

As Magdy descended from the ladder, he looked over at Michael who had a massive frown creasing his forehead as he rotated the hook. With a relieved smile he handed it back to Magdy. He may have been a dedicated monk, but he felt profoundly out of his depth trying to make sense of what he was holding.

Magdy took the hook, handling the heavy object almost like it was made of glass. Like Michael, he proceeded to turn it round and round, albeit more slowly and deliberately. It was immediately apparent to him that the indentations were words written in the Coptic alphabet. As a Coptic historian, he could read the words as easily as he could read Arabic or English, so he immediately began to translate.

"Hmmmmm let's see. The first word is *'Micah.'* This is followed by *'Combatting the scant measure that is accursed'*. Magdy immediately recognized this as the line from Micah Chapter 6 that he had stumbled upon in the Hanging Church when he first tried to get to the bottom of the name of the Order. If any further proof was needed, this was it. They were on the right trail. The Order was undoubtedly active in this monastery in the heart of Wadi Natrun. More than that, it seemed like some of its members had replaced the original hook used by St. Bishoy with a newer one, although it could itself by now be more than a millennium old, to proclaim their presence.

He continued further down the shaft of the hook, as he did so he cast a concerned look at Emad. As a Muslim, he might not like hearing the next sentence, even though Magdy was convinced that he was totally on board when it came to solving the mystery. Below the statement about the 'scant measure' was a tiny version of the 'weighted scale' above the word 'Islam.' Beneath that were the words, *"Mene, Mene, Tekel, Upharsin."*

Initially, Magdy was at a loss to explain what he was reading. Then yet another childhood memory came flooding back. A picture in a Bible storybook of a disembodied hand, writing these very words on a wall. The biblical book of Daniel tells the story of how during a lavish banquet, this sentence announced the end of the reign of the Babylonian king Belshazzar. Magdy cleared his throat, tried to avoid eye contact with Emad, and declared, "The next section has the word 'Islam' and then an Aramaic statement meaning *Weighed and Found Wanting*."

A solemn silence now fell over the room. Even Michael, with his sunny disposition, looked down as he pondered the implications of the presence of this inflammatory object in the cell of one of the greatest saints ever to bestride the sands of Egypt. Magdy finally broke the silence, "There's more. Just give me a moment to translate the last little bit." He stared intently at the final statement as it circled almost to the very top of the hook.

He finally read in a firm voice: "*The Sons of Micah. Strong and Steadfast. Every knee shall bow. Every tongue shall confess...*" He did not need to finish the sentence. Michael did it for him, "*...that Jesus Christ is Lord.*" Emad gave both of them a puzzled look. "Also from the Bible!", Michael said, "The letter from the Apostle Paul to the Philippians." Emad was rather impressed by this; he could not quote chapter and verse of the Qur'an like that. Still, Michael was a monk after all. The clear intent of the words did not escape him. St. Bishoy's hook (or more likely its replacement) was an eloquent statement of the resolve of the Micah Order to re-establish the rule of Christ and an understanding that this would necessarily imply battling the 'scant measure that is accursed'.

Emad was the first to speak. He sounded slightly troubled, "This is an awesome discovery. However, I do not think..."

He never got to finish his sentence.

With a triumphant smile, Abu Bakr, the intern who seemingly had a hotline to the Sheik, swept into the tiny room. "Congratulations Dr.

Almasry!" he said with an exaggerated emphasis on Emad's title. He was swinging a Beretta pistol that he clearly did not know how to use. There could, however, be no such illusions when it came to the two sturdy men who squeezed into the, now tightly packed, room behind him. Abu Bakr motioned towards the muscle-men, "May I introduce you to Yasser and Rafiq? They are here to ensure that no one does anything silly."

"By the way," he said, turning to Michael, "You may want to review your security arrangements. Tattoos can be easily faked after all." He lifted the sleeve of his shirt to reveal a tell-tale Coptic cross tattoo on his wrist.

Emad was numb with shock. How on earth did they know to follow them here? He did not have wait long for his answer. Abu Bakr, who was enjoying his transformation from lowly intern to gun-wielding outlaw, gave Emad what he sincerely hoped was a pitying look, "Did you think that the Sheik gave you that Swiss cell phone only so that you could call him back? We've been tracking your every movement!"

Emad felt like he had just received a super-powered kick in the guts. How could he have been so naïve? Perversely, his thoughts turned to Indiana Jones. He would not have made such an elementary mistake, or would he? Be that as it may, he knew that their moment of triumph had turned into a quagmire from which it would be almost impossible to extract themselves. He was desperately rummaging through the cupboards of his brain for some solution when it became clear that his scope for independent action was about to become severely limited.

Abu Bakr cleared his throat to deliver a little speech that he had probably spent some time rehearsing, and during which he said way too much, "You have found an object that definitively confirms the ancient betrayal of the Copts. It will now pass to the ownership of the Muslim Brotherhood. Dr. Almasry will give it its moment in the limelight at the Capital Broadcasting Center soon enough. We will now take the hook and Dr. Almasry. Do not attempt to resist and do not attempt to follow us. We have brothers in hiding all around the monastery. One false move on your side will bring down the vengeance of Allah."

For a few moments, it was like the entire scene was frozen in time. Brother Michael, staring at the ground so that only the embroidered crosses on his hood were visible. Emad, glaring at Abu Bakr in wide-eyed amazement mixed with contempt. Magdy's eyes half-closed as if in prayer, with the hook clutched to his chest. Then everything unfroze in an instant.

Abu Bakr walked over to Magdy, grabbed the hook, and said, "I'll have that thanks!" in a high-pitched voice that betrayed panic mixed with exhilaration churning inside him. Instinctively Magdy tightened his grip, almost pulling Abu Bakr off his feet in the process. Reflecting on the day's events in later years, Michael often wondered from where the seemingly superhuman strength that Magdy displayed at that moment came. Could it have been a reaction to finally getting a chance to resist those who had his people under their heels? Be that as it may, Magdy's defiance had disastrous consequences.

Abu Bakr's two companions immediately sprang into action. In what seemed like an instant, Yasser had Emad in a chokehold and out of the door. Rafiq bounded towards Magdy and brought the butt of his pistol down on the latter's skull with a sickening crash.

Brother Michael retained only snippets of memories after that. Blood spurting from Magdy's head. The hook clattering to the ground. Someone shoving him roughly to the side. Abu Bakr, running out the door with the hook in his hands and a manic grin on his face. Much later, a brother monk shaking him by the shoulders, simultaneously trying to calm him down and trying to figure out why he was screaming like a madman outside St. Bishoy's old cell.

Chapter 23

There was a strange kind of symmetry to the fact that Magdy's life was ebbing away at the heart of St. Bishoy. Perhaps he would himself have nominated this ancient monastery as the place from where to follow in the footsteps of so many of the Coptic faithful who had passed out of this life before him.

Still, there was nothing serene or peaceful about the scene that Brother Michael observed from a corner of a room in the monastery's clinic. Everybody but him seemed to have a role, some chanting prayers, the local doctor frantically trying to stabilize Magdy, the abbot standing outside the door, trying to get hold of Magdy's wife on the phone. So, Michael decided that the best he could do would be to imprint every part of this scene on his memory. He had an inkling that this death would, in time, be added to the annals of the church, and it needed careful and devout eyes to record it.

Magdy was slipping in and out of consciousness. Blood was still seeping from the wound on his forehead. A priest standing next to him was reading from the Scriptures and praying ancient prayers written for moments exactly like these. Prayers that mingled hoping against hope for recovery, with assurances of a better life should this not eventuate. Michael could see that, even amid the chaos and pain, the words brought Magdy some comfort as he seemed to prepare to quietly slip the moorings of this life.

Then, suddenly, everything changed. The priest began to read the words of Jesus in the Gospel of John, *"I am the resurrection and the life. He who believes in me will live even though he dies."* Magdy's eyes suddenly shot wide open. They betrayed a mix of shock, pain, and elation. He tried to sit-up, but his body was beyond obeying the commands of his brain. Still, he managed to speak in a hoarse, but surprisingly loud voice, "Resurrection...bird...Hana Tadros!" Everybody in the room leaned in closer. Michael came right up to the bed and placed his arm on Magdy's shoulder. No one seemed to mind, so he kept it there.

Magdy never again said anything else. He just kept repeating the same phrase, "Resurrection...bird...Hana Tadros!" Michael gently tried to prod him for an explanation, but nothing ever came. Magdy's intensity never decreased, but the volume and frequency of the words did. Eventually, the sound ceased, but his lips kept moving. A last imploring look up at Michael, a sigh, a smile. Magdy Botros, husband, father, historian, son of the soil, proud Copt, was no more.

Michael's mind was reeling. How could it have come to this? A few hours after receiving a phone call from Magdy about a possible 'find' in the monastery; the caller was dead, and the monastery itself was probably heading into a whirlwind of turmoil. He suddenly became aware of a tear streaking down his face before falling onto Magdy's shirt. The next thing that he was aware of, was the abbot's hand on his shoulder and a soft voice saying, "You'd better come with me!"

They walked to an office deep in the bowels of St. Bishoy, with Michael hardly noticing the stares from little groups of monks who were very aware that something was up. When they arrived, the abbot, Father Reweis, pointed to a chair and quietly asked, "What happened here tonight?" Michael was acutely aware that there was much that he did not know, but he could make some educated guesses as to why the intruders so desperately wanted to get their hands on the hook. They must have been listening in on the entire conversation in St. Bishoy's cell and knew precisely when the prize was within their grasp.

After hearing Michael's version of events, the abbot thought long and hard, even closing his eyes for a full few minutes. When he opened them, there was steel in his voice, "We cannot hide what happened. Some brothers may already have let their families know. The police and the media will soon be all over it." He turned to Michael, "There were three people in that room when they came in. One is dead. One is captive. And there is you! In their rush to get away, they did not '*deal*' with you. You're an eyewitness to what happened and can sink their whole plan. You are not safe here. You need to disappear."

Over the years the Copts have developed sophisticated networks for moving church members around, for those who needed to go under the radar. These networks were typically used for girls who were forced into marriages or for people who had left Islam to become Coptic Christians. Now, a Coptic monk was about to step into this parallel world. They had a short window of opportunity while the Brotherhood raiders were still going to ground themselves. About two hours after Michael's conversation with Father Reweis, a car with black-tinted windows drove through the main gate of St. Bishoy, ready to head back towards the main highway to Cairo.

It would probably have been the easiest option to send Michael to another monastery, but the abbot decided against this for two reasons. Firstly, Brotherhood agents would soon be staking out all monasteries across the length and breadth of Egypt. Secondly, they needed someone to try and figure out what Magdy's last words meant, and especially who 'Hana Tadros' was. The monks of St. Bishoy could not undertake this task as it was almost certain that they would have their moves monitored for the foreseeable future. So, Michael's disappearance would not only keep him safe; it would also enable him to go 'undercover' in search of answers.

A quick phone call and the monk in charge of the monastery's administration was aroused from his sleep and instructed to bring the possessions that Michael had arrived with at the monastery. It felt strange to put on his 'American' clothes again after all this time wearing a monk's habit. Everything still fit perfectly or, if anything, were too big. The strict monastic diet he had been on did have at least some benefits it would seem. One thing that was in his favor was that, in his shock, he did not utter a single word while events were unfolding in St. Bishoy's cell. No one would know to look for a monk with American-accented Arabic. It was therefore decided that Michael would go to a safe house in Cairo and pretend to be an Egyptian-American tourist. A role that, given his background, he could play to perfection.

It felt surreal to see the lights of the monastery dissolving into the darkness. Michael had fully expected to see out his days in this place, and now an almost unbelievable set of circumstances forced him away. How quickly life can change. The previous afternoon, he was sitting in the refectory typing emails to guests planning to come to the monastery. Now there he was, little more than a fugitive from this place that was in many ways dearer to him than any home he had ever known. And who knew if he would ever be allowed to return?

The drive to Cairo was uneventful, if a bit strange. The driver kept making detours through villages next to the highway, presumably to make sure that they were not being followed. As the day began to dawn, they pulled into 17th Street in Maadi where the driver handed him the keys to an apartment. The bawab was obviously used to strange comings and goings, as he merely stuck his head out of his room near the stairs and nodded as Michael's driver escorted him to his temporary home.

It had been a while since anyone had stayed in the Coptic church's Maadi safe house. Cairo dust and sand can seemingly penetrate even hermetically sealed environments, and there was a thick coating on just about every surface in the room into which Michael stumbled. He was beyond caring, however. Without taking off his clothes, he flopped onto the solid wooden bed. He tried for a moment to relive the events of the night, but shock and fatigue overwhelmed his senses, and he was asleep almost immediately.

When he finally woke up, it took him a moment to work out where he was. His first panicked thought was that he was late for prayers in the monastery chapel. Then he heard the unmistakable sounds of suburban Cairo, children playing in the street, a street vendor shouting *'Lemoen! Lemoen'* and a microbus guard loudly trying to rustle up fares. He sank back into the bed, as everything that had happened flooded back into his consciousness. He knew that he was relatively safe where he was, but that did not prevent anxiety from gripping his heart with a cold and re-lentless hand.

It must have been close to midday, as the light was attempting to stream in from behind the blinds. He was suddenly aware of being hungry and thirsty. How strange it was not to be able to walk to the refectory for a meal or a drink. It was disorienting for Michael to contemplate being back 'in the world,' especially after his every move was controlled by the discipline and rhythms of the monastery for so long. He went into the kitchen and found some *El-Arosa* teabags. Soon a very red and very strong glass of tea stood steaming before him; he proceeded to ladle teaspoon after teaspoon of sugar into it. It felt good to have something familiar to hold in his hands. Whatever else may divide them, Egyptians agree that tea should be in a glass, very sweet, and with a paper *El-Arosa* tag on a tiny thread swinging from the side.

For a little while, his thoughts were like a band of wild horses. Over time, however, his immediate priority came into focus. He had to find out who Hana Tadros was, and why her name was on Magdy Botros' lips when he died. Even though he was not in the monastery anymore, he was still a monk, and an order from his abbot had to be obeyed. It was clear that she, whoever she was, must have had something to do with the mysteri-ous quest that brought Magdy and Emad Almasry to St. Bishoy. As such she could perhaps hold the keys to solving the mystery and, one could only hope, help bring the killers to justice.

Someone had left some supplies in the kitchen before his arrival, and he was able to have a quick breakfast, or rather lunch given the time of day, consisting of cheese and bread. He smiled ruefully at the image of a laughing cow, looking up at him from the round cheese container. He wondered whether he would ever be able to laugh again after witnessing a brutal murder and having to leave the place where he was convinced he would spend every day of the rest of his life.

A quick shower cheered him up a bit. However, he was thrown into turmoil when he looked at the mirror afterwards. If he went out like this, without his monk's habit, his luxurious beard would immediately cause him to be mistaken for a Brotherhood sympathizer. Given the sensitivity of his quest, it would not do to look like either a monk or a fundamentalist. The beard had to go. Whoever stocked the apartment before his arrival must have had the same idea. There was a packet of disposable razors amid all the other toiletries. What followed was messy, and not a little painful, but after more than half an hour he saw a face he hardly recognized anymore. 'Mike from California', was staring back at him.

Going back to his room, he reached into his bag to pull out a pair of jeans and a t-shirt he had forgotten he owned. He slowly got dressed. When he had finished, he could not shake the feeling that he was still half-naked. Would he ever again wear the long black robe that defined his identity during his years at St. Bishoy?

Anyone who saw Michael walking down a tree-lined street towards the Maadi Metro about half an hour later would not have bothered to shoot him a second glance. He was just another Egyptian going about his business. If he spoke to anyone, they might have noticed his American-accented Arabic but, given that so many Egyptians lived abroad, even that would not be remarked on as too out-of-the-ordinary. No one would guess that less than 24 hours earlier he was a resident of one of the oldest monasteries in the world.

In the end, it was not all that hard to track down Hana Tadros. By then, the news of Magdy's death had reached the Coptic Museum, and the abbot of St. Bishoy had warned them that a monk, who may not look like a monk, would come to make inquiries. As Michael was escorted into the administrative section of the museum, he felt like he had gate-crashed a wake. The shock of losing such a gentle man in such violent circumstances permeated the atmosphere, as people tried to make sense of what had happened and of what this meant for the future.

The receptionist, Mrs. Salib, seemed most composed and took Michael to an empty office to answer his questions. He briefly told her what had happened and related Magdy's final words. He could see her dabbing at her eyes as he spoke, but she quickly checked herself. In the end, her efficiency and attention to detail came in very handy. She managed Magdy's diary, and it was merely a matter of going back through his appointments to track down Hana's number. As she handed it over on a piece of paper, she gave Michael a steely look and said, "He was a good man. One of the best I've ever known. Please see to it that he did not die in vain!" Michael did not quite know what to make of this but found himself solemnly nodding.

As he crossed the street from the Coptic Museum to the Metro, Michael looked with new eyes at the layer upon layer of security that sealed this area off from the rest of Cairo. Every person who entered had to go through airport-style checkpoints, and there were enough heavily armed troops and police around to start a small war. "Would even this be enough when the storm breaks?" he gloomily mused as the train towards Maadi pulled into Mar Girgus station.

Michael figured that the safest place to see Hana would be in the safe-house apartment. Surely someone must have made sure that it was safe from both physical and electronic threats. On the way there he quickly ducked into KFC. As he bit into his chicken, he felt for the first time that, for this American monk, there were at least some perks to not being in the monastery anymore.

When he got to the apartment, Michael sat down at the dining room table, took out the little slip that Mrs. Salib gave him, and dialed the number. Almost immediately, a female voice answered. He could tell that the speaker had been crying. It seemed that the news of Magdy's death had reached Hana as well. Michael briefly explained who he was and then asked, "Would you be able to come and see me in Maadi as soon as you can?" He could sense her hesitation and swallowed hard before saying: "Hana, I was there when he died. He mentioned your name several times before expiring!"

There was a long silence on the other end of the line before Hana, in a trembling voice, said, "When can I come?" He replied, "Please come immediately if you can sister!"

Less than two hours later, there was a soft knock on the front door. As he walked over to open it, Michael could not help but be at least a little nervous. He had spent years in an exclusively male environment; he was not entirely sure that he knew how to be around women anymore.

Hana had been crying. Her eyes were red and swollen, and she had a look of utter desperation on her face. Michael awkwardly motioned for her to sit down at the kitchen table. Hana wasted no time, wanting to know everything about Magdy's final moments. When Michael told her about the dying man's reaction to the priest reading about the resurrection, his constant repetition of 'Resurrection...bird...Hana Tadros', she began to sob.

Michael was at a loss to know what to do. Finally, he decided that he was first a human being, then a monk. He took her hands in his and just sat with her for a few minutes. This seemed to comfort her, and she gradually began to fill in the gaps in his knowledge of what exactly was going on. When he heard about the Sheik's plan to incite a religious war on the back of Emad's proposed television appearance, it was as if the future turned into a menacing and gaping chasm.

They were silent for a moment before the inevitable question raised its head. Michael said it first, "What are we going to do?"

Michael was dumbfounded when Hana answered: "I think we'd better get in touch with the Micah Order!" Before he could say anything, she pulled out her phone and dialed the number that Magdy had told her to call should anything go wrong. It was time to speak to the man who convinced Magdy that a version of the Micah Order was still alive and well in the 21st century. She felt strangely reassured when a voice on the other side of the line said: "Samuel Mounir here!"

That evening found a little group gathered around a Maadi kitchen table: a monk, a trainee archaeologist, and a Coptic activist. All of them desperately trying to discern a way forward. It took Michael a while to get over his astonishment at the continuing existence of the Micah Order. He had to keep forcing himself to close his mouth as he listened to Samuel float one seemingly crazy idea after the other. Sadly, no matter where their thoughts turned, it seemed as if the Copts were heading into yet another vale of tears, and there was nothing that they could do about it.

Hana eventually became so quiet that Samuel and Michael almost forgot she was there. Her words, when they finally came, cut through the fog, "I don't think the riddle was solved. There was nothing on the hook about the '*Qibla of the Arabs*' or how it would bring defeat to the Saracens. The only thing that we can learn from the hook is to keep searching at St. Bishoy. I believe that Magdy tried to tell us, tell me, something about the next step when he died. We don't have a choice. We'll have to go to Wadi Natrun."

Both Michael and Samuel stared at Hana in open-mouthed astonishment. Was this brave young woman really prepared to go straight into the mouth of the lion? A place whose perimeter, by then, must have been bristling with Brotherhood supporters watching every movement of those entering or leaving. The glint in her eyes told her that this was indeed precisely what she was proposing.

Samuel rested his gaze on her for a few moments before cracking a wide smile. Turning to Michael, he said: "Hope you still have your robes brother, looks like you're going back!"

Chapter 24

Emad sat on a bed, staring at the wall. He, a respected archeologist at the Ministry of State for Antiquities, could now give his address as follows: Bedroom, Secret Brotherhood Hideout, Al-Zikry Automotive, Near Al-Sayyeda Zeinab Mosque, Cairo (Prisoner).

Inevitably his thoughts turned to the night before.

The drive from Wadi Natrun to Cairo had been the most uncomfortable of his life so far. After what they did to Magdy, he knew that he was in the company of men who were ready to unleash extreme violence if they deemed it necessary. Yasser and Rafiq barely spoke to him during the drive, and their silence made them seem even more menacing. What were their plans for him? He knew that he was considered 'useful' to the Brotherhood for the moment, but what would happen when his usefulness came to an end?

As the traffic thickened on the outskirts of Cairo, Emad struggled to keep images of Magdy falling to the ground, with a look of horror and pain on his face, from replaying in his mind. He could still hear the clang of the hook as it hit the ground. An object that he thought would represent the end of their quest, but that may instead have caused the first casualty in the catastrophe that was about to hit the Copts. What happened to Magdy, was he okay? He had no way of finding out, but he despaired of anyone surviving such a blow.

The area around the Sayyeda Zeinab mosque was swarming with devotees of the saint as usual, even though they reached it in the middle of the night. As he looked out over the crowds, Emad half-remembered that many of the faithful believed that it was very beneficial to pray near her tomb all through the night.

Emad could see that Rafiq, who was driving, was deeply irritated by the expressions of *shirk* (idolatry) around him. Gesticulating wildly for people to get out of the way, he edged the Land Cruiser towards a side street near a row of restaurants. "This is not good!" Emad thought as he prayed that he would not somehow become a victim of Rafiq's lousy mood. His apprehension deepened as Rafiq stopped the car in a narrow alley, in front of a nondescript workshop.

Without a word, Rafiq got out a key and lifted the shutters of the workshop. Just like Yusuf before him, Emad could not help but be impressed by how cleverly the modern and comfortable space, in which he was now sitting, had been carved out from such mundane surroundings. As he was shown to his room, Emad also realized that this was, unfortunately, a perfect place for holding someone against their will. The front-shutter was the only way to get in and out. The 'hideout' at the back had no external doors or windows. He also noted, to his dismay, that Yasser sat down at the reception desk and seemed to settle in for the night, but not before he made sure that Emad had no way of communicating with the outside world. He was not going anywhere without their express permission.

He woke after a few hours of drifting in and out of sleep as the horrors of recent events kept rushing unbidden into his consciousness. Sitting up on the bed, after giving up on getting any rest, he finally permitted himself to complete the thought that he was about to utter when Abu

Bakr stormed into St. Bishoy's cell: The hook was significant, but it could not be what they were ultimately looking for. There must be something else, something more.

In some ways, the hook made everything worse. It definitively confirmed the existence of a secretive Coptic order dedicated to the overthrow of Islam, while not shedding any new light on exactly how the 'Saracens' would be overthrown. So, it could provide plenty of ammunition for the enemies of the Copts, while not providing them with much by way of defending themselves. As he thought about the fact that the price for the release of his fiancé would be his wielding of the hook against the Coptic people on live television, he felt sick to the pit of his stomach.

Laying back on the bed again, Emad fervently wished that he had the means to get back to Wadi Natrun. Surely, there must be more to discover? Yet, the reality was that he could not go back to St. Bishoy. The Brotherhood now had what they wanted, a way to indict Copts throughout history for their supposed disloyalty. And they had him. They would seek to get his face on television as soon as possible, and they would keep him cooped up, without any contact with the outside world, until that time.

The usual workday had started by now outside Emad's luxurious prison. He could hear engines being revved and spanners clanging to the ground. Mundane sounds that provided the backdrop to the desperate thoughts of someone who was not sure if there would ever really be a 'normal' again.

CHAPTER 25

Shiny billboard, desert, grandiose estate gatehouse, more desert, roadside mosque, yet more desert, repeat. It felt like the same scene was playing on a loop as Michael, Hana, and Samuel sped towards Wadi Natrun along the Cairo to Alexandria highway. Nobody said anything much. They had no idea what to say. Nothing in any of their lives up to that point had prepared them for the feeling that the fate of a people may be resting on their shoulders.

It was perhaps Michael whose emotions were the most turbulent, veering wildly between elation and utter dread. Elation because he was going home, after only a very short time away. Dread, because 'home' had become a place of death and intrigue. The intrigue was deepened through discovering that there was, after all, a part of the history of the monastery that had remained hidden to him up to that point.

Back in the kitchen in Maadi, they floated idea after idea on how to get back into the monastery. They could not simply drive up to the monastery gate as it was bound to be watched with eagle eyes. Each idea was shot down in flames as being too impractical or dangerous. In desperation, they finally decided that Michael should call the abbot, tell him about Hana's desire to continue investigations, and ask how they could get in.

After Michael explained their predicament, the abbot, Father Reweis, was quiet for such a long time that Michael began to wonder whether the connection had been cut. When he finally spoke, it was with the voice of someone who had decisively crossed a formidable obstacle. He was all in. "Go to the shed on Bolous Adib's property," he said. Michael knew the place well. Mr. Adib was a local farmer who sometimes did odd jobs for the monastery. He had no idea, however, of how going to his place would make any difference in terms of getting them back into St. Bishoy. Father Reweis continued: "Someone will meet you inside the shed and take you into the keep."

A lot of things suddenly made sense. Michael had always prided himself on knowing the monastery inside out, but that was not exactly true. Like many other Coptic monasteries that had to withstand the onslaughts of Islamic invaders, St. Bishoy had a keep; a fortified tower that could act as a refuge of last resort in case of attack. Michael had been told that the monastery's keep was built over a well and in the past contained food supplies, in the form of dried beans that could keep the monks going for several months. He was convinced, however, that the keep was now full of rubble and off-limits due to being unsafe. Apparently not. It seemed that the abbot had a card up his sleeve and maintained a role for the monastery's place of final refuge.

Michael guessed, correctly as it turned out, that a secret tunnel connected the keep with the outside world. Many Coptic monastery keeps shared this feature, being equipped with tunnels with inconspicuous exits some distance from the monasteries. So it was, that they turned down a dusty back street when they reached Wadi Natrun village. Michael directed Samuel, who was driving, to a nondescript walled compound. As soon as they stopped, a gate swung open, and they were waved inside with urgent hand gestures. They were obviously expected.

Once inside they were hustled into a shed at the back of the property. There they were greeted by a gaunt-looking monk whom Michael recognized as brother Zakaria, St. Bishoy's head of security. He motioned to the little group to follow him. Reaching a large wardrobe, he pushed it aside to reveal a perfectly circular hole in the ground. Knowing that he would soon re-enter the monastery, Michael suddenly felt intensely self-conscious about being beardless and dressed in civilian clothes. He could sense Zakaria's restless urgency and did not even think to ask if he could change into his habit; they needed to get inside!

Zakaria gestured towards the hole and said, "Climb down. Once you reach the bottom of the stairs, follow the passage. I'll bring up the rear." Samuel, whose face looked like a child's at Christmas, practically jumped at the opportunity. He felt in his bones that he would soon be walking in the millennia-old footsteps of the members of the Micah Order. Hana followed, with much more uncertain steps. She knew that she would be stepping into the inner sanctum of an all-male domain where her presence may very well be resented. To make things worse, there was a weight of expectation on her shoulders to provide archeological wisdom and direction, and she had no idea whether she would be able to deliver.

For his part, Michael could feel tears welling up in his eyes as he climbed down the ladder. He felt like someone who had just received a pardon after being sentenced to a long stint in prison. He was genuinely thankful that his exile from his beloved St. Bishoy could be measured in days rather than years. Still, he knew that if their mission to wrench some meaning from Magdy's final words was not successful, there may one day not be a St. Bishoy to come back to. With a look of grim determination, he turned towards the passage that would lead them straight into the monastery's keep.

The narrow passageway that they entered was not designed with comfort in mind. Some LED lights provided basic illumination, but visibility was not their main problem. In places, they had to go down on all fours to get through particularly tricky sections. Still, the whole experience was probably preferable to being at the receiving end of Brotherhood attention at the front gate.

After what seemed like an eternity, they emerged into a dimly lit room. A large icon of St. George dominated it, its golden paint gleaming in the soft glow of yet more LED lights. They all got the message immediately. In a place where the occupants expected to be in great peril, it seemed only natural to invoke the aid of the great soldier-saint. With his emotions veering wildly between trepidation, faith and determination Michael walked over and softly kissed the icon. He also reached into a small bag that he had slung over his shoulder before entering the tunnel and pulled out a black robe which he slid over his head. Brother Michael was back where he belonged.

Just as they were about to think about their next steps, they could hear Zakaria coming down the tunnel. He gave the little group standing in the middle of the keep a satisfied look before shutting a heavy steel door. It was strangely ironic to think that this ancient system for helping beleaguered monks to survive and escape was now used to confound a contemporary foe.

As they left the keep to walk across the courtyard, Hana was deeply conscious of the astonished looks of the monks at the strange spectacle that they presented. Not only because a lost and beardless brother emerged as if from the dead, but also because seeing a woman in this part of the monastery was about as common as seeing a polar bear in the desert.

After being stared at for several minutes, they were finally shown into the abbot's office. Father Reweis had them sit down before ordering some tea. For a few moments it felt as if the events of the past few days melted away with the soothing familiarity of pouring tea and cupping the warm glasses in their hands. Father Reweis finally spoke. Despite the gravity of the situation there was the hint of a smile in his voice, "Well, we don't know what we're looking for, let alone where to look for it. Do any of you have any idea where to start?"

Hana cleared her throat and softly said, "I think we need to analyze Magdy's final words. Surely he was trying to tell us something." Father Reweis nodded. The fateful words with which Magdy Botros ended his life was burned into all their brains. Still, he softly repeated them: "Resurrection...bird...Hana Tadros!"

Hana blushed as he said her name. She had already figured out that Magdy probably mentioned her because he left Samuel's details with her. She was the only one who could notify the modern-day Micah Order of what was happening. Still, she could not help thinking that those in the room with her would interpret the words as indicating that she could bring some specialized skills or archeological know-how to the table. She did not quite know how to deal with the weight of expectation that this brought, as she was as perplexed as the rest of them. However, she had been racking her brain, so she decided to share what she believed she knew.

She started hesitantly at first but gained confidence as she saw the men around her giving nods of assent as she went on, "It seems obvious that this monastery was a place to which the Micah Order withdrew during a period of intense persecution. While here, they left definite clues to confirm their presence. The most obvious of these was the hook. With it they signaled their intent to continue with their struggle against *the scant measure that is accursed.*' But there must be more. The parchment in the Fustat jar that led Emad and Magdy here in the first place made it clear that there is something in Wadi Natrun that will lead to the defeat of the enemies of the Copts:

> *At the place of the resurrection*
> *She that walks will finally soar*
> *The Saracens will be pulled apart*
> *As the sons of Micah awaken*

As he was dying, Magdy must have realized what this referred to. He spoke of the resurrection and a bird. We need to figure out somehow where his thoughts turned. Whatever or wherever it is, it must be in the oldest part of the monastery because the jar with the initial clues was buried in Fustat before 1186. So, I suggest we start by attempting to identify the parts of the monastery that existed back then."

Even as she was saying these words, an image presented itself to Hana's mind as if from nowhere. A colossal bird, running along the ground before suddenly, and improbably, soaring into the sky. She could not help laughing at the absurdity of it all. While dying, Magdy had left the perfect clue! Her thoughts must have taken over her facial expression because everyone else in the room was staring at her. She chuckled and shyly said, "I think I've got it! Can we go to the original St. Bishoy Church?"

A few moments later, they crossed the courtyard towards the church in the middle of the monastic compound. Upon entering, they all stood for a few moments, taking in the sanctity of the place. Hana looked up and saw Michael staring at her in deep admiration. She smiled, sincerely hoping that she was not about to make an utter fool of herself. As they stepped into the sanctuary, Hana led the way towards the front of the church. When she reached the *iconostasis,* she lifted her eyes upward. There, hanging from the roof, was a large ostrich egg.

The presence of the ostrich egg in St. Bishoy's church was not something out of the ordinary. Just about every Coptic Orthodox church in the world has one, encased in an ornamental metal holder, hanging above the altar. The egg is a symbol of the resurrection of Jesus Christ and its presence in the church is, therefore, a potent reminder to believers that they serve a living Lord.

For the second time in just a few days, a small group stood with their eyes riveted to the roof. The egg in the St. Bishoy church was in a particularly ornate holder, reflecting its position in one of the most sacred spaces in the Coptic world. Michael broke the silence, "Better get that ladder again!" he said, with a sheepish grin on his face.

In the end, the ladder that they had used in St. Bishoy's cell did not cut it. It reached only about halfway up to where the egg hung. Zakaria asked Michael to come with him so that they could get a taller ladder from the monastery's main workshop. Once this was in place, there were a few moments of embarrassed silence. Given what had happened to the last person who mounted a ladder in the monastery, who would go up this time?

Hana finally stepped forward. A surge of confidence of which she did not quite know the source, was rising inside her. "I guess I'm the archeologist around here" she said with a hint of irony in her voice. She was a little mortified when everyone nodded gravely. They were taking her, a mere intern, very seriously. "Way to go, putting your foot in it!" Hana thought as she gave the little group a weak smile.

With a great deal of trepidation, Hana mounted the ladder. It all made sense. The egg is a symbol of the resurrection. An ostrich is a bird that does not fly. It all checks out. But what if this was a dead-end?

A dead-end is precisely what it felt like when she finally came face-to-face with the egg. Unlike the hook there was nothing on the egg to indicate that it was a significant object. It did not contain any writing that she could see. The ornamental holder did not offer much hope either. It contained some stylized patterns but nothing more. Disappointment rolled over her like a tidal wave. She had been so utterly confident that this would be the key to unlock the solution. She looked down, grief written all over her face.

Was this the end of the road? Was Magdy's death ultimately in vain? She did not have to say anything. Her expression was eloquent enough. Looking down at the group below: Samuel, Zakaria, Father Reweis and Michael standing with their heads bowed, sharing her disappointment, nearly pushed her over the edge. She tried very hard not to embarrass herself by crying. It was no use; she could feel the tears welling up deep inside her. It was while she was trying to keep these tears from surfacing that she saw it. As she rapidly blinked her eyes, an image jumped up at her from the floor.

The floor of the church was covered in mosaic tiles. It did not seem like they were organized in any pattern, except for two dark lines that demarcated the edges of the central aisle. However, seen from above, from *the place of the resurrection*, a pattern was visible. Hana could not believe that she had missed it going up the ladder, but there was no denying it. When looked at from her current position, the floor contained the image of a weighted scale!

Hana gasped, amazed at how what seemed like a random collection of tiles morphed into the image that they were, by then, so familiar with when viewed from on high. She was getting quizzical looks from below. The change in her expression and demeanor did not go unnoticed. "What's happening?" Michael shouted. She almost did not hear him. Her brow furrowed in concentration. She noticed that the egg was directly above the left-hand side of the scales.

Hana slowly descended the ladder. Once she reached the ground, she got down on her knees, staring intently at the mosaic tiles directly below the ostrich egg. After a minute of this, she finally found what she was looking for. There was a very thin line in the tiles.

By then, the four men in the room were huddling above her, sensing that she was on to something significant. Hana finally looked Father Reweis straight in the eye with an expression that was somewhere between horrified and amused, "I don't know how to ask this of you Father," she said, "but would you perhaps know where we can get a crowbar?"

The abbot gave her a shocked look, before silently giving Zakaria a nod. After a few minutes, Zakaria came back into the room, carrying a crowbar and two spades. He gave Hana an expectant look. She pointed out the nearly invisible line on the floor and said, "I think there must be something under this!"

Zakaria gave Father Reweis a concerned look. What he was about to do seemed almost sacrilegious. Father Reweis hesitated for a moment but finally gave another nod.

Everyone in the church flinched as Zakaria brought the crowbar crashing down on the floor. Once the shock of the first strike abated, Hana gave a triumphant smile, "Did you hear that? The floor is not solid. That sounded like someone beating a drum!" Sure enough, after a few more hits, they could see a hole opening up.

"Careful now," Hana said, "We don't want to damage whatever is down there!" She directed them to all get down on their knees to pull on the stone that was still covering the emerging hole. Working in unison, they could feel it moving ever so slightly, causing them to redouble their efforts. When they were finally able to lift the stone, the strangest sight confronted them. Two enormous eyes were staring up at them.

The eyes were painted on a small sarcophagus. Hana immediately recognized it as being in the 'Fayoum Style.' Thousands of similar sarcophagi have been discovered at Fayoum, an oasis south of Cairo. All of them contained hyper-realistic (except for their huge eyes) portraits of the people whose remains they contained. These people were all upper-class Romans who had lived in the area during the time of the Roman occupation of Egypt. Given the demographics of the later Roman Empire, it is quite likely that some of the 'Fayoum faces' had belonged to some of the earliest Christians in Egypt.

Hana knelt over the hole and stared at the soulful eyes painted on the sarcophagus. They seemed to tell her that their quest was at an end.

After widening the hole some more, Zakaria and Michael gently lifted the sarcophagus up onto the floor of the church. It was much smaller than any sarcophagus that Hana had ever seen, about the size of a small watermelon, and could not have been used to bury anyone, not even a child. Perhaps this was never its intended use.

Her suspicion was confirmed when she had a closer look at the portrait. This was no anonymous Roman-Egyptian. The image was that of St. George, the ultimate warrior for the cause of God. In his hand, he was not holding a sword or even a bible, but a set of scales, the left-hand side much heavier than the right. Hana could feel a surge of excitement rushing through her veins. Hard on the heels of that, her professional training asserted itself. How could they open this in a way that would ensure that it, or its contents, were not damaged?

Ultimately, it was a much less sophisticated operation than the last time that she had opened an ancient artifact. She asked for a blunt knife from the monastery kitchen and got to work on the line that separated the upper and lower parts of the sarcophagus. Even though the situation was beyond urgent, she paced herself by using slow, methodical movements. After what seemed like an eternity, she could feel the two parts beginning to separate. Following some more work with the knife, she finally asked Michael to hold the bottom part, and began to wiggle the top of the sarcophagus, somewhat unnerved by St. George staring up at her as she was doing so.

When they were sure that everything was ready, she finally lifted the lid. She felt utterly elated, it was her first real 'find,' and it could be of momentous consequences.

Everyone realized that they had been holding their breaths when the contents was finally revealed. Exhaling in unison they saw that the sarcophagus, thankfully, did not contain any remains. Inside there were three plates made from gold leaf.

Hana leaned over to have a closer look. The plates contained Coptic letters. Her eyes were drawn to the one that was on top. She began reading. She gasped. This was it. The topmost letters spelled:

"God's verdict on the Saracens."

CHAPTER 26

Emad was conscious that he kept blinking his eyes as he walked into the studios of the Capital Broadcasting Center. After two weeks of having his field of vision restricted by the back wall of his room at Al Zikry Automotive, it felt strange to be confronted by the bright lights and expansive lobby of the TV station's Cairo headquarters.

He tried to look down to keep a sense of vertigo at bay. This also had the advantage of helping him to ignore the many curious faces staring at him. The owners of at least some of those faces were probably aware that he was there for the much-heralded 'big interview.' An impression likely enhanced by the fact that two burly men in sharp suits closely shadowed him. He knew that he would have to go through with this, come what may.

The reason behind the two-week delay in his appearance on CBC was that the channel wanted to launch an extensive media blitz to prepare viewers for the fact that some bombshell revelations were on the way. Back in his room, Emad watched with increasing horror as the television continued to blare out an over-the-top ad for his appearance, "We are about to reveal an archeological discovery that could change the way we see Egypt forever. Don't miss this CBC exclusive exposé, Thursday evening at 8!" Accompanying the words were images of great archeological discoveries, mingled with the earnest expression of Mustafa al-Tarek. He was one of CBC's most famous stars, and Emad assumed that he would be conducting the interview.

As a station employee pointed them in the direction of an elevator that led somewhere into the heart of the building, Emad wondered at what stage he would get to see Maryam. He stuck to his guns in conversations with the Sheik to make it clear that he would not say a word if she was not present. So, when Rafiq came to pick him up, he specifically asked him if she would be at the studio. He interpreted the grunt he received in reply as affirmative. This meant that he would soon lay eyes on his fiancé after they had been separated in the most dramatic of fashions.

In the end, their reunion was a little anti-climactic. As he entered the pre-interview lounge, there she was, sitting on a sofa sipping a soft drink and talking softly with a young woman beside her. He was surprised to see that a black veil tightly framed her face, very different from the loose-fitting ones that she wore in the past. The reason for this was not hard to work out. Behind her stood the Sheik, positively beaming, and her brother Yusuf, looking decidedly uncomfortable.

Maryam's face lit up when she saw Emad. She jumped up and ran towards him. Then, remembering who she was with, she suddenly checked herself and demurely offered Emad her hand. "So good to see you dearest!" she said while vigorously shaking his hand. She was smiling, but Emad noticed her casting a rather contemptuous look at the person who was directly responsible for their separation.

The Sheik was savoring the anticipation of what he firmly believed would be his moment of triumph. "Welcome 'Brother Archeologist'!" he shouted across the room, sheer joy radiating from his voice and demeanor. Emad was in no mood for joviality, but he did want to get this over as quickly as possible, so he decided to at least be more-or-less civil. "Mr Ramadan," he said with a tight smile and a nod.

Next to greet him was Yusuf. Emad thought that he had the look of some-one who had the stuffing knocked out of him. Gone was the swagger and bravado of the 'soldier for Allah.' What happened next was entirely unexpected. Instead of shaking his hand, Yusuf embraced him and soft-ly murmured the word 'brother' as he did so. Emad had very little time to ponder the change that had come over his future brother-in-law. The moment Yusuf released him from his embrace, a small feminine hand was reached out to him with the words: "So good to meet you Dr. Almasry!"

The hand belonged to the petite and very sharply dressed young woman who had been chatting with Maryam a few moments earlier. "My name is Fatima Shoukry, and I'll be managing your appearance," she said. Fa-tima shot an uncertain look in Yusuf's direction, "I also happen to be a childhood friend of Yusuf and Maryam." Emad gave a start. Maryam had told him about how a friend of hers kept Yusuf out of trouble by re-peatedly interviewing him during the time of the Rabaa protests. And, here she was in the CBC studios, intimately involved with the interview he was about to give. Did Maryam have a hand in this? Given the furtive glances being exchanged, he would not be surprised if this was the case.

Fatima was about to launch into some instructions and tips on what to expect when she was interrupted by the Sheik. "Excuse me, Miss Shoukry, would you mind giving us a moment?" he said. He was charm itself as he said this, but everyone could hear that it was a command, not a request. Fatima hesitated for a moment, but then relented on seeing the tiniest nod from Maryam. This all but confirmed Emad's suspicions that his fiancé had something to do with the fact that CBC was carrying the interview.

Fatima nodded and said, "I need to be back in here in 5 minutes!" Once she left, the atmosphere changed immediately. There they were, six peo-ple, bound together in a conspiracy in which not all of them were willing participants, each bringing a different set of emotions to this strangest of gatherings. Rafiq and Yasser made a table in the corner their own and were making appreciative comments about the range of food and drink laid out for the station's guests. The rest of them sat on the sofas in the middle of the room, facing each other. Yusuf stared down at the floor, clearly wanting to be somewhere else. Emad and Maryam looked at each other, both desperately wishing that they were alone. The Sheik, taking charge, finally spoke up.

"Today is one of the most important days in the history of Egypt!" he began. "Mustafa al-Tarek, who will interview you, already has possession of the hook that the treacherous followers of the cross installed in their wretched monastery." He looked intently at Emad, "Your task tonight will be to explain what it is and what it stood for. You can leave the rest to us!" Emad felt as if he was going to be sick. He had known, of course, that this moment would be coming, but the stark reality that violence might follow from words coming out of his mouth was almost too much to bear.

It was almost as if the Sheik could read Emad's thoughts. He continued, in a very formal tone, "I regret that we are not gathered here as people with a united purpose. Still, I thank you for your cooperation. Even if it had to be accompanied by a measure of coercion. May I strongly urge you to keep your commitments. If you don't the consequences could be severe." He made a casual gesture towards Rafiq and Yasser, his armed enforcers, and the message could not have been more explicit. "However, if you cooperate, you will find that I'm a man of my word and you'll be able to leave this place, freed from any further obligations to me, although I hope that this whole experience will eventually bring you closer to the true worship of Allah. Sister Maryam here has certainly taken encouraging steps in that direction!" Emad gave Maryam a puzzled look, but she merely blushed and looked down.

Readying a final rhetorical flourish, the Sheik looked directly at Emad. "Dr. Almasry, I know this is difficult for you. I presume that you believe that you will be the cause of much violence and bloodshed. However, I want you to sleep soundly at night. You will be nothing more than the messenger. The Copts have brought what is about to happen onto their own heads!" He was about to elaborate on this, his favorite theme, when there was an insistent cough at the door. Fatima clearly could not wait any longer. There was a nation out there, getting ready to tune in.

Emad wanted nothing more than to spend a few moments with Maryam, to fill her in about what happened with him and to ask about her experiences. It seemed, however, that this would have to wait for later. If there was indeed a 'later'! Fatima touched his elbow and pointed to a side room. "Dr. Almasry, if you would be so kind, it is time for your makeup!" she said. Emad did a double-take. He had never been 'made up' and was not so sure that he wanted to start now. Sensing his hesitation, Fatima broke out in a broad smile. She was used to dealing with men who felt that this kind of insult to their manhood was a bridge too far. "Look at it this way," she said with barely concealed amusement, "You can either submit to this, or look like a shiny beach ball with all the studio lights trained on you. Your call!"

Emad could hardly believe that it was still possible to find humor in this situation, but he could not help grinning broadly as he walked towards the makeup studio. This lasted only for a moment. "If only we had more time!" he thought for the thousandth time. There must have been something more at the monastery. Yet, it seemed that whatever it was, it would now forever remain a mystery. Not only that, he was about to speak words that could tip his country into murderous chaos. Would he have the courage to describe what the hook stood for? Would he have the courage to step back, remain silent and face the consequences? He felt utterly helpless, like a drowning man being swept forward by a raging torrent.

His thoughts were rudely interrupted when the door of the makeup studio clicked behind him. A young woman motioned him to a chair. Sensitive as he was by then to such things, Emad immediately noticed that she wore a tiny silver cross around her neck. She tried to smile warmly at him, but Emad could not help but think that she looked utterly terrified. "My name is Rania Ayad," she said her voice quivering. Emad nodded, "Emad Almasry," he responded. These words seemed to open a floodgate, her eyes filled with tears and she looked at him with desperation etched on her face.

After a few moments, Rania took a deep breath and more-or-less composed herself. "Dr. Almasry," she began, "I'm only a makeup artist, and

I feel overwhelmed by all of this. But I have a message to deliver to you from something called the Micah Order. I understand that this message could mean the difference between life or death for some of my people." Emad stared at her in wide-eyed astonishment. Somehow his bewilderment seemed to give her confidence. She bent over to pick up a black shopping bag made of cotton, with something heavy in it, and placed it in Emad's lap, "There is a letter in there for you to read. While you do so, I'd better get going!"

The next few moments were utterly surreal. Emad was trying to concentrate on a letter that might radically alter the course of his life, and those of millions of others, while Rania was fussing about, trying to get him ready for the interview. The letter contained only a few lines, but what lines they were:

"Dear Emad,

We are exploring every possible option for getting this to you. If you read this, we have been successful. I'm afraid Magdy did not make it. Even in death he kept up the struggle, and he had a final message for me. It led us to what is in this bag. Inside this sarcophagus you will find a message written on gold leaf, as well as an Arabic translation. If you could bring this up during your interview, it will make all the difference in the world. May God give you strength.

Hana

PS. You will probably be in mortal danger after the interview. If you can get out, go to the Church of St Simon the Tanner. You will be safe there."

His mind still reeling at the news of the death of his friend, Emad looked into the bag and was momentarily startled by a massive pair of eyes staring up at him. He carefully opened the sarcophagus and took out the piece of paper that contained the translation. As he read, it was as if an icy hand grabbed hold of his heart. "What on earth was this?" he wondered.

When he reached the last few lines, he realized that he had been holding his breath for the whole time. As he exhaled, there was a loud rap on the door. With questions and contradictory emotions jostling for attention in his mind, he heard someone saying, as if from the other end of a long hallway, "Dr. Almasry should be on the set in 10 minutes! Could we hurry things along please?"

As if operating on autopilot Emad bent down and put the small sarcophagus back in its bag before getting up to face Rania, "Thank you. Thank you for everything!" he said, half-lifting the bag as he did so. Her response was a weak smile tinged with sadness. It took her a few moments to compose herself, her fingers nervously playing with the tiny cross around her neck, "Dr. Almasry," she finally said, "I have a strong suspicion that it will be us who will be thanking you for many generations to come."

Fatima, who had come to fetch him, immediately noticed the black bag that Emad was carrying as he came out of the makeup room. "I need it for the interview," he said, before she could say anything.

They were together for less than a minute as they walked down the hallway to the studio, but this was enough for Fatima to say to Emad, "I know that this is perhaps the most difficult thing that you have ever done. Remember, Maryam and myself go back a long way. If there is anything I can do to help, just ask." Before he had time to respond, they were in a world of blinding lights, miles of wires and banks of flashing screens.

In the middle of it all, master of all that he surveyed, stood CBC's superstar interviewer: Mustafa al-Tarek. "Welcome Dr. Almasry," he beamed, his perfectly white teeth radiant in the bright studio lights. He pointed Emad in the direction of a leather chair in the middle of the studio floor. It was part of an ensemble that included another chair and a small table. As he came closer to the table, Emad did a double take. On it, atop a black velvet cloth, was the hook that had cost Magdy Botros his life.

Emad was only vaguely aware of Mustafa al-Tarek pumping his hand with all the energy of someone who had just been told that he had come into a substantial inheritance. He continued to nod his silent assent as the course of the interview was mapped out. He would later reflect that this was probably the closest that he ever came to an out-of-body experience. It was almost as if he was watching from the outside as a colleague, whom he vaguely knew, was trying to make sense of multiple sensory and neurological inputs. Not quite knowing which thought to explore and which to discard as useless under the circumstances.

This feeling of unconnectedness continued even as Mustafa indicated that they were about to begin. As they sat down the interviewer suddenly arched his eyebrows when he saw the black bag Emad was carrying. Despite everything, Emad somehow had the presence of mind to mutter "Prop."

The beginning of the interview made for a strange bit of television, "Dr. Almasry, can you please tell us a bit about your background?" Silence. "Dr. Almasry? Dr. Almasry?" Emad looked up to see the expression of utter horror on Mustafa al-Tarek's face as he saw his 'interview of the century' descending into a train-wreck. He dredged the initial question from who-knows-where inside his memory and slowly began to speak about his childhood interest in archeology and his work at the Ministry of State for Antiquities. All the while Mustafa al-Tarek, consummate professional that he was, seemed to indicate that this was the most exciting life story that he'd ever heard.

The interviewer had clearly been thoroughly briefed by the Sheik. He worked hard to help Emad to settle into a very unfamiliar situation. He walked him through the initial investigation of the clay jar, the link to St. Bishoy and the eventual discovery of the hook. In looking at the hook on its velvet cloth, Emad tensed up again. The Sheik had warned him not to say anything about the violence associated with its discovery. Yet, he felt almost overwhelming internal pressure to point fingers at those who had taken his friend's life. Under different circumstances, he might have given in to this temptation, but his time in the makeup room changed all that. He felt a rock-solid resolve rising in him, a resolve to gain his revenge in another way.

By this time Mustafa al-Tarek was like a predator ready to descend on its prey, "Dr. Almasry I truly admire your skill and ingenuity to solve such a complex archeological problem. Leading you to this!" He paused for a moment to pick up the hook and angle it towards one of the cameras. "This is a strange object to regard as a major archeological discovery! Would you mind explaining its significance?" It was crunch time. In looking towards the back of the studio, Emad could see nothing but a ridiculously bright bank of lights, but he could imagine the Sheik sitting there, leaning forward, anticipating the answer that would grant him his wish to reshape Egypt.

Emad collected his thoughts and began his answer slowly and deliberately: "The hook was placed in the cell of St. Bishoy by a group known as the Micah Order. Some of their members also buried the clay jar in Fustat, probably during a period of intense persecution. I would imagine that they hoped that it would lead future members of the order to the St. Bishoy monastery once things settled down. The 'riddle' that took us so long to figure out was a means of protecting their identity during hard times, in the hope that later generations of Copts would be able to figure it out and continue the work of the order."

Mustafa leaned forward in his chair; deep concentration etched on this face, "So this 'Micah Order.' It seems obvious that it was, or is, a kind of Coptic secret society. But I'm still not clear as to what they were up to. What was the objective of the order?" Emad met Mustafa's gaze, conscious of beads of sweat forming on his upper lip: "The order was established to combat and, if possible, defeat Islam in Egypt. Its symbol was the 'weighted scale' that appears on the jar and the hook. The left-hand side represents Islam, *Weighed and found lacking.*"

Off to the side, Emad heard an audible intake of breath from some of the station personnel watching the interview. If this were anything to go by, much of the television-watching public in Egypt would, by this point, also be looking at their screens in shock and surprise. Some feeling visceral anger rising in them, others dreading what the future might hold.

Emad exhaled. The words had been said. Mustafa was playing the moment for all that it was worth, an expression of deep shock plastered all over his face. "So, you're saying," he said, attempting to sound as incredulous as possible, "that there was an organized Coptic resistance movement that survived until long after the end of the Islamic conquest and it was based at one of the holiest sites of Coptic Christianity? Would this not have been a terrible violation of the pact of protection granted by the Muslim rulers? Would you go as far as calling it a betrayal?"

The flame was being held to the kindling. Emad was expected to fan it into an irresistible blaze. At that moment, while mentally composing his answer, he thought of Magdy, of Hana, of Michael.

He leaned towards the camera, straining to find the right words. They came. "It could perhaps have been portrayed as an act of betrayal if the Micah Order fought with conventional weapons. However, I could find no evidence that this was the case."

Surprise was written all over Mustafa's face. This was not quite part of the script. Still, it could make for memorable television, so he asked the obvious follow-up question: "So if this Micah Order did not fight with conventional weapons, what did they fight with?"

In response, Emad reached under his chair to pick up the black bag, placing it on his lap. Several people in the studio, including the interviewer, strained forward to get a closer look. Emad took a deep breath and began, "Their primary weapon was history!"

"History?" What do you mean by that?" came the inevitable perplexed reply. Emad placed the sarcophagus next to the hook. The attention of everyone in the room was immediately drawn to St. George's oversized eyes which appeared to be sizing them all up.

"When I left the monastery," Emad shot an accusing look at where he believed the Sheik must be, "I was convinced that the hook did not represent the end of our quest. Fortunately, some of my colleagues were able to follow the trail to the end and discovered this sarcophagus." As he said this, he was vaguely aware of an angry argument and even some pushing and shoving taking place behind the studio lights and cameras, but he pushed on regardless.

"It contains what the order would have regarded as their ultimate 'secret weapon' against Islam. It was hidden during a time when its members were apparently being hunted down. A bit too well hidden perhaps, because it only came to light again here in the 21st century!"

As Emad finished speaking, Mustafa put his hand in the air in a gesture that almost resembled pleading. He desperately wanted to regain control of a situation that had gone spectacularly off-script, but that nevertheless had the potential to be the interview of the century. He was aware of the commotion towards the back of the studio, no doubt because someone wanted to terminate the interview. He sought out the producer and gave him a firm nod of the 'Let's do this!' kind before turning back to Emad.

"This is fascinating Dr. Almasry. You mentioned 'history' and 'secret weapon.' I'm somewhat perplexed, and I'm sure I'm not alone in this regard, as to what the connection might be?"

Emad carefully opened the tiny sarcophagus. The golden plates that he took out glittered in the bright studio lights. "This," he said, "contains a statement that the Order hoped would one day fatally undermine Islam in Egypt and beyond."

Mustafa gulped. He was either about to lose his job or become one of the most famous television journalists ever. He pushed on, "Would you mind sharing the statement with the nation?"

Emad unfolded the pages containing the Arabic translation of the words on the plates and began:

"We, the Members of the Order of Micah, followers of the cross, are ready to take our place among the martyrs. We welcome this

opportunity to add to the great suffering of our people. It is our prayer that what we bury in this sarcophagus may one day be gloriously resurrected to aid later generations in striving for the sake of the gospel.

The Saracens came into our beloved Egypt, hungry for land. The Romans and our own people did their best to drive them back, but God in his inscrutable wisdom allowed them to gain a foothold. From this foothold the Arabs proceeded to declare themselves overlords of this blessed land. As if this was not enough of an insult against our people, who had lived here on the banks of the Nile for many centuries, they also began to proclaim that they knew the way to heaven. They are now telling people that it is through a pathway of submission to God, known as Islam.

We fear that the spread of this new teaching, in the name of which we are being hunted and killed, will bury Egypt in error and turn multitudes from the truths proclaimed by our fathers. Especially because the Muslims, as they now insist on being called, are removing all traces of their deception.

Our own struggle is almost over. We cannot hold out for much longer. God willing, there may come a time when brothers and sisters yet to come can continue what we started. It is our prayer, dear reader from the future, that you are one with us.

We want you to know that the religion that the Saracens are now forcing on our people was also invented by them. When they came here, they prayed towards the east from where they came. They spoke about the brotherhood of all believers in the one God and even minted coins on which the sacred symbol of our most holy faith, the cross, appeared. They had no book, no prophet, no message. All that they wanted was our land.

This all changed when one of their leaders, Abd al-Malik, decided that he could better control the lands that they overran in their greed if he convinced people that this was being done in the name of God. Suddenly everything changed. Where they had once prayed towards the east, they now ordered everyone to pray in an entirely different direction to a city in the emptiness of the Arabian desert. They tell us that this was the 'mother of all cities'. That people came from far and wide to worship there and that it was one of the great trading centers of the Arabs. This is a lie. We have been trading with all the world from here in Egypt, and there is no record that a city ever existed at the place the Arabs now swear is the very center of the world. For more than a century they waged war, even on their own people to get them to change the prayer directions in their mosques.

They also swear to high-heaven that God gave them a book. They had no book when they came here. We are certain of this. Some of them had half-remembered poems. Others some of our stories or tales from the people of Israel. They put these together in a new book, fighting all the time about what should be included or excluded, and now claim that these are the very words of the King of Heaven.

To add insult to injury, the Saracens began to boast that they acted in the name of a great prophet, whom they call Muhammad. They never mentioned him when they first came here. He is nowhere to be found in the writings of our fathers or of the Romans as they spoke about the accursed time when we were being overrun.

Our fathers also never mentioned the book, Mecca or that the people who overran them wanted to be called Muslims.

There is more that we can say to you, dear reader, but look for yourself. Look at the original prayer directions of their mosques here in Egypt and other places, see how they do not point at their new city of Mecca. Study their book, see how it is cobbled together from Christian, Jewish, pagan and other sources. Read our fathers, read the Romans, the Syrians, the Greeks and the Persians. See how none of them ever confirm the existence of the 'ancient' city towards which they pray.

These truths are dangerous. We are being hunted down because we know them. Soon there may be none of us left. Many of our people may begin to pray towards that place in the desert. But we bear testimony that the qibla towards which the Arabs pray is not the one they prayed to when they came here. Their very buildings betray them.

If the Saracens are still here, share this message with the world as we have strived to do!"

As he finished reading, Emad became aware of an eerie silence. Every single person in the studio, including Mustafa al-Tarek, was staring at him in open-mouthed amazement.

The silence was not to last. Towards the back of the studio, someone started to shout, in a tone that mixed panic with rage, "The bastards, the bastards!"

CHAPTER 27

Deep in the heart of a Coptic Orthodox monastery, about two hours from Cairo, the abbot thumbed the "off" button on his television's remote. As the picture faded, he turned to the small group assembled in his office, tears streaming down his face. He did not need to say the words but felt that he still had to utter them as an expression of sincere gratitude, "Thank God. It worked. It reached him!"

Father Reweis, Samuel, Michael and Hana had engaged in long and heated debates about what to do with the sarcophagus after its discovery. Ultimately the choice came down to its preservation on the one hand and dealing with the immediate crisis of the exposure of the Micah Order, on the other.

Preserving it would not have been that hard. There are many places in a monastery, or if needed, in the wider Coptic community to hide a precious object. Still, making it disappear again would make no difference when it came to the fact that Emad was due to go on live television, more-or-less with a gun to his head, to speak about the discovery of St. Bishoy's hook.

In the end, it was Samuel, modern member of the order that had first placed the object in the St. Bishoy monastery, who persuaded them to go on the offensive. "They intended it as a weapon," was his simple yet eloquent argument.

Once this was decided, the seemingly impossible challenge was to get the sarcophagus to Emad. At least they knew where the blow would fall. Abu Bakr foolishly gave that part of the game away on the night when Magdy died. Samuel was confident, given the interconnectedness of the Coptic community, that there had to be someone 'on the inside' at CBC that they could contact before the broadcast. The problem was that they were all marked people, none of them could leave St. Bishoy to find someone able to deliver one of the most precious packages in Coptic history. So, it was decided after yet more soul-searching, that Samuel would phone one of his friends in the order to meet him at the exit to St. Bishoy's keep and take the package to Cairo.

They had this one shot. A terribly long shot. Yet in the end it had found its target against impossible odds. They all looked forward to hearing the story of how the package had made it into Emad's hands, but for the moment they could bask in the afterglow of knowing that it did. They knew in their bones that the revelation of the contents of the statement would provoke so much astonishment and debate within the Muslim community of Egypt, and beyond, that there would be little time or energy left to focus on the Copts. They could breathe. There would be no mass attacks while Islam struggled with fundamental questions about its reliability and legitimacy.

They also knew that one guaranteed response would be for the Brotherhood to try and destroy the sarcophagus and the plates, claiming that it was all a hoax, a modern forgery. It was, therefore, of the utmost importance to get the objects out of Egypt, to be dated and preserved by international scholars. Working out how this could be done was for another day, however. For now, they could rejoice in what had been achieved.

They sat quietly for the longest time, lost in thought. Hana was the first to speak. Father Reweis had insisted that she stay at St. Bishoy's guest house until Emad's television appearance, so this little group had met in this office every day for the past two weeks. She had participated fully in the process of coming to terms with the enormity of the discovery and working out what to do with it. Now there was no reason for her to stay at the monastery any longer. She looked at each member of the group before speaking, "I will never forget my time with you all. I strongly suspect that nothing more meaningful and exciting will ever happen to me. I guess the time has come to take my leave of all of you. Thank you, brothers, for believing in me. I'll go to my room and then make plans to go back to Cairo in the morning."

Father Reweis nodded; he knew that some of the monks were already asking questions about why she had been allowed to stay at the monastery for so long. It was probably for the best that she went back home, especially now that the danger had passed. The time would come for international recognition. For the moment it was better that she disappeared into the relative obscurity of being a graduate student at the University of Cairo.

It was a strange, almost solemn, parting of ways. Hana walked around the room. Shaking the hands of the men whose destinies had been so closely tied up with her own over the previous few days, each of them murmuring words of thanks and appreciation in return. That was until Michael diverged from the script. Instead of taking the hand she offered him he suddenly stepped forward and enveloped her in a bear hug. For a second, Hana was too startled to know how to respond. Then, for the first time, she cried as he continued to hold her in his arms. She cried for Magdy, for her people, about how close they had come to disaster, for the fact that there would be many more trials. It felt right to be with this man who had become a dear friend, allowing her grief to wash over her.

Finally, remembering where she was, and who he was, she suddenly let go. Michael had an embarrassed look on his face. Even in extraordinary times, monks were not supposed to embrace members of the opposite sex. There may be a reckoning, but he felt he had no choice. It is what 'surfer Mike' would have done.

They looked deeply in each other's eyes for a moment before Hana, not entirely trusting her emotions, quickly turned around and headed for the door.

CHAPTER 28

In the studio of the Capital Broadcasting Center, the scene resembled the aftermath of an explosion: Shouting, people milling about, a few staff members sitting with their heads in their hands. Emad was vaguely aware that he had to get out of there, with the sarcophagus and plates, and fast. He felt paralyzed as he replayed in his mind the events of the past hour, and his role in them.

In the end, it was Maryam and Fatima Shoukry who saved the day. Their little chat on the sofa when Emad entered the room turned out to be quite a bit more than two old friends catching up. By the end of it, Fatima knew that it might be necessary to help Maryam and Emad get out of the building. The 'might' had, of course, definitively morphed into an utter necessity.

So it was, that as Emad stood half-dazed in the middle of the floor, he felt a firm hand on his shoulder, "You had better come with us!", a voice said. Only it was not the voice of one of the Brotherhood heavies, Rafiq or Yasser. He turned around to see Fatima hurrying towards the lifts, with Maryam and Yusuf in tow. He shoved the sarcophagus into its bag and followed after them. Once they were all in the elevator, it was clear who was in charge. Fatima was in her element, as well as on home territory.

She turned to Yusuf, and Emad could not help but notice that she blushed as she did so, "Did you bring the keys?" Yusuf smiled and patted one of his trouser pockets. Emad, still very much used to the 'old Yusuf', could not quite understand what was going on. Why was he fleeing 'his people' with them? Maryam read the look on his face correctly and softly said, "It's okay; you can trust him."

As the elevator descended, Fatima had just enough time to outline her plan. The Range Rover in which Emad, Yasser, and Rafiq had arrived at CBC was still in the guest parking lot at the front of the building. Yusuf took its keys from the table in the lounge where Emad's 'companions' sat before the interview. He would get into it and drive off the moment any of the Brotherhood members come out of the building. That way he would be able to act as a decoy. In the meantime, Fatima, Maryam, and Emad (with his precious cargo) would go down a few more floors to the underground parking lot where her beat-up old Fiat Uno was parked. Hopefully so much attention would be focused on Yusuf that they could slip away unnoticed. It was by no means a foolproof plan, and it held some danger for Yusuf, but it was the best that Fatima could devise at such short notice.

Maryam looked at her friend, who was the very reason why she suggested that the interview should be at CBC, with profound admiration. Most Egyptians would see a small woman, dressed to the nines and perhaps dismiss her as 'deficient in intelligence and religion' (as the prophet Muhammad once described a group of women). Maryam, however, saw someone who was into her second stint of literally putting her life on the line for her friends. She was about to say something when the elevator door pinged. They had reached the ground floor.

If only for a brief few moments, Fatima's iron-lady masked slipped. She stepped forward to grab Yusuf's arm, "This is where you get off. Please be careful *habibi*!" She poured so much emotion into that last word that no one could miss the underlying meaning. Yusuf gave her a slightly sheepish look before giving her the briefest of hugs.

As he walked through the lobby, Yusuf barely noticed the little groups of people earnestly discussing the bombshell that Emad had dropped on the Muslim world just a few minutes before. Instead, he tried to remain firmly focused on the task at hand. So much had happened since he had originally believed that he was being called up to fulfill a vital role in the global jihad. In the meantime, holed up in the City of the Dead with his sister, his certainties had steadily abandoned him, to the point that he was now acting directly against his former comrades.

In the end, it was personal. The Sheik, someone who for him was the embodiment of a successful 'Soldier of Allah', cynically betrayed his trust to get to Maryam. He realized that the prophet had said, 'War is deceit,' but had always understood that this should be used against the enemy - not your own loyal followers. For her part Maryam had always shown him nothing but devotion. Even during the rockiest parts of their relationship. So, he was going to stand with her — the sister who had saved his life.

As he reached the front door of the CBC building, Yusuf heard an angry commotion behind him. Someone upstairs had realized that the birds were trying to fly the coop. He quickened his steps, praying that he would be able to reach the Range Rover before whoever was pursuing him realized that he was on his own. Once inside, its tinted windows would give little away.

He ran across the parking lot and was able to slam the door of the Range Rover shut, mere moments before a group of wild-eyed men burst out of the building. Watching from inside the vehicle, Yusuf saw that Yasser and Rafiq was among them. The men stood for a few moments. Not sure what to do, or where to go first. They were, however, startled by the turning of the Range Rover's ignition. Yusuf would have burst out laughing at Rafiq and Yasser's expressions if his situation was not so desperate. Once they got over their initial shock, they both began to pat their pockets, only to confirm the obvious, which was that neither of them had the keys to the vehicle they came in. By this time, Yusuf was well on his way out of the parking lot.

In his rearview mirror, he could see the men frantically rushing to another car. He floored the Range Rover's accelerator and felt it surging into the main road in front of the CBC headquarters. Almost immediately, he was confronted with the stark reality that Cairo is one of the most congested cities on the planet. He tried to weave through the traffic, but there was precious little room for maneuver.

To his dismay, he saw that the newly commandeered vehicle containing Rafiq and Yasser was also desperately trying to navigate the snarling traffic at speed. Yusuf ruefully thought that this must be one of the worst places on the planet in which to make a getaway if you are being actively pursued.

With a mix of curses, prayers, and shouts he willed the car forward, but the erratic set of lights behind him kept gaining on him. The next moment, the sound of his desperate screams for the vehicle in front of him to get out of his way was joined by an almighty bang as his rear-window shattered into a million pieces. This was followed in short order by what sounded like a swarm of angry bees inside the Range Rover. Yusuf had only half a second to work out that he was being shot at before the first bullets slammed into his body.

Death came quickly to Yusuf Abbas. As his life slipped away against the backdrop of unbearable pain, one of his last thoughts was that he was thankful to be dying for a cause, even if it was not the one that he swore he would give his life for. After that, a moment of utter clarity as to what might have been, a gasp, and he was gone.

CHAPTER 29

The loud clanging of a bell yanked Emad from a deep, dreamless, sleep. For a moment, he had no idea where he was, and his first sensation was that of an overwhelming stench that threatened to smother him. Gradually the events of the previous night filtered back into his consciousness.

The first image that surged unbidden into his mind was a study in anguish. He would never forget the look of despair on Fatima's face as they watched Yusuf walk into the night, while Maryam and he had remained in the elevator with her. At that moment, as Fatima pushed the button for the basement level, he involuntarily tugged at the handle of the bag he was holding in his right hand. Besides concern for their safety, they just had to get it and its contents away from the studio, and eventually out of the country.

Once they reached the basement, which contained a large parking lot, Fatima rushed them over to her little Fiat Punto. As they got in, she turned to Emad and almost plaintively asked: "Where to?" Emad gave her a bewildered look. How was he supposed to know? Then it hit him. On the note that Rania, the makeup artist, gave him it said to go somewhere if he managed to get out. He fumbled in the bag for a bit until his fingers closed on a piece of paper. "We need to go to the Church of St Simon the Tanner," he said after scanning the page. "Never heard of it!", said Fatima, looking over to Maryam and Emad for a glimmer of recognition. Emad shook his head; he had no idea either. The irony that three Muslims had to get to a Christian church, that they had never heard of, for safety was not lost on him.

In the end, technology came to the rescue. Fatima took her phone and typed the name of the church into Google Maps. She frowned for a moment and then said, "This is weird. It looks like it is deep in the Mokattam Hills." She handed the phone to Emad. Looking at the map he suddenly knew exactly where they were supposed to be heading. Cairo's famous 'Cave Church'. He just never knew that it was named after someone called Simon the Tanner. He assumed that the name had something to do with a story that the Copts tell about this part of Cairo. "I know the place," he said, "Let's go!"

Fatima drove up the parking lot ramp to go back to street level. There was a moment of tension when the guard at the exit stared intently at them. Perhaps he was wondering where he had seen Emad before. However, after a moment or so, he recognized Fatima and waved her through. As they drove past the front of the building Maryam craned her neck to look for the Range Rover. It was not there, Yusuf got away. But how far did he get?

The Mokattam Hills are just beyond the center of Cairo and provided the sandstone out of which much of the city, including the pyramids, were built. The top of the hill was occupied by the suburb of Mokattam, one of the most exclusive areas of Cairo. The contrast with the lower slopes could not be starker. It played host to a community of 30,000 people who are commonly known as the *zabaleen* (or 'garbage people'). This part of the Mokattam Hills is often known as Garbage City. For decades now, the *zabaleen* have been bringing waste, which they collected in Cairo, into this area to recycle and process. This meant that they lived in houses overflowing with trash.

Some of the waste coming into this living trash heap like cardboard, metal, etc. could be sold. Whatever was somewhat edible could be fed to the pigs that was kept by the community. However, in 2009 the government ordered a massive cull of the pigs in the area, ostensibly to prevent an outbreak of swine flu, but probably also because pigs are generally not welcome in a Muslim country. This cull led to even more hardship, as the pigs made a significant contribution to the livelihood of the people in the community, and it took years for the herd to recover its numbers. It also left Cairo significantly dirtier as the *zabaleen* were far less likely to collect organic waste to take back to their neighborhood without large numbers of pigs to eat all of it.

The fact that they kept pigs provided a vital clue to the identity of the residents of the Garbage City. More than 90% of those living in the area are Coptic Christians. An alternative name translates as 'City of the Christians.' It is one of the only communities in all of Egypt where the vast majority of residents are Christian, something that many of the *zabaleen* appreciate - even if they live in miserable circumstances.

From the perspective of many of these Christians, the very best thing about their neighborhood was the presence of the largest Coptic church in the world, in terms of seating capacity. This was the church towards which Emad, Maryam, and Fatima were now heading.

What makes the Church of St Simon the Tanner unique is that it was constructed inside a massive overhanging cave with a capacity of 15,000 people. The cave resembles a stadium, reaching deep into the sandstone cliff. Emad was vaguely aware, thanks to a half-remembered lecture on Cairo's archeological landscape, of the history of the church and the legends that the Copts wove around it. He found this story very ironic, given their present circumstances. This was because the Copts firmly believed that the cave had its origins in an epic Christian-Muslim struggle.

According to the Coptic hagiographies (saint's lives), the Muslim Caliph Al-Muiz (reigned 972-975) challenged the Coptic Pope to prove the truth of the Christian faith or face severe consequences. He confidently stated that the Copts did not actually believe the words of Christ. "Did Jesus not say," he asked, "That those who have faith as small as a mustard seed will be able to move mountains?" The Pope had to agree that this statement was indeed from the Gospels. In response, the Caliph gave the Pope three days to prove that Egypt's Christians had this kind of faith. If nothing happened during that time, he would force them to embrace Islam.

Faced with what amounted to an existential crisis, the Coptic Pope gathered some of the holiest among the Coptic faithful together for prayer and deliberation. It was Simon the Tanner who finally said that he would go to the Mokattam Hills to pray to the Lord for deliverance. After saying "Lord Have Mercy!" three times and making the sign of the cross towards the mountain, it moved. This happened, so devout Copts believe, right in the presence of the Caliph and caused him to relent.

Whatever one thinks of this story, the fact is that a church dedicated to St. Simon the Tanner had existed in the Mokattam Hills for more than a millennium. As large numbers of Christian *zabaleen* had moved into the area, this church was enlarged to serve as one of their parish churches. Towards the end of the 20th century the decision was made to utilize a vast cave, supposedly created during the 'moving of the mountain' as a church and as a shrine to Simon the Tanner. Hence, the present visually striking 'mega-church' that now occupies the site. Surrounding it are several smaller churches and shrines, clustered together around this site of uncommon sanctity.

Most Cairenes would know about the existence of the 'Cave Church,' but very few Muslim residents of the city have been there or know its real name. The Copts do not particularly encourage visits by non-Christians to the site, and you must inch your way through congested alleyways containing mountains of decaying waste to get there.

As the Fiat sped along Saleh Salem Street, one of Cairo's busiest thoroughfares, the eyes of its passengers were drawn to the brightly illuminated Cairo Citadel, built by the scourge of the Crusaders, Saladin. The

Citadel dominates the approaches to the Mokattam Hills and the entire skyline in this part of Cairo. Its splendor and statement of Islamic dominance through the impossibly tall minarets of its mosques stand in stark contrast to the 'Garbage City' almost on its doorstep. Very few words were spoken in the car. They were each doing their best to process the events of the evening. As they did so, they were all stalked by their own fears. Who knew where this was leading? Thankfully, there was little time for reflection. As soon as they left Saleh Salem Street, the challenge of driving in the home of the *zabaleen* imposed itself.

Pursuing the little arrow on Google maps, Fatima had to push the Punto down increasingly narrower alleys, all of them overflowing with all sorts of waste. Fires were burning here and there, adding to a stench that threatened to suck the wind from their lungs. She had to reverse the car several times to let donkey carts piled high with junk pass. All the while, they were attracting stares from the residents who obviously knew that they were outsiders. The worst moment came when they drove past a hole-in-the-wall butchery where a pig was being slaughtered. It was still in its death throes, and its blood flowed, in copious amounts, under the wheels of their car. As Muslims, they had barely even seen pigs, let alone been present while one was killed.

After asking for directions several times, they finally pulled up before the massive steel gates of the church compound. Several soldiers were sitting behind a barrier off to the left, but the gate itself was manned by a burly man in civilian clothes. "Can I help you?" he asked, in a none too friendly tone. Fatima did not quite expect this level of access control, and meekly asked if they could be let in. The man gave her, and the other occupants of the car a suspicious look. Emad later learned that they were expected at this point to show a cross-tattoo or ID documents which stated that they were Christians. For the most part Muslims don't visit the site or have to declare a clear purpose when they do. Fatima was still trying to come up with a response when the guard took a good look at Emad.

Emad was just about to start squirming under the guard's stare when a flash of recognition flashed across the latter's face, "Weren't you on television a little while ago?", he demanded. Upon Emad's affirmative nod, the guard rushed over and flung the gate open. "Get in! Quick!" he motioned. Once they drove through, he stepped inside himself and bolted the gate. A few minutes later they were sitting in the office of the bishop in charge of the compound.

Bishop Yakoub was utterly bemused by the situation, "You are, of course, very welcome," he said, "but why did you come here of all places?" Emad briefly explained about the Micah Order and about the note Rania gave him, instructing him to go to the Church of Simon the Tanner. The bishop furrowed his brow, "I guess if you need to disappear from the radar of Muslim pursuers, this is the place to be!" He coughed uncomfortably, suddenly remembering that his guests were Muslims themselves. "Besides," he continued, "as a community we are deeply in your debt. So, welcome to your temporary home!" Emad exchanged relieved looks with Maryam and Fatima. They were safe! At least for the moment.

As soon as the realization sunk in that the threat of mortal danger was gone Emad realized how utterly exhausted he was. He was, therefore, very thankful at being shown to a room in the guest house and was asleep almost before his head hit the pillow.

It was in his room in this guest house, in a Christian compound at the heart of an inhabited garbage dump that he now found himself. He sat down on his bed, thankful for the opportunity to process some of the events of the past few days and especially the previous night. How quickly things change. Yesterday morning this time, he dreaded the fact that he was expected to go on live television to implicate a community in what would be regarded as ancient treachery. Instead, he ended up presenting a challenge to the faith of more than a billion people, among whom he counted himself.

Entirely unbidden Emad's mind wandered back to that moment when, in another place and time, he had pulled up a map of the Fustat mosque on his computer. Back then, his archeological sixth-sense had told him that something was not quite right. He dismissed the idea as soon as it occurred to him, but a line from the statement he read in the studio the previous night came back to him:

"Look at the original prayer directions of their mosques here in Egypt and other places, see how they do not point towards their new city of Mecca."

That was it! How could he possibly miss it? The entire Fustat mosque complex was oriented due-east, and not to the southeast where Mecca is. Those who pray there face a *qibla* (prayer direction) that is out of sync with the orientation of the building. *"The qibla of the Saracens shall betray them,"* said the riddle on the jar. The meaning of that enigmatic sentence now became crystal clear to Emad. He knew that the prayer direction was supposedly changed from Jerusalem to Mecca during Muhammad's lifetime, but this mosque was built long after Muhammad's death and still did not face Mecca.

Back at the studio, as he sat in Rania's chair, he had to make a snap decision on whether he would read the translation of the message on the golden plates on air. His decision was almost entirely based on the extraordinary journey that the sarcophagus and plates had taken to get to him. He had no opportunity to seriously consider the claims about the origins of Islam that it was making. He was merely thankful that it provided him with a chance to shunt the runaway train bearing down on the Copts into a siding. Pondering its accuracy was not high on his list of priorities at that moment. Although, even under the harsh glare of the studio lights he had thought that the claims were, at the very least, interesting and worthy of further exploration. Now, in the light of a new day and against the background of his initial reaction to the Fustat satellite photo, he was willing to wager that what the plates were saying may possibly be accurate.

Emad got up and paced the room, deep in thought. He could feel his identities as both a Muslim and an archeologist engaging in a fierce tug-of-war inside his brain. What was he to do? Almost automatically, his eyes were drawn to the black bag, where he had placed it on the table next to his bed. Questions raged inside him. Should he be faithful to his calling as an archeologist, by making sure that the contents of that bag were properly investigated? If he wanted to do that, he would somehow have to get the sarcophagus and the plates it contained out of Egypt.

He immediately realized, however, that successfully transporting what must at that moment have been the most talked-about archeological artifact in the world across an international border would be akin to completing one of the twelve tasks of Hercules. He would also be committing professional suicide, as he would be guilty of smuggling if he removed it from Egypt without proper authorization.

He was still racking his brain for possible solutions when a soft knock on the door interrupted his thoughts; it was Maryam. He could instantly see that she had been crying. Before Emad even had a chance to speak, she stepped forward and clung to him, "It's Yusuf," she said, desperation rising in her voice, "There has been no word from him since last night!" Emad immediately understood. This was not good! Still, he tried to conjure up a flicker of hope, "The Sheik presumably still has your phones. How would he have reached you?"

"I spoke to my parents," Maryam said, "They have been worried sick about us, so they were so relieved to hear from me. But they have not heard anything from Yusuf either!" Emad did not know what to say. Could it be that Yusuf had walked into harm's way as he left that elevator? He hoped that his presence would at least be somewhat comforting after such a long period of enforced separation. He motioned towards a chair, "Sit with me for a bit," he said with a tender smile.

The two of them sat in silence for a while, replaying the events of the previous evening in their heads. When the silence became too heavy, Emad switched on the television. If he thought that this would provide a bit of distraction, he could not have been more mistaken. No matter which channel he flicked to, he was on it.

His interview the previous evening was front and center on every single news bulletin, even the international ones. Programming alternated between clips of him reading the translation of the plates and interviews with scholars who, it seemed, had been working on questions related to the early origins of Islam for years and had now been plucked from relative obscurity.

Click.

Al-Jazeera: "We now welcome Dr Gunther Klostermann from the University of Erfurt in Germany. Dr Klostermann, what do you make of the claims that were aired on Capital Broadcasting Center in Cairo last night?" An older gentleman cleared his throat. "In the 1970's I was granted permission by the Yemeni authorities to examine the text of what is possibly the oldest Qur'anic manuscript in the world. It was found in the Grand Mosque in Sana'a. My examination led me to the conclusion that this 'oldest Qur'an' differs markedly from the text that Muslims recite today. Ever since then I've been fascinated by the question of whether the early history of Islam was correctly reported in the classical Islamic sources. Sources that were, after all, written down centuries after the events that they supposedly describe. This find raises some fascinating questions, and I would deeply appreciate the opportunity to investigate it further!"

Click.

BBC: "In an interview earlier today, Professor Gertrude Thorpe, formerly from Oxford University pointed to her research which indicates that Mecca could not have been anywhere near ancient trade routes or functioned as a religious center. She even went as far as challenging anyone to produce a single pre-Islamic reference to the existence of a city at the location where the modern city of Mecca is located. She stated that she viewed this find as a vindication of her thesis that the original holy city of Islam must have been somewhere else."

Click.

CNN: "We asked Samuel Edwards, author of a book entitled *'The Geographical Context of the Qur'an'* for his views on the find. Over to you Sam!" "Thank you. In my work, I analyzed every single geographic reference associated with early Islam. These include places, tribes and geographical features in the Qur'an. The reality is that the place that is being described simply could not have been where Mecca is located. All of the references are very far to the north, and the Qur'an describes its audience as living in a location where they practiced livestock farming and cultivated all sorts of crops. This would have been impossible at the location of modern Mecca, which is located in one of the driest spots on the planet. The plates that Dr. Almasry read from last night strongly support my theory that Islam had its origins somewhere else, possibly the ancient city of Petra. I just hope that international scholars will get the opportunity to study it."

Click.

Russia Today: "In a statement Dr. Bjorn Lichtenberg, author of *'Reading the Qur'an with Syriac Eyes,'* stated that large parts of the Qur'an only made sense if it is understood as containing a significant Syriac substratum. Its Arabic was therefore profoundly influenced by a language spoken much further to the north, in the part of the world now primarily occupied by Syria and eastern Turkey. Dr. Lichtenberg firmly believes that this latest discovery will be of significant help in cutting through later additions to get to the real history of early Islam."

Hammer blow after hammer blow striking against ancient certainties. Emad switched the television off and glanced over at Maryam. She gave him a plaintive look, barely managing to stifle a sob that arose from deep inside her. Emad was not at all sure, at that point, whether her tears were only for Yusuf.

CHAPTER 30

Emad spent the earlier part of the next day wandering around the church compound, marveling at the many biblical scenes carved into the rock face. Entering the cave church, he sat down in one of the hundreds of rows of seats that stretched deep into the belly of the mountain. The knowledge that he was a marked man, and his inner struggle about what to do with the sarcophagus and the plates, gelled perfectly with the sense of humility that the scene inspired. He felt tiny and very lost.

He was sure that the Brotherhood did not know where he was. If they did, an attempt to forcibly enter the compound would have been made by now. Still, he knew that they would deploy all available eyes and ears, especially at the international airports, to ensure that he did not take the plates out of the country.

As he was pondering his options, he suddenly became aware of someone next to him. It was Bishop Yakoub, who had been looking for him. "Please come with me," the priest said softly, "There's something I want to show you." Emad got up, and they walked up toward the light at the entrance of the cave. Squinting in the bright Cairo sunlight reflected off the sandstone cliffs, they crossed the main entrance road and entered the cafeteria. Emad was a little startled by this. It looked just like any of a thousand places where you could get a cheap meal in Cairo, although admittedly it was at least somewhat unique because it sold pork dishes.

Bishop Yakoub motioned him over to the window at the back of the room. It gave those inside a panoramic view of the 'Garbage City.' What Emad saw next, almost took his breath away. Looking back at him was one of the largest, and one of the most unique, murals in the world.

The French-Tunisian artist El Seed spent years gaining trust and getting permission from the residents of the Garbage City to paint a work of art across no fewer than 50 buildings. To make things worse, he had to keep the project secret from authorities because of a crackdown on street art after the revolution. The mural is called 'Perception' and it contains a quote from the Egyptian church leader Athanasius of Alexandria (AD 296-373), in stylized Arabic that stretches and curls over the walls of the buildings. Seen from up close, sections of the mural looked like carelessly splashed paint, but from a more distant vantage point, like from the window of the cafeteria, a coherent and beautiful picture emerged. This is proper, given that it is all about 'Perception.' The quote from Athanasius that it contains also deals with this very theme: *Anyone who wants to see the sunlight clearly needs to wipe his eye first*".

Emad stood transfixed for a few moments. Bishop Yakoub broke the silence, "This mural means so much to the people living there. It invites those who stand where we are to see them as much more than a bunch of garbage collectors. We need to 'wipe our eyes' to see that these are people with the same hopes, dreams, and fears as the rest of us."

Bishop Yakoub continued, "Do you know much about St. Athanasius?", he asked. Emad gave him a quizzical look. He did not quite expect the conversation to turn to Christian theology. During his time at St. Bishoy he did hear the name mentioned a few times in discussions about the history of the monasteries at Wadi Natrun. This was because St. Athanasius was a friend and patron of St. Anthony, the original 'Desert Father'. Other than that, he admitted, his knowledge was sketchy.

Bishop Yakoub, looked Emad straight in the eye before solemnly declaring, "St. Athanasius teaches us about courage in the face of adversity. Especially adversity that comes because of the rejection of accepted certainties. He was the patriarch of Alexandria during a time when our church was being torn apart with debates about the nature of Christ. It would have been the easiest possible thing for him just to accept whatever the authorities wanted him to preach and teach. But he refused, he wanted to 'see deeper', to stand for truth no matter what the consequences. What it got him was a life of exile and countless death threats. He persisted, and here he is", Bishop Yakoub motioned towards the mural, "Continually encouraging us to not simply believe what society and those in power want us to believe."

Emad nodded. Bishop Yakoub did not have to say much more.

At that moment the last bit of doubt about what to do with the sarcophagus and the plates dissolved. He should do everything in his power to get them to a place where they can be properly studied, without the possibility of destruction hanging over them.

This resolve did not bring clarity in terms of *how* such a thing could be done. Nor did it bring relief from the stark realization that as a known 'smuggler' of ancient artifacts out of Egypt, he would probably never work in his chosen profession in his homeland again. It did mean, however, that he was fully committed to seeing this through. The personal and professional consequences could sort themselves out later. He turned to Bishop Yakoub, "Could you please get in touch with someone named Samuel Mounir? The abbot of St. Bishoy monastery should be able to help you find him. Please ask him to come here."

It did not take long to arrange for Samuel to come to the cave church complex. He had been waiting impatiently for a phone call after seeing Emad on television, knowing that he might yet have a part to play.

As Samuel stepped into Bishop Yakoub's office that evening, he rushed over to enfold Emad in a bear hug. Emad rather wished he hadn't. Not because he was not glad to see him. It was just that Samuel, with his customary flair for the dramatic, had disguised himself as a garbage collector and came to the Cave Church on the donkey cart of one of the *zabaleen*. The result was a weapons-grade assault on Emad's sense of smell. He nevertheless smiled broadly, returned Samuel's embrace and kissed him on both cheeks.

The meeting with Samuel was bittersweet. The awareness that their association that had started out as a bit of an adventure, had eventually led to the death of a friend was an invisible presence throughout. There was also the feeling that they were at a literal dead end. The only road into the St. Simon the Tanner compound ends at a cave. If they had any hope of success they would have to turn around and face the world. A world in which some people had already made it abundantly clear that they were prepared to kill and maim to uphold their version of the truth.

For the next four hours, Emad and Samuel paced up and down between the Cave Church and the heavy steel doors at the entrance to the compound. Countless ideas were floated and quickly discarded. They could almost imagine the Sheik, probably holed up in one of his hideouts, issuing orders to scuttle the very plans they were making.

Samuel was especially frustrated. The Micah Order had plenty of experience in moving people about, but none when it came to archeological artifacts. Yet, here was a situation in which flesh and blood and perhaps the most sought-after objects in the whole world had to be moved across international borders at the same time.

In the end, it was Samuel who unwittingly provided the solution when he said in a desperate voice: "We need someone on the outside, to help us!" As he did so, he made a gesture that Emad immediately understood as denoting 'someone very far away'. At that moment her name popped into his head. A name that, he had to admit, did not occur to him even once during the cut and thrust of the past few weeks.

Lucy.

Emad felt slightly ashamed at the fact that he had given so little thought to how someone he once considered one of his closest friends would react to recent events. She had to be aware of what was going on. How could it be otherwise? His interview was replayed regularly on all the major international networks. Surely, she must know and must be extremely worried about him. She may also, through years of connections made at the SOAS library in central London, be able to help.

Emad's resolve to get in touch with her as soon as possible was followed by the realization that he had no means of doing so. The Sheik's men had confiscated his phone and he could hardly log into his Ministry for Antiquities email account. Doing so would give away his approximate location through an IP traceback. It was then that he remembered his good old Gmail account that he had used while he was in London. It had been ages since he checked it, but he was confident that it would still be active. He used to log in now and then, in moments when nostalgia seized him, to go over the sometimes silly, sometimes serious, messages he had exchanged with Lucy.

A few minutes later, Emad and Samuel were seated in his room, hunched over Samuel's laptop. Emad had to chuckle when Samuel pulled his high-powered machine from his tattered and smelly bag. This particular 'garbage person' was on the technological cutting edge.

As Emad opened the browser, he paused for a second. Would it not be possible to use even this old email account to track him down? As if he was reading his mind, Samuel reached for the mouse and clicked a few icons. "You're on a VPN now, and it would be pretty hard to trace you!", he said. Even the ancient Micah Order had to keep up with the latest in cybersecurity.

Emad's fingers trembled slightly as he typed in his login details. He was not sure what to expect. Would she even want to hear from him under present circumstances?

He need not have worried.

As soon as the first page of his email account loaded it was clear that Lucy had been trying very hard to reach him. There were a series of messages whose subject lines ranged from excited, hopeful, worried and finally, desperate:

"I saw you on TV, you're famous! Awesome!"
"They say you've gone missing? Wanna come out of hiding?"
"Seriously Emad this is not funny! Let me know you're okay. Please!"
"Emad, just send me a single line, I beg you! I can't bear thinking about what may have happened to you."

For the second time that day, Emad felt slightly guilty that he had not given Lucy and her reaction to his current notoriety any thought. Still, it would not do to dwell on the state of his social interactions during a time of chaos and upheaval. At least he could try to make amends by making Lucy an offer that she could not refuse - involvement in the final chapter of this extraordinary saga.

He clicked 'Reply' on her final message, the desperate one, and started to type:

"Dear Lucy, I am touched that you have been so concerned about me. I am well. Or at least as 'well' as you can be with half the country looking for you. At the moment I am in the proverbial 'undisclosed location' not quite knowing the way out of here, especially while carrying a rather important package. I feel horrible asking you this, especially since we did not have regular contact recently, but I'm in a bit of a pickle, so here goes: You are probably the best-connected 'archeological librarian' out there. You wouldn't by any chance know of anyone who could assist an old friend in a tight spot? Your friend, Emad

PS. I'm sure 'Indy' would send his greetings. He now lives on a shelf above the desk in my office, although it's been some time since I last saw him, or my office for that matter."

Emad hesitated for a second before pressing 'Send.' He hoped that he had struck the right tone. He tried to keep things light, while at the same time making it clear that he could seriously use some help. Admittedly it was a long shot, but if anyone had someone who could help in her list of contacts, it was Lucy. He smiled at how ironic it was that the one thing about Lucy that sometimes irritated him, her far too trusting acceptance of people who were interested in archeology for ulterior motives (he used to call them 'mercenaries' back in London) might now prove his salvation.

Lucy must have been constantly checking her email, because it was hardly 15 minutes before her answer came:

> *"Oh my goodness Emad! I'm so glad you are safe. You would not believe how my heart raced when I saw your message. As for helping you. I already had several calls from Rhys Davies to offer any assistance you may need, should you ever get in touch. I realize that you will probably be extremely reluctant to accept his help. Please Emad, do it, if only for my sake! You need to get out of there. Love, Lucy"*

Emad's emotions veered between utter elation and profound horror. If anyone could get him and the sarcophagus out, it would indeed be Rhys Davies. Emad knew this because he was convinced, along with just about every other Egyptologist out there that Davies was knee-deep in smuggling artifacts out of Egypt to sell on the European black market.

Working with him would feel like selling his soul.

CHAPTER 31

Decisions. We make them, big and small, every single day.

On the second evening, after Emad had dropped his bombshell live on television, the urgent necessity to make decisions came knocking at the doors of several people. People whose lives had been irrevocably changed by a clay jar, caked with dirt, found under the soil of old Fustat.

Where would they have been, what would they have done, if that jar was still safely under the ground? That's a question that none of them had the luxury to consider. They had to deal with the chessboard as they found it and make their moves accordingly. Moves that would not only change their lives, but that would also have ripple effects reaching into the lives and hearts of many who were doing nothing more on that night than going about their business.

Alone in her room at the postgrad residence at Cairo University, Hana Tadros picked up her passport and locked it in a drawer in her cupboard. She spoke English; she had a valid British visa after a recent conference. She would be granted asylum in any number of western countries if she told her story. She just had to get on a plane. A new life awaited. Still, she resolved that her passport would remain in the drawer. She knew that the choice she was making would condemn her to a life of looking over her shoulder. Yet, this was her home. Not just hers, it had been the home of her people for countless generations. She wanted to be here, shouldering a tiny bit of the responsibility of carving out a place in the sun for the Coptic people. There would be times of pain and fear, but the fear of losing a connection to something infinitely precious was greater. *"Blessed be Egypt, my people,"* she muttered, and she felt those ancient biblical words acting as a balm on her beating heart. She opened her laptop and clicked a few buttons until the printer sprang into life, pushing out a picture of the St. Bishoy monastery. Hana tacked it up above her desk. It would be a reminder of the place where her life was irrevocably changed. It would also remind her of someone. Someone who called this place home. Someone she was not allowed to miss.

What would Hana have thought if she knew that in that very same monastery another decision, one that was in some ways a mirror image of her own, was being made? Brother Michael stood with his hand raised, ready to knock on the door of Father Reweis. He had slept very little the previous evening. Just a few days ago he was devastated when he believed that he would have to leave St. Bishoy forever. His return felt like a rebirth. But there he was, about to request permission to travel back to America for good. Magdy's dying moments continued to replay in his mind every time he closed his eyes and the desire to honor his legacy by somehow continuing his work took hold of him and would not let go. Over time it came to him: He may not be an archeologist, but he knew how to tell a story. Part of the problem for the Copts was that so few people in the outside world were aware of their existence, let alone their plight. Michael as an American citizen from a Coptic background, who was at the heart of some of the dramatic events that had all the world talking, could help change that. He could be a voice for his people. He had to do it, even if it meant leaving this place that had captured his heart behind. His hand descended, and the silence of the monastery was broken by his knock on the abbot's door.

Maryam's room in the guest house at the Cave Church complex was just down the hall from Emad's, but she had the surreal feeling that the physical distance between them was increasing as he drifted towards places where she could not follow. At the heart of this feeling was Yusuf. Where was he? This brother of her, who so firmly believed that his actions in pulling her towards ever-stricter obedience to Islam were expressions of profound concern. Yusuf, who provided a way out when all they could see were dead ends. Where was he? How could she go with Emad with uncertainty gnawing at the core of her being? And where would their journey end? Emad's appearance on CBC had already undermined the faith of many. After his interview a massive debate had erupted, and it was sweeping like a tornado across the Muslim world. People were openly declaring their apostasy from Islam. Was she ready to join them? Would going with Emad, would marrying him, mean that she had to? Of course, she sometimes struggled against the restrictions Yusuf imposed on her, but she could also see how his faith gave him a deeper purpose. Embarking on a road away from Islam would feel like doubly deserting him. Leaving the place where her brother might still be and betraying his faith. Still, she deeply loved Emad. She thought back to that time in the dingy flat near Helwan when it seemed that their dream of starting a life together might be just a little closer. How was she to know then that he would become a poster boy for skepticism and doubt? She had spent the past few weeks trying to outfox the Sheik. Was his brand of Islam and extreme skepticism really the only two options? Should she not at least do her best to find a kind of middle ground? Sobs tore through her body at the realization that the time for a decision was drawing ever closer. Each sob pulled in the direction her broken heart was moving, until clarity finally came. Even if her faith was built on airy nothings, she still wanted to believe, if only for Yusuf's sake. She sat up straight, wiped her eyes and began to work out how she would break the news to Emad that it was over between them.

Across the city, in a back room at Al-Zikry Automotive near the Sayyeda Zeinab mosque, the Sheik looked at the ultra-modern space that he had created with a rueful smile. What was supposed to be the command center for the final victory against the Copts had turned into 'Damage Control

Central'. His mood shifted between red-hot rage directed at Egypt's Islamic scholars in their public response to recent events and white-hot rage aimed at Emad. The scholars, those very people who should be shoring up Islam, were doing nothing more than referring to historical sources, Ibn Ishaq, Al-Tabari and the *hadiths* (traditions). These were sources that had been committed to paper hundreds of years after the life of Muhammad. In the process the scholars were merely confirming what the critics were saying, that there was very little by way of contemporary primary sources to support Islamic beliefs. There were only secondary sources written hundreds of years after-the-fact. The Sheik despaired at where Islam would be, and where the Brotherhood would be, if it had to depend on such feeble defenders. Still, he believed. He had to. Belief, submission, was at the core of who he was. It was for this reason that his more profound rage was directed at the man who was supposed to deliver the Brotherhood's long-planned masterstroke, but instead struck at the movement's heart while an expectant nation looked on. Sheer hatred stiffened the Sheik's resolve. If it cost his last breath, Emad Almasry would be found and made to pay dearly. The war would go on, and the retribution would be terrible.

As for Emad. His decision on that night was both the easiest and hardest that he ever had to make. He had already resolved that he would get the sarcophagus and plates out of Egypt, come what may. So, in a sense his mind was made up. However, the fact that following through on his resolve meant teaming up with someone involved in the black market revolted him to the core of his being. He was one of the 'good guys' after all. He had dedicated his life up to that point to safeguarding his country's ancient heritage. And now? If he followed through, he might rightly be labelled a smuggler himself. Still, there was nothing to be done; he had to do this. He just never thought that the price would be quite this high.

He could feel the tears stinging his eyes as he composed an email to Lucy to ask her to get in touch with Davies on his behalf.

CHAPTER 32

The Cairo to Alexandria highway was much the same as the last time that Emad had traveled on it. Only this time, he was not on a quest to solve an impenetrable ancient riddle. This time, he was a fugitive. More than that, he was a fugitive with a broken heart.

As the billboards next to the highway flashed by, he sat back in his seat to reflect on how he got there.

Rhys Davies must have been waiting for Emad to get in touch with bated breath. Almost as soon as he replied to Lucy's email to say that he would be willing, if that's the right word, to work with Rhys; he had an email from him. It did not say much. It merely directed Emad to open a Telegram account and to contact him on that. Emad was vaguely aware of the existence of Telegram, a messaging app with some serious encryption. There have been a few cases in Egypt where militant groups used it for internal communication, knowing that the authorities would find it very hard to 'crack' their messages. He could understand the need for such a tool in his present circumstances, but it only increased his unease about the world he was now entering.

Then there was Maryam. Never in his wildest dreams did he think that their journey would end due to his work as an archeologist, but it had. Or perhaps, to be more accurate, it had ended due to where archeology was leading him. There were, of course, tears aplenty, but her mind was made up. She would stay in Egypt, where she could continue to look for her brother and where she could feel safe in the faith that same brother cherished.

Not for the first time, Emad thought that life would have been so much simpler if an ancient clay jar remained undisturbed under the soil of Fustat. That may indeed have been the case, but there was no turning back the clock, and it was his task to let the contents of the St. Bishoy sarcophagus say what it must to the world. If only the price was not so high. He had lost friends. He lost Maryam. He might be leaving his beloved Egypt for the last time, and he was about to put his professional reputation on the line. Still, he was somehow at peace with himself and with the world. He was now part of something much bigger. He knew that he would probably one day look back on these days as the most exciting and meaningful of his life. That was enough for the present. Besides, there was still the small matter of skipping the country.

He looked at himself in the rearview mirror of the rickety truck in which they were driving towards Alexandria and could not help smiling. Staring back at him was a picture of what he would most likely have become if the path of education did not lead him out of Upper Egypt. He wore a loosely wound turban, a thick, full-length cotton *galabia* and the five o'clock shadow of four days ago. To any observer, he was just one more Upper Egyptian *fellah* heading to the north to seek better prospects. Thankfully he could play the role to perfection; he merely had to channel his father or his uncles. The biggest challenge was to make sure that he never slipped out of the 'street Arabic' of the south or let anyone have too close a look at his hands; hands that had not seen much physical labor in recent times.

Emad's interactions with Rhys Davies were indeed enlightening. Not least because he now had a deep understanding of how ancient objects were smuggled out of Egypt by hiding them in plain sight. If the circumstances were different, he would have been fascinated by the ingenuity of it all. As it was, he just wanted this to be over.

It had taken many messages on Telegram to get to this point. From the start, Davies had made it clear that he was not in this for 'love and charity' as he called it. He had big dreams for a book with a host of media tie-ins, and he wanted to make sure that a significant proportion of the royalties would go his way. Emad, who at that stage would have agreed to pretty much anything to get out of Egypt, readily consented. They were in business.

Next, they had to work on getting out of the Cave Church complex without being spotted. Samuel and the modern Micah Order came into their own at this point. Helping people to adopt new identities was their bread-and-butter. In no time at all, Emad had new identity papers, and the process of turning him back into a salt-of-the-earth Upper Egyptian peasant started in earnest. That was the easy bit. Emad was confident that he could comfortably slip into an alternative version of himself. But how on earth would the 'new Emad' be able to travel with the hottest bit of ancient history in the world?

He, once again, recalled his Telegram conversations with Davies:

> *Emad – They will be watching every international airport with eagle eyes. There's no way I'll get through.*
> *Rhys – Who said anything about flying?*
> *Emad – Are you crazy? Both the western desert and Sinai are swarming with militant groups! I'd be dead before I even get close to any border.*
> *Rhys – Not so fast. I'm not about to throw you to the wolves. You're heading to Europe. There's a bit of it a mere 500 miles north of Egypt. Hope you don't get seasick?*
> *Emad – You want to get me out by boat!?*
> *Rhys – Indeed! There's a weekly cargo service between Alexandria and Limassol in Cyprus. You're going to be on it soon.*

So, that's how he did it. The anti-smuggling unit of the Ministry for Antiquities focused on making sure nothing of value left Egypt through its airports. Davies' approach was to bypass the airports altogether. Over the years his Egyptian agents became regulars on the Cairo-Limassol cargo run by taking Egyptian art to be sold at a craft market in the Cypriot capital, Nicosia. The objects they sold there were mostly reproductions of classical pieces or modern Egyptian handicrafts. It was all above board, except when something quite a bit more ancient somehow made it into the consignment. With Cyprus being part of the European Union, such an object could then be taken anywhere in Europe without any further customs checks.

Emad had to acknowledge that there was a kind of twisted brilliance in Davies' arrangements, but he did have his doubts whether they would be able to slip the sarcophagus into all of the bric-a-brac heading to the Nicosia craft market. Davies was way ahead of him, however. One of his messages read:

> *"Emad, you're going to have to trust me on this one. You'll have to tell me where you are, so that I can send my associate Farouk to you. He will need some time with the sarcophagus."*

So it was that a short man with thinning hair and thick glasses was brought to St. Simon the Tanner in the dead of night. He looked like the last person who would be suspected of being part of an international smuggling ring, and perhaps this was precisely the point. Blending in and being invisible was half the game. The only thing about Farouk that looked slightly out of the ordinary was the enormous black backpack that was slung over his shoulder. Every trade has its tools, and this was no social visit.

Farouk said very little as Emad showed him to his room, where he kept the sarcophagus. His silence was probably because he recognized that Emad was from 'the other side' and did not approve of his choice of career, even if it was of short-term benefit to him.

Emad stood at the door as Farouk got to work. It was indeed hard for him to remain civil towards him. The fact that he was Egyptian made his involvement in the black market just that little bit harder to stomach. He was not plundering somewhere 'over there'. Instead, he was stripping his homeland of some of the objects that made it special and unique. Still, beggars can't be choosers, and this man, whom he would gladly have helped send to prison just a few short weeks ago, now represented a way out of his current predicament.

What Farouk may have lacked in the ethical sphere, he made up for in skill. He knew what he was doing. From his backpack emerged brushes, bowls, plastic sheets and a host of other mysterious objects central to his trade. He started by placing a white plastic sheet on the ground and laying the tiny sarcophagus on it. Then he took photos of it from every conceivable angle. His next step was to make a silicone mold of the object. Emad was, at least, heartened to see that he took the utmost care in the way he handled it and amazed at the evident skill with which he went about his work. That was it for the evening. Farouk packed everything back into his backpack and disappeared into the night.

Two nights later, he was back there again. This time his bag was even bulkier. The reason for this soon became apparent. He had brought with him a replica of the sarcophagus. As soon as Emad had a good look at it, he realized that it was not a precise copy. It did have the right shape, the mold that Farouk took saw to that. However, the color was a bit off, and the paint strokes were too rough. No expert would ever be fooled into thinking that it was the real thing. The replica sarcophagus looked like it was hurriedly produced to supply consumer demand. Emad soon realized that this effect was exactly what he was trying to achieve.

Farouk did not take the time to explain his methods, but his intentions became evident once he asked Emad to take out the original sarcophagus. He placed it on the ground again and gently slipped an ultra-thin silicone sleeve over it. The sleeve was also produced using the mold he made and fitted the original sarcophagus perfectly. "I'm going to be here for a while," he muttered as he took out some paint and brushes. Over the next few hours, he painstakingly painted the sleeve to look precisely like the less-than-perfect copy he brought along. In the process, he transformed the original sarcophagus by making it look like a hurriedly produced knock-off. Emad was deeply impressed with Farouk's work, in spite of himself, and wondered aloud how many pieces had been smuggled out right under the noses of the authorities using this method. Farouk only shrugged. As far as he was concerned Emad was still very much on the other team and he preferred to keep his cards close to his chest.

So it was that Emad and Farouk were trundling towards Alexandria in a truck that had seen much better days. In the back, the truck was piled high with papyrus scrolls with garish designs, hundreds of scarab beetles, clay models of Egyptian mythological figures and even small obelisks covered in hieroglyphs. These were all items that sold well at the Nicosia craft market. There were also some new items in stock, 30 replicas of the small sarcophagus that had caused such a stir on Egyptian television a few nights before.

As they got closer to Alexandria, they passed the sign for Wadi Natrun. Emad said nothing but he longed to stop there for a moment to pay his final respects to Magdy before leaving. He consoled himself with the fact that he might soon be able to tell the world about the courageous and crucial role that Magdy played in unearthing the sarcophagus and plates.

As they left the highway and turned towards Alexandria's city center, Emad tensed up. He had always liked Alexandria. Until quite recently it retained its place as a city that belonged to the world rather than to a single country. The status of the city as a multicultural melting pot only came to an end in the 1950s when President Nasser had nationalized the property of the tens of thousands of Europeans, especially Greeks, who still lived there. However, more than two millennia of Greek influence had left its mark. Even though Alexandria is now totally Egyptian in terms of its inhabitants it is still the least 'oriental' of Egypt's major cities. It is also now, laying claim to its ancient intellectual heritage again. A replacement for the 'Great Library of Alexandria', destroyed during the Muslim conquest of Egypt was, rather belatedly, inaugurated in 2002.

They were not there to take in the sights, however. Their mission was powerfully brought home to Emad as they turned into the harbor precinct and the characteristic smell of diesel fumes and fish hit their nostrils. Emad suddenly felt nauseous. Not because of the smell, but from the realization that his fate, and that of their precious cargo, would be determined at this place and on this very day. As they entered the harbor, they passed some deep basins where massive container ships, the workhorses of the global economy, were being unloaded. Farouk steered the truck deeper into the port towards an area where some much smaller vessels were moored. One of these would take them to Cyprus, if they were allowed to leave port that is.

Emad looked over at Farouk. He had probably done this many times before, albeit probably never with a cargo quite as precious. He tried to look nonchalant, but Emad could see from the way he furiously worked a piece of gum inside his mouth that his nerves were on edge as well.

They had to pass a customs post before reaching their vessel. "This is it," Emad thought, "Could this be the place where it all ends for me?" He should have been confident. Samuel had worked hard to help him craft a new identity. Farouk was a veteran of this journey. Still, it would take only one tiny flicker of suspicion for them to be exposed.

This part of the port was very run down and did not see much action compared to the rest of the harbor. Emad wondered whether it was perhaps a kind of outer darkness for those whose careers in the customs service were not going anywhere. Was this why Davies and Farouk had chosen this route? Had they found the soft underbelly of Egypt's border protection system?

Farouk stopped the truck at a boom gate next to the customs post and honked the truck's horn. A low rasping sound, reminiscent of classic *cops and robbers* movies, resulted. A few moments later, the door opened, and an officer wearing a uniform that looked like it had its glory days in the 1990s sauntered over. Almost immediately, his face broadened into a smile of recognition, "Ah Farouk, welcome! So, it's that time of the week again is it?" Farouk returned his smile and handed him a packet of cigarettes, "Always good to see you Officer Rahman!" The gift was accepted with profuse expressions of gratitude that had the air of regular usage about them. Except, this week was a little different.

The tiniest hint of a frown appeared on the officer's face as he saw Emad in the passenger seat. "Where's Tariq this week?" he asked. Tariq usually came along every week to help unload the truck and to assist at the market. Farouk was prepared to explain his absence and answered in a somber tone of voice: "His father passed away suddenly, and he had to go to his village to help set the family's affairs in order. Khaled here will help me until Tariq gets back." Officer Rahman nodded sympathetically and motioned towards Emad, "I'll have to see his papers, rules are rules!" This was Emad's moment to shine. He laid his Upper Egyptian persona on thick, addressing the officer with exaggerated expressions of respect as he handed over a passport in the name of 'Khaled Khalili.' Watching the officer study his passport was some of the longest seconds of his life.

Samuel's people had done an excellent job. The passport passed the test with flying colors, "Have a nice trip. Don't let him work you too hard!", the officer said with a twinkle in his eye, as he handed the passport back to Emad. He continued, addressing Farouk, "I'll have to check your cargo, because..." Before he could continue, Farouk interrupted him: "... rules are rules!" Despite the tension gnawing at his insides, Emad had to chuckle at what was obviously a well-practiced weekly routine.

"Be my guest," Farouk said as he got out to unlock the truck's back door. Emad, still seated in the passenger seat, could feel the truck move as someone got into the back. For the next few moments the steps of Rahman's boots on the metal floor reverberated through the cabin. Then it stopped, and there was a deathly silence for a while. Fate turned on moments like these. The silence was broken by steps rushing back to the back of the truck, and a loud summons, "Hey Ahmed, come and have a look at this!"

Emad froze. Was this the end of the road? He mentally got ready to make a run for it. He was not going down without at least giving himself a fighting chance. Officer Ahmed was not happy with having his daily routine interrupted in this way. As he walked towards the truck his face had a single message, 'This had better be good". His colleague did not disappoint. He pointed to the crate holding 29 replica sarcophagi (and unbeknownst to him, one genuine article) and burst out laughing, "Look at this! Is this not Egypt at its very finest!? Only a few days ago we were all talking about this, and this jackal," he motioned towards Farouk, "is already cashing in!" Officer Ahmed stared at the cargo for a moment with the expression of someone who did not quite get the joke, then turned around and walked back to his desk without another word. Farouk and Emad both burst out laughing. If Rahman had been a keener observer, he might have noticed that there was more than a bit of relief mixed in with the hilarity.

Officer Rahman, still smiling broadly, signed the proper forms and waved them through the boom gate. He was, of course, totally oblivious to the fact that he had just let the catch of a lifetime slip through his fingers. Emad now understood what it must feel like to get a stay of execution. He looked over at Farouk, who dealt with the relief by softly running through a list of Arabic obscenities under his breath. Bottom-line: They were going to make it!

It took an hour or so to unload the truck. Emad enjoyed the physical exercise of carrying items up the gangplank of the *Khufu*, the small cargo vessel that would take them to Cyprus. He could feel his blood, frozen in his veins a few minutes ago, coursing through his body. Carrying the sarcophagi, especially, the one on which all the others were based, felt especially strange. Here he was, the archeologist who had presented it to the world, carrying the most wanted object in Egypt for all the world (or at least for some dockworkers) to see.

An hour or so later the *Khufu* was leaving the harbor behind. Emad stood on deck and looked back at Alexandria. Centuries ago, the tallest lighthouse on the planet, one of the seven wonders of the world, would have greeted him. Now, it was just the Alexandria waterfront, made up of mile upon mile of European style apartment buildings. He could have been looking at Marseilles or Nice. Would this sight, so unlike the Upper Egypt of palm trees and water buffaloes that he had grown up in, be his last view of his beloved homeland? Only time could answer that question. For the moment he was content to feel waves of relief breaking over him.

He had no idea what was waiting for him on the other side of this journey. Would he and Lucy pick up where they left off? Would he ever work as an archeologist again? Would he even have somewhere to sleep that night? All of those questions could wait. For the moment he could rejoice in the fact that with a little help from his friends and former enemies he had outfoxed the Brotherhood. What had been found in Wadi Natrun would be verified and trumpeted the world over. That was the sweetest revenge he could hope for.

And his faith, not only his, but that of more than a billion people? What if their quest to solve a riddle on a Coptic clay jar provided the thread that would cause the tapestry of Islam to unravel? What if it proved that the history that Muslims are taught from their earliest days was nothing more than a mirage? What if people go looking for pre-Islamic evidence for the existence of Mecca and the search turns up exactly nothing? That, too, is a bridge that he would have to cross when he got there. He knew, even then on the deck of the *Khufu*, that he would not hide from the implications of whatever the search for the earliest origins of Islam might reveal.

Many hours later, the *Khufu* sailed into the port of Limassol. Cypriot customs officers came on board a short while later. Farouk's consignment looked just the same as it did every week, give or take a few new products, and they hardly gave it a second look. After they had gone, Farouk produced a padded backpack and placed the 'real' sarcophagus in it before handing it to Emad. He was to be the one who would carry it into the wider world. The weight of the backpack as he put it on seemed to be increased by the knowledge that it contained an object that had already started to sway the course of history.

Farouk insisted that they stick to his regular routine, even though they were, by then, probably beyond the reach of the Brotherhood. So, their next task would be to participate in the unloading of the vessel before taking their part of the cargo to the Nicosia market where Davies' agents would meet them.

There was, however, something else to get out of the way before the *Khufu* could be unloaded. Emad noticed that many of those who were on board with them had formed up on the quay to offer thanks to Allah for a successful voyage. Passengers and crew alike stood in two rows, facing Mecca, as the familiar strains of the Islamic call to prayer filled the salty air of the harbor. Emad, who was still on board, looked down at this scene with a mixture of sadness and compassion.

As the prayer-leader made his first prostration towards what was supposedly the 'mother of all cities', Emad could almost feel the words that he was carrying on his back demanding to be heard, to be weighed, insisting that things could not simply be as they used to be.

Emad was no less thankful to be there than those below, possibly much more so. Strangely, the memory of Athanasius, that strong rock against popular opinion, came to him at that moment. He faced in his own direction, away from the two lines of the praying faithful, and muttered the word *'Shukran!'* (Thank You!) into the wind.

Author's Note

The *House Built on Sand* is a work of fiction. The main characters, the weighted scale, and the Micah Order were products of my imagination. However, buildings, locations, and historical events were accurately described.

It is, furthermore, certainly the case that serious questions can be asked about the reliability of Muslim accounts of the early history of Islam. Some of these questions played a central role in *The House Built on Sand*. If you are interested in reading more about this subject, please read my non-fiction work: ***"The Mecca Mystery – Probing the Black Hole at the Heart of Muslim History"*** at: www.meccamystery.com

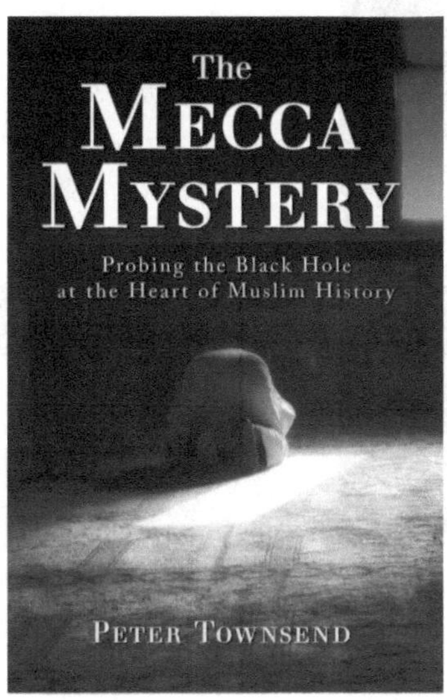

I am constantly working on new projects. If you would like to keep up-to-date, please visit my website: https://www.petertownsend.info

More from Peter Townsend

*Questioning Islam – Tough
Questions and Honest Answers
About the Muslim Religion*
An exploration of the truth-claims
of Islam www.qi-book.com

*Nothing to do with Islam? –
Investigating the West's Most
Dangerous Blind-Spot*
An analysis of the link between
Islamic teaching and violence
www.ntdwi.com